THE ARKADIA SAGA COMPLETE SERIES

TIFFANY SHAND

Copyright © 2021 Tiffany Shand

All rights reserved. No part of this book may be reproduced.

ISBN: **9798527655902**

DEDICATION

For Mum

ACKNOWLEDGMENTS

Editing by Dark Raven Edits

CHOSEN AVATAR

PROLOGUE

Aurelia ducked as the sound of explosions roared through the city. The shining white stone towers that once touched the sky were now blackened, broken and burnt. Their windows long gone, and their walls crumbled. "This wasn't supposed to happen," she muttered. "I never meant for this!"

Airships hovered overhead, lighting up the sky with fire. The great city her people had built and treasured for centuries was falling before her eyes, and around her hundreds lay dead or dying. People coughed, and hands reached out for her as she moved past them. She was their avatar, someone meant to help them. But she knew she had very little time left. Her people would punish her for breaking the balance of magic by creating a device that had brought so much death. Magic prickled against her skin and she knew she had only minutes before the curse took effect. She would die today, no matter what happened. It was her punishment, her fate.

I never meant for this to happen, she thought. *Yet, nothing can change it now.*

"You've lost, avatar," Esme, Queen of the Esrac, smiled. Her long blood red hair and teal skin gave her a menacing look, and her fangs glistened like metallic points. "Surrender now, and I'll let you live."

Aurelia wiped a tear from her cheek as she shook her head. What was left to live for? Her family, friends, her beloved – all dead. She could sense it. Now the city had fallen. "You should know I'll never surrender, Esme," she hissed.

"I hoped you would say that."

Aurelia shot to her feet as Esme came at her.

The runes surrounding the gate—the very device she had created—flared to life, forming a glowing field of static around it. Fire flared in Aurelia's hand, and she hurled it at the Esrac Queen.

Esme stumbled backwards, falling into the glowing wall of energy. Her talons gripped the sides of the gate to prevent the magic from pulling her through.

"What are you doing?" Esme screamed.

"Sending you and all your kind to a realm where you'll never harm anyone again," Aurelia replied. "You will never escape the hell I'm sending you to. You made a big mistake coming here and waging war on my people."

She hurled another ball of glowing blue fire at the Esrac. She knew she'd made a mistake creating a doorway between the worlds. It was one that had cost so many people their lives, but she'd fix it. She might not have the power to destroy the Esrac, but she'd make sure they never hurt anyone else.

Esme's claws scraped against the sides of the gate as she fought to hang on. "You can't do this."

"I'm the one who first set foot in your world. I'm the reason the Esrac came here, I'll make damn sure you never come back."

Screeches rang out as, one by one, every Esrac was dragged through the gate. Esme still hung on to it, refusing to let go.

"You can't leave me locked up forever! My followers will wipe out every avatar in this world so there will be no one left to control the gates and keep me out. Your precious city of Arkadia is already falling. You may have won this battle, but you haven't won the war."

"Go ahead. I'll be there to stop you. Even death won't hold me." Aurelia shoved Esme through the gate, watching the runes turn dormant as she did.

Aurelia slumped back against the wall as she drew her final breaths, knowing she had performed her duty. Their world would be safe from the Esrac. For now, at least.

CHAPTER 1

Ella Noran pushed her long black hair off her face, smudging dirt over her cheek as the midday sun beat down on her. She brushed the dirt off and sighed. Digging by hand was tedious work, but it was the best method of finding potential artefacts, and far less invasive than using any tech. She had to find *something* to prove to Griffin it would be worth excavating the area. He insisted this part of the old city wouldn't be worth exploring, since scans had shown no potential artefacts. But she disagreed.

A faint whisper carried on the breeze came from behind her. She turned around, half expecting one of her team members to be there. No doubt Eric would try to play a practical joke on her again.

"Eric, if that's you, then stop it. This isn't funny!" she snapped.

No one there.

She frowned, certain she'd heard something, but shook her head. She didn't believe the multitude of legends that said the city held some kind of monster. Most of the teams who'd come here over the years had soon returned empty-handed, using wild stories to protect their reputations. But Ella wasn't superstitious like the rest of them. Those stories were almost as absurd as the rumours. Yet it had taken months to convince the Senate to agree to an expedition.

Glancing at her link, she saw she'd already been in her spot for over an hour and had found nothing but layers of dirt. It was already past noon, but she had a few more hours before heading back to the citadel for dinner with the rest of the team.

A low growl made her jump and scramble for her stunner. Its high voltage energy would deter any would-be assailants. Excavating the old city so close to the border where rebels lived had made everyone on the team uneasy, but she had felt bravest. Eric had stayed with her for a while before flying back to Celestus to get more supplies. He hadn't been happy about her digging on her own. He agreed that as long as she had a weapon with her, she could take care of herself. She doubted the rebels would be interested in an archaeology student digging through dirt, anyway. What possible use could she be to them?

It's just the wind, she told herself. *Stop being so on edge.*

She slipped the stunner into her belt. More whispering and the sound of chanting filled the air with words she couldn't understand, yet she found no one there.

What is going on?

Ella glanced around for her dust bunny, looking for the tell-tale signs of his snowy white fur.

"Fidget?" she called. "Fidget! Where have you wandered off to now?"

She knew he'd come back. He always did, but he always seemed to get up to mischief.

"Fidget, don't do anything stupid or you'll go back in your cage." The last thing she needed was for him to get stuck somewhere.

"Food?" chirped a voice. A pair of pointed ears appeared through the long grass, followed by the rest of the dust bunny.

Ella rolled her eyes and breathed a sigh of relief. "No, you're not having more food. I'm not wasting supplies on your never-ending appetite. We didn't come all this way for me to feed you all the time. If you're that hungry, go look for some food on your own."

His ears drooped, and he gave her his best 'but I'm starving' look.

"Come help me dig. We've got to find something useful to show Master Griffin, or he'll never take me seriously." She cursed as another strand of hair fell over her face before scooping it back behind her ear. "I need to prove this area is worth excavating."

As much as she wanted to find artefacts, she also hoped she'd find some trace of what had happened to her father here.

Fidget sat grooming his fluffy white coat, wagging his long tail behind him. Sometimes he helped, but dust bunnies had limited attention spans.

"I'll give you treats after," she promised. "Come on, just dig down a few feet for me. I need to know if there's something down here or not." She held up her scanner. There were signs of metal in the soil, but it didn't tell her what kind.

Fidget perked up at the sight and used his paws to burrow through the dirt. This was the place she kept seeing in her dreams. She knew it was insane. Still, she hadn't been able to shake off the feeling something important was hidden here, so she'd decided to investigate for herself.

Again, she found nothing but rocks and empty earth. Sighing, she rose, pushing her hair off her face again as loose strands escaped from the knot she'd tied it in. "Maybe I'm going mad letting dreams lead me here, but they felt so real. We've only been here a few days, and I still feel like there's something for me to find. Maybe excitement made me act on dreams about things that don't exist."

Ella knew following dreams seemed like complete madness, but she couldn't get this area out of her mind. She kept seeing another building in her recurring dream, but so far, the scans hadn't shown much.

She muttered a curse as Fidget started tossing stones everywhere. "Stop that!"

She made a grab for the dust bunny as he continued burrowing his way through the small trench.

A stone landed by her feet, but she ignored it. Maybe Griffin was right, and she should stop searching here, even though it had been home to their ancestors a thousand years earlier. Her theory about this being a potential hotspot for their excavation hadn't gone down well with him. He wanted to focus on what they could find in the citadel, which was still in good condition.

Ella glanced back to see its rising towers in the distance. Despite being abandoned and uninhabited for over a thousand years, its spires still reached toward the heavens and watched her like silent witnesses. It almost felt like the eyes of the ancestors were watching her every move.

Ella knelt as Fidget's white form disappeared beneath the earth. "Come out of there. I…"

She pulled out her maglight and pointed it down the hole. Something small glinted in the low light. She frowned as she picked up the object. A stone with a silver rune carved into it. It flashed as she rolled it between her fingers.

"Fidget, you did it! I can't believe you found something." She grinned and pulled more stones out of the hole. "Good boy, I'll give you a whole pack of treats later."

Ella turned on her keyno—a golden, orb-shaped device—to record everything as she examined each stone. It hovered above her head.

Fidget reappeared; his furry coat covered in dirt. He held a silver stone between his paws. This one looked to have a gold rune carved into it.

Oh, no! Ella groaned. Fidget loved shiny objects almost as much as he loved food.

"Fidget, give me that." She held out her hand.

"Mine," he squeaked.

"Yes, but won't you let me see it first?" Ella put her hand into the pocket of her tunic and pulled out some honey drops. "You can have these."

Fidget stared up at her with beady black eyes looking at the treats. "Mine," he said finally. He took off, his long tail dragging behind him.

"Fidget, come back!" Ella grabbed the other runes, shoving them into her bag and rushing after the dust bunny. The keyno whirled behind her, following like a silent companion. "Fidget!" she yelled, running downhill. She dropped her bag as she went, but didn't bother stopping to pick it up again. She'd collect it later.

The dust bunny proved too quick for her. They were hunters in their natural habitats and could move a lot faster than people.

Ella skidded downhill, almost tripping as earth fell away with each footfall. "Fidget, come back here. Please, you'll get lost."

She scanned the embankment, but found no sign of him anywhere. Sweat poured down her face from the heat of the midday sun. She sighed. It was pointless to keep chasing him. He'd reappear before she left. He always did, almost as if he could sense her movements.

A chortling sound made Ella turn to see Fidget waving the stone at her as he stood on the edge of the embankment. She had to get it. Unlike the other runes, that one looked like it had been made from pure gold. She didn't care about its monetary value, but it could prove historically priceless.

"Come here!"

She scrambled down the embankment. She'd get that stone, then head back to the citadel to show Master Griffin what she had found so far. Fidget waved again, then vanished from view with a yelp as he went down the embankment.

CHAPTER 2

"Mum said this animal would be the death of me. I should've listened to her," Ella muttered. "This is what I get for trying to turn him into a house pet!"

She ran, or at least tried to, before losing her footing on the loose earth. "Fidget!"

As Ella reached the edge of the cliff face, the ground beneath her fell away.

She screamed, falling through the air for several seconds, until she hit the edge of the cliff again. Rocks and brambles cut into her arms, legs, and face as she rolled down the embankment, making her cry out in pain. She tried to grab onto things as she descended, but kept losing her grip.

Ella yelped as she landed on the edge. A deep cavern filled with blackness loomed below. She winced, clutching her face as blood dripped down her cheek.

"La." Fidget appeared beside her; the stone still clutched in his front paw.

"What are you doing?" she grumbled and scrambled up. "It's going to—"

The earth beneath her feet gave way. She shrieked, clawing for something to hold on to. She fell through darkness for what seemed like forever until she finally landed hard on solid earth, and the air left her lungs.

Her head throbbed. Her face, arms, and legs all stung. Ella closed her eyes, wanting the nightmare to end.

Groaning, she rolled over onto her side, relieved she could still move all her limbs. Nothing seemed to be broken, and she managed to sit up without too much pain. Darkness surrounded her, so thick and heavy it felt like a living thing, watching her, waiting for her to do something.

She raised her hand. Light flared to life like tiny stars between her fingers as beautiful, coloured flames burst forth. Ella prayed her keyno wasn't hovering around. Magic wasn't supposed to exist here. Only people living on the other side of the border were supposed to possess it. It came from their strange pagan goddess.

Her father had always warned she couldn't show her gift to anyone. If they found out, her people wouldn't hesitate to put her to death, just as they did with anyone suspected of possessing magical talent. She never used the magic—not intentionally—but she'd always wondered where her strange power had come from. Part of her had hoped coming to the old city would provide answers.

She also hoped it might give her answers as to why, and how, her father disappeared ten years earlier. No one had ever been able to give her or her mother an explanation as to why he'd vanished without a trace. Legend stated that their ancestors had not only possessed magic, but used it for incredible things, like wandering into different realms. As much as she doubted it, she clung onto her hope something similar had happened to him, and he was still out there somewhere.

The fire rose higher from her hand, hovering above her and creeping through the blackness. Cuts and abrasions covered her arms. She noticed a deep slash on her shoulder, but it had clotted with blood and dirt. Her trousers were torn, too. She glanced around for signs of white fur. Her heart skipped a beat as she began to panic. What if he'd been hurt?

"Fidget!" Her voice echoed through the darkness, and she moved the flames lower to examine the dark earth surrounding her. Finally, she spotted Fidget sitting a few feet away. He chortled and waved, scurrying over to her. Dirt and bits of bramble clung to him, but he appeared unharmed.

Ella breathed a sigh of relief, but admonished him. "Fine mess you've gotten us into!"

She used her light to scan the space, but saw nothing but blackness. Too thick for the flames to penetrate. Rocks covered the ground, and she looked up to see how far they had fallen. As she stared, faint slivers of sunlight crept down through the darkness.

Fallen earth and pieces of trees covered the steep cliff face, and there was nothing but sheer hard rock all the way up.

"Too bad my magic can't help us," she grumbled as she tore off a piece of her tunic, tying it around her arm as best as she could. "How are we gonna get out of here? Really, Fidget, why do you have to be such a…"

Her voice trailed off as dread washed over her at the thought of being swallowed further into the darkness. Something inside her warned her to stay put, but she knew she had to find a way out.

Ella twisted her link and tried to engage a call. "Eric, are you there? Luc, come in. Please, if you guys can hear me, answer." Despite their recent break up and her desire to stay away from him, she'd have been glad to talk to Luc now. Even if it meant hearing him lecture about being so reckless.

She waited, but only static greeted her. She guessed she was either too far underground for the call to work or she'd damaged the link during her fall. She twisted the device again. After a few more attempts, the link's light finally engaged as a thin blue glow emanated from her wrist. It didn't do much to cut the darkness, but the light gave her a little more comfort. Now that her eyes had adjusted, she could just make out the outline of a large cavern a few feet in front of her.

Ella moved along, careful not to trip on any fallen debris. Fidget scurried alongside her. She expected to find an empty void filled with nothing but rocks and dirt, but up ahead she spotted something white glistening in the darkness. Goosebumps covered her arms as she approached.

Odd, she thought, but she didn't believe in omens or superstitious nonsense.

She pressed her link a few more times to increase the intensity of the beam. Rubbing away at the stone of the cavern with her fingers. Whiteness appeared underneath the dirt. She couldn't be certain, but it looked exactly like the stone used back at the castle. Maybe this section had fallen away and become buried at some point in the last thousand years?

Ella felt a rush of excitement. Maybe she'd found what she'd been looking for. Cursing the fact that she didn't have any tools with her, she continued to rub away at the dirt, praying she wouldn't damage anything by using her bare, bloodied hands. As she ran her fingers along the stone further up, she felt odd shapes.

Something glittered in the low light, reflecting in the orbs of her floating fire. She realised more runes were etched along the walls as she shone her light closer. They were just like the ones she'd found outside.

"I take back everything I said. Well done, Fidget!"

Ella moved further along the wall, using her fingers to trace every shape. The runes vanished, revealing a gap and a door that seemed to block it. She brought her fire down closer and saw that it was indeed a stone doorway, yet there seemed to be no sign of a handle.

Something gold glistened in the low light at the edges of her vision. She turned to find her keyno on the floor and grabbed it, relieved to find it still working. She checked to make sure it wasn't recording before stowing it away. The last thing she needed to worry about was having to explain how she conjured floating fire.

"Fidget, this is incredible. I wonder what this place was?"

She rubbed her hands together, feeling a rush of excitement, and examined the doorway. Trying to find an opening, but found nothing. Next, she ran her hands along the other side of the wall, touching each of the runes one by one. As she touched the last rune in the first row, something hissed and vibrated. With a loud groan, the door swung open. Ella coughed as a wave of dust swirled around her.

She called her fire closer, so she could examine the space inside. Art had been carved along the walls, depicting various people accompanied by strange symbols that she had seen before in the old city. She and her friend Sam, the historian on their expedition, were still trying to figure out what they were, hoping to use them to decipher the written language of the ancients. Ella knew they were close to making a breakthrough. As she scanned the other walls, she noticed more people who she guessed were the ancestors. Some looked as though they had green skin, but others had pale white skin and wore long, flowing robes. The green-skinned people seemed to have large, ominous teeth. That made her shudder, but she shook off the feeling. None of the images she had uncovered in other parts of the city had depicted anything like this, preferring instead to focus on the ancestors' way of life and the deeds they had done.

Ella fumbled with her keyno, relieved when its bright white light broke through the darkened room. The darkness seemed somehow thinner here than the heavy shroud that had surrounded her outside.

"I can't wait to start researching. I knew there was more down here. I just knew it!"

Examining the floor further, she found the bones of what appeared to be a woman, judging by the size and shape of the skull. Another body lay nearby. She suspected there may be more. Something bad had happened here.

She couldn't wait to test the bones back in her lab. Having actual remains of the ancestors was a dream come true for someone as obsessed with her heritage as she was, and even Master Griffin would be impressed.

"La, home," Fidget squeaked as he followed her in. "La and Fidget go home." He wrapped his tail around her foot and clung to her leg, frightened.

Ella frowned down at him, surprised by his fear. He never seemed afraid of anything. "I'm trying. We need to find a way out that doesn't involve trying to climb up the cliff."

She moved through the room, checking the walls as she went. With a flick of her hand, she made her fire bigger and brighter, but kept it away from the keyno's line of sight.

Fidget's fur slicked back and his tail raised. His eyes turned bright blue as he went into defence mode and hissed a warning, "Bad."

Ella ignored him and waved a hand, spotting what looked like an archway carved into the back wall. Runes were etched around it, and a circle with a wavy line through the centre had been carved above.

On closer inspection, there was no gap for entry, let alone a handle.

A door that led nowhere?

"This is incredible," Ella breathed. "I wonder what the ancients used it for. Maybe—"

"Bad," Fidget hissed again, louder this time. "Home."

"Soon. Maybe this thing is a transportation device to help us get above ground," she mused, moving closer to the wall. Had it been used for decoration or ceremony?

White fur blurred in front of her as Fidget stood in her way and growled.

Ella drew back, alarmed. She'd never seen him act like this before. "What is wrong with you?" She put her hands on her hips, frowning. "You know not to interfere when I'm working."

She moved past him, and the runes glowed brighter as she touched the wall.

"Bad, bad, bad," Fidget repeated, tugging at her trouser leg with his tiny paw.

"Ella?" a voice called. Seconds later, the figure of a man appeared.

"Who…Who are you?" Ella gasped.

The man's form wavered, making it almost impossible for her to see what he looked like.

"Help me!" The man reached a hand out. "Please, I'm dying."

Ella tried to see through the swirling golden light that surrounded him and stumbled. She reached her hand out to touch the glowing wall, and static jolted through her, first shooting up her arm, then flinging her across the chamber. An image of a dark-haired woman crying flashed through her mind. She hit the ground hard, her head knocking against the wall.

Ella winced, clutching her head as she sat up.

What was that?

She looked up, but her vision started to waver.

A blur of darkness emerged from the archway, which glowed with golden light again. Glittering emerald eyes stared at her, and Ella caught a glimpse of long white hair. Fidget hissed at the shape, his fur slicking back as he growled in warning.

She screamed as the blur drew closer and threw a glowing ball of purple fire at it. The creature growled and vanished in a flash of light. As darkness dragged her under, Ella thought she heard the whisper of voices and a chorus of low growls before everything went black.

CHAPTER 3

Something dragged her from the depths of her centuries long hibernation. Blackness wrapped around her like a blanket that offered no warmth or comfort. What had woken her? What had interrupted her slumber?

She tried to rise, but her limbs felt stiff and weak when she attempted to use them. Hunger gnawed, so harsh and deep it seemed to rip through her stomach. It was all she could think about; all she could feel. Her body was tightly cocooned in dark and sticky fibres, rendering her as helpless as a child tucked away in their mother's womb. Long, vine-like tendrils were attached to her hands, trailing away as they connected to the rest of the pod. She shoved them away in disgust, pulling her hands free.

She tried to focus, to remember where she was. Her pod, she remembered, the structure that had kept her nourished and secure for all these years. She shook her head, trying and failing to recall why she had chosen to be in here. How long had it been? Why couldn't she move?

It took a moment for her thoughts to clear. *Esme*, yes. That was her name. She ran a hand over her chest, feeling an echo of pain where something had struck her, the near fatal injury that had forced her into her pod. Esme shook her head. That injury had been a long time ago—*lifetimes* ago—yet the pain of it still echoed through her body.

It does not matter, she told herself. *I am safe now.*

Her stomach panged with hunger again, and she looked around her impatiently.

Where were her helmsmen? Why hadn't anyone brought sustenance for her yet? Had the fools forgotten?

She needed nourishment, strength. The blood in her veins felt just as stale as the dryness in her throat. When she opened her mouth to call out, only a low growl came out.

Damn it!

She needed to feed. She needed blood. She used her claws to rip through the fleshy surface of her pod, yanking it open until a large enough hole formed for her to crawl out of.

Esme landed on the floor in a heap, muttering curses. Around her stood walls of dark stone, and cold, hard earth lay beneath her. Her breath misted before her eyes, but the cold didn't bother her. On her hands and knees, Esme crawled across the ground. Someone would pay for not being there to greet her. She was their queen, for goodness' sake! How dare they leave her to wake up alone without any blood?

As she crawled on, a knot of dread began to form in the pit of her stomach. This shouldn't have happened. She shouldn't have woken yet. She had programmed the pod to wake her when it was time to leave this place, when her helmsmen had found a way out of this hell realm. Getting to her feet to stagger into the passageway, she dug her claws into the wall for support. Her helmsmen lay in their pods, still deep in hibernation. Each male lay in a black pod with its tendrils connected to them, keeping them alive just as her own pod had done.

Ripping off one of the lids, she placed her hand on the chest of one man and gasped as she drained the blood out of him, feeling some warmth flooding back through her cold veins. It didn't feel as good as feeding from someone warm and living, but some of her strength returned.

The male's body disintegrated to dust.

Esme straightened, able to move freely now. Flashes of awareness returned as the blood flowed inside her. Someone had opened the gate. At first, she thought herself to be dreaming—it could be difficult to distinguish between a dream and pod slumber—but no, she'd felt it.

For the first time in a thousand years, the doorway, her only escape from the hell she'd been forced into, had finally opened. She ran through the corridor until she reached the gate room. The runes on the wall still glowed with light as she approached. She threw herself at the gate, screaming when a blast of energy repelled her, sending pain through her every nerve ending.

"No!" Esme cried. "No! Let me pass!"

She scraped her claws along the runes, written in the language of the Arkadians who had cursed her and her brethren to spend eternity in this prison. She had to get free. Then would she have her revenge on the people who had sent her here. She didn't know how much time she and her brethren had spent hibernating in this awful place. Their pods nourished and maintained their bodies, keeping them alive through long centuries of sleep.

Esme cursed, trying once again to break through, but still the wards held in place. She couldn't pass through the gate unless an avatar opened it for her. One of them must have been out there to open it.

She raised her hand, trying to tap into the gate's power. The ancients may have stopped her from going through it, but she could still see what lay on the other side. If one of her men had gone through, maybe she'd still be able to see him. If he had caught the one who opened the gate, she'd take great pleasure in watching him torture the avatar. All the Arkadians deserved to pay for what Aurelia had done.

The gate clouded over, shimmering like a mirror. Beyond lay a darkened room. A young woman with a mass of long curly black hair stood there, her face and body marred by blood and scratches. Esme's fangs and barbed hand ached to reach out and drain the woman dry.

But it wasn't the woman's blood that caught her attention. She *knew* this woman and recognised the pale skin and dark eyes of the one who had cursed her to this realm.

Aurelia.

Her hands clenched, black blood seeping out as her claws dug into her palms. She screamed, cursing the woman's name.

How could it be her? She should have died centuries ago. Even the Arkadian avatars couldn't survive like her brethren could.

The woman breathed a sigh of relief. "I think that thing's gone, whatever it was," she said. "By the ancestors, what have I done? Master Griffin will kill me when he finds out. What am I going to do, Fidge?"

Esme frowned. This one seemed nothing like the avatar she knew. She'd never seen Aurelia whimper like a child and couldn't understand it. The woman looked the spitting image of the avatar Esme despised. Esme continued watching her moving around and talking to a strange white animal with pointed ears.

Not Aurelia, someone else. But why does she look like her? Still, she has to be an avatar to have opened the gate.

The woman picked up a gold shaped ball at her feet. "Fidget, we've got to find a way out of here." She glanced toward the gate, almost as if she could see Esme watching her from the other side.

Esme raised her hand, trying to use her weakened senses to discover how powerful this girl was. She sensed the woman possessed the same raw power as Aurelia and the Arkadians, but based on her childish naivety, Esme doubted she knew how to use it.

Her lips curled into a glistening smile. *An avatar with no idea how to use her power or protect herself!*

Esme couldn't have hoped for a better opportunity. This was what she had been waiting for. The centuries of sleep hadn't been in vain. The time had finally come for her to get revenge on the avatars, as well as on the Arkadians and the Valan who had helped imprison the Esrac here. All of them would pay for what they'd done to her people. It was their turn to suffer, and she'd make sure their agony lasted longer than a few painful moments before death. She'd bring them to the brink of death but revive them over and over until they begged her for mercy.

One way or another, you will free me from this prison, Aurelia. I will have my revenge on you and your people. I won't stop until I've drained you all dry.

CHAPTER 4

Luc was pulled out of his meditation, yanked away from the peace and serenity that came with it as alarm bells went off inside his mind. After being awake half the night helping his teammate, Eric, and Master Griffin move rocks out of the way, he'd hoped to have a couple of hours of relaxation before he went to sleep. Meditation could be just as rejuvenating, he'd learned from long nights when sleep had proved impossible, if not even more so.

He stood up, glancing around the whitewashed walls of his chamber, and gasped as realisation dawned. One of the gates had been opened. He'd felt it, like being jolted from a deep sleep.

He pulled on a shirt as he raced from his room and headed down the hall toward the chamber where Master Griffin had set up his office. He stopped midway as a chill ran across his senses, and dread overtook him.

No, this can't be happening. It couldn't.

Pushing the feeling aside, he ran faster and pushed the door to Griffin's chamber open. Piles of books and paperwork were scattered across the desk. Another table contained rocks and other artefacts they'd found in their expedition so far. No sign of Master Griffin himself.

Luc muttered a curse, running a hand through his short, dark hair. He hurried back down the hall, taking the lift to another part of the castle. The ancient mechanisms groaned as they lifted him up to the next floor. Despite Eric's assurances, Luc still felt uneasy using it, but he didn't have time to search every part of the castle on foot. He ran through the empty corridors of the castle, checking each room as he went. Griffin had mentioned wanting to explore the third floor of the citadel when the team had breakfast together that morning, so there was a good chance he'd be there.

Luc gasped for breath when he reached the double doors on the third floor. He pushed the doors open, and Sam's eyes narrowed as he came in. With her short blonde hair and piercing blue eyes, she looked nothing like the librarian she was.

"Is there something you wanted, Luc?"

She gave him an annoyed look. He knew she hated it when he interrupted her time with Master Griffin. Sara worshipped the ground the man walked on and was eager to learn everything she could from him. Working alone with him was her life's dream come true.

"Master Griffin, I need to talk to you. It's urgent," he puffed.

Griffin, scratching his head of shocking white hair, rose from where he had been sat on the floor holding his scanner. He wore his dark blue university robe and had deep creases around his eyes. "Luc, I thought you were taking a few hours off. Is something wrong?" Griffin pushed his glasses up to the bridge of his nose. "Is it Ella? I haven't seen her since breakfast this morning."

"You know, Ella, she loves to go off and do her own thing," Sara remarked.

Luc had no idea where Ella was, nor did he have time to worry about her just now. He had to talk to Griffin, then go and find out what happened to the gate.

"Master, I need to speak with you—in private." Luc glanced over at Sam, who gave him a disapproving look. "It's urgent."

Griffin sighed, set his scanner on the table, and followed him into the hall. "What is it?"

"One of the gates has been opened." Luc hissed. He glanced around, half expecting Sara to have followed them, or Ella to appear, though she would no doubt be off exploring some remote part of the city. His heart twisted just thinking of her. It had been hard enough coming on this expedition after their recent breakup.

Griffin took his arm, leading him back to his office and not saying anything until he closed the door behind them. "You're sure?"

Luc nodded. "I felt it, and I think something came through."

As one of the Valan, he could sense the presence of the Esrac—the age-old enemy of his people.

Griffin rubbed his stubbled chin. "That's impossible. The gate was sealed centuries ago, and there hasn't been an avatar born in almost fifty years. How could anyone have opened the gate?"

"Maybe there is one out there. There must be." Since the avatars had designed the gate to act as a transportation device, only someone with the power of an avatar could open it.

"Then who is it?" Griffin demanded. "I've searched the descendants of the ancients for almost years. The last known avatar died decades ago, and no one since then has shown signs of such magic. No Valan has sensed anyone with the potential to be an avatar, either."

"Does it matter? If one of the Esrac came through, we must find and kill it." Luc's adrenaline flowed in anticipation. The one thing he trained for his whole life had happened.

"Esrac aren't easy to kill, you know that." Griffin sighed. "I'll—"

"I'll go to the second gate and see what I can find," he said. Griffin opened his mouth to protest, but Luc cut him off. "I can handle this, Master. I've been preparing for it my whole life. You'll be safer here, and we need to make sure the others don't notice anything." He glanced behind him. "Do you know where Eric is?"

"He flew back to Celestus to get more supplies and equipment. I don't expect him back for at least another hour." Griffin glanced at his link. "Sara will stay here with me; Eric should be safe enough. You must contain the situation quickly, Luc. We can't afford to have anyone finding out about the Esrac."

Luc nodded. He knew the importance of containment better than anyone, he'd find any Esrac who'd come through. He didn't know who the avatar might be, but he'd worry about that problem later. Finding and killing the Esrac was much more important.

"Do you know where Ella is excavating?" Luc asked. It would help if he knew where everyone was when he searched for the Esrac. If the Esrac fed on one person, they would be much harder to kill.

"She said she was going to have a look around the lower part of the citadel, but knowing her, she could be anywhere." Griffin pushed his glasses back onto the bridge of his nose. "I'll keep trying her on the link, don't waste time looking for her. Your first priority is to kill any Esrac and ensure that the gate is still sealed."

Luc pressed the button on his link. Despite Griffin's assurances, he had to know his teammate was safe. "Eric, where are you? Is Ella with you?"

"Jeez, I've only been gone a couple of hours!" Eric said. "You haven't broken something already, have you? I sometimes wonder how you people manage to survive without me."

Luc rolled his eyes. "Just tell me where you are."

"I'm flying over the citadel now. I'll be inside in a few minutes."

"Good, I need a lift. Hurry back." Luc disengaged the call and pressed the link again. "Ella, are you there?"

This time, static greeted him.

Damn, why does she never answer her link? That girl might have a brilliant mind, but she has no concept of time or safety.

She often got herself into trouble through wandering off without telling anyone, and Luc sometimes wondered why Griffin tolerated such behaviour.

"We'll fly out to where the gate is buried. Don't worry, I'll make sure Eric flies straight back after he drops me off," Luc told Master Griffin.

Master Griffin shook his head. "Have Eric go and search for her first. If something came through that gate, she might be in danger."

"I will." Luc nodded. "I'll make sure he doesn't stay close to the area near the gate. The last thing we need is for them to find out about it and what may come through it."

"You're to tell no one of this, are we clear, Luc?" Griffin warned. "Don't you dare let the others stumble across it. Secrecy is just as important as hunting down and killing the Esrac. If anyone finds out about this, we'll both be killed."

"I won't." He bowed his head and hurrying away.

Returning to his room, he gathered a pack and filled it with supplies. He slipped his sword into its holster, making sure it was concealed underneath his jacket.

Time to face an ancient evil that hasn't walked this world for over a thousand years.

Luc hurried down to the courtyard, where he found Eric waiting in his Pegasus, a small aircraft capable of carrying up to four people. It was cylindrical with an angled front and rear, metallic silver, and had two retractable thrusters that helped it to fly. He crossed the grass to the side of the craft and sat down in the front passenger seat.

He pressed his link, trying to call Ella again, but she still didn't answer. He sent her a voice message instead, telling her to stay within the city walls and to get to the third floor of the citadel to see Master

Griffin as soon as she could. A mixture of fear and annoyance gripped him. He didn't have time to go looking for her.

"You haven't seen Ella anywhere, have you?" He glanced over at Eric. "Did she tell you where she was going this morning?"

Eric shrugged and shook his head, his numerous earrings jangling as he did so. "Nope, I haven't seen her. You know what she's like."

The engines whirred to life with a faint hum as Luc let out an exasperated sigh.

"So where are we headed?" Eric asked as he brought the Pegasus's system online. "I'm surprised you called. I thought you'd want me to unload the supplies first."

Luc keyed in the coordinates himself, careful not to let on how urgent the situation was. "I don't know how long I'll be there, so just drop me off and I'll call you when I need to fly back."

Eric frowned as he glanced at the screen. "That's close to the border. Why would you want to risk going there? You could be attacked by rebels."

Luc didn't give a damn about the rebels, they were no threat to him. The rest of the Republic might consider the people who lay beyond their borders as dangerous, but Luc didn't agree. The worshippers of the Arkadian goddess, who still believed in magic and the ways of the ancestors resided there, refugees from the modern, anti-magic society of Aldden, which had chosen to shun their past. Even the Valan had been forced into hiding after a century of keeping the peace.

"I can take care of myself. I have to run an errand for Master Griffin."

Luc ran through the plan as the craft took off. He'd get there, check to make sure the gate remained sealed, and survey the area to find out what had come through. He had to make sure whatever it was didn't have the chance to harm anyone.

He watched Eric weave through the streets, his green eyes scanning the landscape even as his long blonde hair fell in front of them. His bright clothes almost made Luc's eyes ache. "You know the area?" Luc observed.

"You'd be surprised at some of the places I have to fly to when I'm working," Eric remarked, guiding the ship over the spiralling stone towers of ancient Arkadia. "If you're scavenging at this hour, it must be to find something interesting. Shouldn't you be off shift now?"

"I told you, I'm taking care of something for Master Griffin." Luc crossed his arms and leaned back in his seat. "That's all you need to know."

"Ah, top-secret crap, I get you. Listen, about Ella, she is—"

"It's over between Ella and I," Luc said firmly. "We broke up weeks ago."

He didn't want to talk about Ella any further, so he pulled out a small leather-bound notebook filled with information about the Valan's old enemy—everything Master Griffin had taught him about them, anyway. He'd never fought a real Esrac before. He scanned the book, checking to see if they had any weaknesses that he might have forgotten about. He knew he had to avoid their hands, since their touch could drain the life out of anyone. After they fed, they became stronger and much harder to kill.

He'd have to be focused, ready, and clear minded when he faced his first Esrac. He couldn't believe their age-old enemy had come back into their realm. The ancestors had banished them in an effort to prevent them from ever hurting humanity again. By sealing them in another realm and locking down the gate, they had thought the threat had ended once and for all, but Luc and the other Valan knights had always known they would come back sooner or later. No realm was strong enough to hold Esme, the Esrac Queen, forever, and when she broke free, she would want her revenge on them for almost killing and then banishing her.

Luc stayed silent for the rest of the flight, lost in his thoughts as he tried to come up with the best plan if he faced one. It took a few minutes to get from one side of the ancient city to the other, but to Luc it felt like an eternity.

As they neared the destination, Eric continued his interrogation.

"What are you looking for in here? Did Ella find something?"

Luc frowned. Eric knew better than to be nosy. Although they'd known each other for a few months, they weren't friends, and this was their first excavation together. Eric had come along with Griffin as the engineer and pilot, while Luc had come as their military support. Although he was a member of Celestus' troopers, he had been temporarily relieved to come along on the expedition and make sure the others stayed safe. The excavation was taking place close to the border, which the rebels had been known to cross over to attack those on the other side. Although they were technically in peacetime, it was only a matter of time before the Chancellor declared war on the rebels again and try to eradicate them. Luc pitied them. They were fighting for a better future, a chance to use the gifts the goddess had given them.

"Just looking around." Luc glanced out of the window as the canopy of trees they were passing over ended in a clearing and found himself straining to scan it. Down there might be an enemy, he was one of the few capable of fighting. There were only a few of the Valan left now the Republic had enforced laws forbidding the use and teaching of magic. Both the law and the reduced population made it much harder for elders to train potential knights in the old ways.

"For what? Maybe I could help," Eric suggested.

Luc's eyes narrowed. Eric was good at fixing things, and not much else. The archaeological side didn't interest him like it did Sara, Ella, and Master Griffin. He would be of no use, and the risk of him seeing the gate was too much for Luc to even consider his help.

"You need to get back to the city, unload the supplies, and keep an eye on the others."

Eric shrugged. "I've got time; it would do me good to get some fresh air."

"I can manage. You'd only slow me down." Luc drummed his fingers on the armrest and tried not to let his impatience show. He needed to get down there and start looking around, not have to worry about what the others were doing. He couldn't afford to have them at risk as well.

Eric paused. "It's in the middle of nowhere. You could get lost or hurt. Anyway, Master Griffin doesn't want us going out this far, part of the city has fallen away in this area."

Luc tried not to sigh. He didn't have time to waste arguing.

"Just bring the ship down so I can be on my way."

Eric swung the ship around and peered down, looking at something.

"What are you looking at?" Luc asked, unclipping his belt and rising to look out the window too. Below, steep hills and fields stretched out before them, but nothing appeared out of place, and there was no sign of any Esrac or anyone else around. His heartbeat slowing again, Luc let out a terse huff.

"I don't want to damage my ship," Eric said defensively. "You might be able to come and go as you please, but I don't have that luxury. My chief will have my head if I crash it."

"Just land anywhere, I'm sure Master Griffin will cover any damages you might sustain."

"So, it *is* important then?" Eric raised his eyebrows.

Luc crossed his arms. "Why are you stalling me? You need to get back to the city and drop off the supplies. Go looking for Ella while you're at it."

Eric shrugged. "Why aren't you looking for Ella? I know the two of you broke up, but aren't you the least bit worried about her?"

"You are trying to stop me from going out there. Why?" He gave the engineer a hard look. "Of course I'm worried about her, but I have something more important to take care of first."

Eric avoided his gaze, saying nothing.

Luc moved to the console and scrolled through the ship's recorded flights.

"Hey!" Eric snapped. "You can't be touching those." He tried to shove Luc out of the way, but Luc held firm.

He scanned the data and spotted an unscheduled visit a few hours earlier. "Who did you bring here?" he demanded.

Eric shook his head. "No one. I just..."

"You're a lousy liar. You'd never come here for anyone except—" He ran a hand through his hair. "Ella. She's out here, isn't she? On an unsanctioned dig too, no doubt."

It was just like her to wander off and do her own thing, even though she knew the dangers of being so close to the rebel border. What she didn't know was there were countless other unknown dangers out there, too. One's people weren't supposed to know about.

Eric's jaw tightened. "There's no harm in her looking around. She had a stunner with her. She can take care of herself."

Not unless she's the one who opened the gates. By the ancestors, why did it have to be her?

"Land. Now," he ordered. "If something happened to her, I'll —" His fists clenched.

Eric guided the ship to the ground, landing it with a thud that suggested he had forgotten all about potential damage.

"What do you mean?" he demanded. "Is Ella in trouble?"

"Stay here and be ready in case we have to make a quick getaway."

Without another word, Luc shoved the door open and hurried out into the unknown.

CHAPTER 5

Ella opened her eyes, reeling. She'd attempted to climb out of the chamber, only to fall from the wall soon after. She'd been desperate to get away from that strange doorway in case anything else came through it.

Okay, climbing walls isn't a great idea.

She scrambled up, rubbing her injured shoulder. Her excitement about the incredible find had long vanished. Glancing around, she saw no sign of the glowing emerald-eyed monster she'd seen earlier. Fidget had stopped hissing, and his fur had returned to normal, which meant the monster had to have found a way out. "Fidge, that monster has gone, hasn't it?"

"Gone," Fidget said and scurried off.

Ella's eyes widened. She hadn't expected him to understand what she meant. Dust bunnies only had limited vocabulary. It confirmed her suspicion Fidget was a lot cleverer than he let on.

She checked her link, but the device still refused to engage. Typical. She'd hoped to call Eric for help, or even one of the others. It might be embarrassing to admit she'd gone off without permission and gotten herself into trouble, but at least she would have helped to get her out.

She twisted the link again. "Eric, are you there? Anyone? Come in, please."

She waited, but heard the hiss of static. She sighed, then twisted the link for a third time and gritted her teeth.

"Luc, are you there?" She didn't want to talk to him, but she didn't have any other choice. Even his help would be better than being stuck down here with that strange doorway and the monsters it housed. "Master Griffin? Sam?"

More static.

Glancing back at the now dormant doorway, she shuddered, not wanting to go near it again. It wouldn't make a very good means of escape either, since she had no idea where it led. For all she knew, she could end up surrounded by more of those monsters.

She thought back to the drawings she'd seen earlier of green skinned people. Maybe that drawing had been put there to tell people to stay away?

Master Griffin's warnings about never touching ancient devices flashed her through her mind now.

Guess I should have listened to him.

Yet the strange doorway had called to her. She doubted she could have ignored it, even if she tried.

Maybe Master Griffin had been right about her curiosity getting her into trouble. She always let her excitement over finding something potentially incredible get in the way of her better judgement.

"There must be another way out of here. The ancestors wouldn't have created one chamber to have no means of getting out again."

She ran a hand through her hair. This place looked intact, and she hoped there would be an exit she could access. Other than the strange doorway, she'd found nothing but walls with no other entry points. Going back through the doorway she'd fallen in front of didn't seem like an option either.

"Home," Fidget chirped.

She glanced over at him, standing in a golden circle on the floor. Whatever had come through the doorway must've used something to get out, unless it had somehow managed to jump fifty feet up a steep cliff face.

Ella paced, trying to come up with something else.

Eric and the others would realise she'd vanished sooner or later, and would come looking for her. But how long would that take? She was a long way from where she'd left her gear. It could take hours for them to locate her. She hated the idea of being stuck down here for days on end. She had no supplies and doubted even Fidget would be able to scurry back up the cliff face.

"Home," Fidget repeated and stamped his foot.

Sighing, she walked over to him. Examining the circle earlier hadn't revealed any indication of what it did. It could be decorative, for all she knew. Maybe it was a ceremonial tool used during the ancestors' rituals to their mother goddess?

Kneeling, she ran her hand over the cool metal, which held no sign of any runes.

"Fidget, I don't know what this is."

"Home, home." Fidget said again, jumping up and down on the platform.

Ella glanced back at the strange doorway and shivered as goosebumps crept over her arms. Weird, it almost felt like someone was watching her every move. Could there be someone else on the other side? She guessed it was possible, given that someone had come through earlier. How many more monsters were there, and where had they come from?

Ella brought her fire down from where it had been following above her head as she examined the wall next to them. On it sat two square crystals, one red, one green. *Almost like buttons…*

"Hmm."

She frowned. *Could this be a way of getting out?*

"Worth a try. Fidget, come here."

She patted her uninjured shoulder, and he scurried up her arm before settling, his tail wrapped around her neck like a scarf. She gripped her keyno and pressed the red crystal.

Nothing happened.

She tried the other crystal, but still nothing happened. Ella shook her head, wondering why she was doing this. Fidget might be good at sensing danger, but she doubted he could find them a way out of there.

Maybe they didn't work anymore? Frowning, she tried pressing both crystals.

Nothing.

"Home, La." Fidget tapped her cheek with his paw.

"I'm trying," Ella grumbled.

She stepped into the circle, pressing the green crystal again.

Three giant gold rings shot up out of the floor, flashing with blinding white light. Her head spun, and breath caught in her throat as she felt her body float upwards. All before she had time to consider what was happening. Her stomach flip-flopped as she reappeared above ground and the rings fell from around her, disappearing back into the earth. Ella sank to her knees, putting her hands out in front of her and touching the warm, hard ground. Bile rose in the back of her throat, but she gulped it back down again. Fidget jumped off her shoulder and rubbed against her arm as if to reassure her.

Laughing, she ruffled Fidget's fur. "Good boy, I'm sorry I ever doubted you. I owe you a whole bag of treats when we get back to the castle."

Touching her link, she said, "Eric, I need a lift back to the castle. How soon can you get here?"

"I'm already here," Eric replied.

"Great, I'll just get my gear—"

"Luc is here too; he's looking for you. Are you okay?"

"I… Luc?"

What was he doing here? He was the last person she wanted to see.

"Something about doing something for Griffin," Eric replied. "He said you were in trouble. I've got your location on my link, I'll be there in a few minutes."

Not bothering to reply, Ella raced off toward the site where she'd begun her excavation, her dust bunny scurrying alongside her as she ran. She'd grab her gear, then come up with some excuse. She knew she couldn't tell anyone about the strange creature she'd seen, not until she got back to the city and had time to do some research, at least.

Griffin had bought a comp unit with him, so she would have access to the archives and databases back at the University in Celestus. She'd figure out what it was first, and then deal with the creature on her own. She'd be in enough trouble already for doing an unsanctioned excavation. She wasn't about to let the others help and find out about her magic. If they did, she had no idea what they might do. Griffin was the head of the university and a member of the Senate—the very people who hunted and killed magic users.

Shaking her head to bring herself out of her thoughts, Ella watched the landscape for signs of the others. She didn't want to see Luc under any circumstances, as things had been awkward between them since she'd ended the relationship. She'd been sick of the way he always seemed so distant and secretive with her, but she needed to get back to the city fast. If she had to travel with him, so be it.

She scrambled up the hill, heart pounding as she went.

Finally, her fallen gear came into view. Glancing around to make sure no one else could see her, she raised her hand. Her pack, scanner and other items all floated into the air at her command, hovering there. She could only move small objects, but it did come in handy sometimes. *In,* she thought. All the items shot inside her pack, then the bag flew into her arms.

At least magic is good for something.

It didn't take her long to find the Pegasus. To her relief, she only saw Eric on board.

"What the hell happened to you?" Eric called as he opened the door for her. "You look awful. You're bleeding."

"I fell and rolled down a cliff, but I'm fine," she insisted. "Where's Luc?"

"Out looking for you. Guess he was right about you being in trouble." Eric pulled out a med kit. "Here, let me—"

Ella spun around as a familiar chill went down her spine. The same chill she'd felt when that creature had appeared.

Luc!

The creature could attack him, and she had no idea what it was capable of.

"Fidget, stay here." She turned and jumped from the ship without bothering to unfold the ramp, racing back toward the cliff where she'd fallen. He must have come here either for that strange doorway or the creature that had come through it. She engaged her link and tried calling him, but he didn't reply.

She opened her mouth to call out for him, then stopped.

The thing was nearby. She could feel it. The same coldness she'd felt back in the underground room crept over her again.

Luc, where are you?

She closed her eyes, trying to feel his location. She's always been able to sense him, whether it was magic or because they had once been emotionally involved. She didn't know. She felt his presence close by, coming toward her.

"Ella?"

She froze at the sound of his voice, then opened her eyes. Seeing him again made her both relieved and annoyed. With his short dark hair, athletic body, and piercing grey eyes, he looked every inch the warrior. Her heart still skipped a beat whenever she saw him—something she hated. She didn't want to feel anything for him anymore, didn't want to think about what they could have been to each other.

"Ella, what did you do?" Luc glared at her.

Ella crossed her arms. "Hello to you too."

She couldn't believe it. Here she was worried about him, and he didn't seem the least bit happy to see her!

"You're bleeding." He reached out to touch her cheek, but she backed away. Letting him touch her would make things more awkward between them.

"I'm fine. It's just a few scratches. Why are you here?" she retorted, pretending she didn't know the reason.

"What did you do?" he repeated.

"I came to look for ancient artefacts, but I didn't find anything." Her heart started pounding in her ears. What would he do when he found out what she'd done? Would he and the rest of the team turn her in if they found out she possessed magic?

"What about your injuries?" Luc ran his hand down her arm, examining the cuts and scrapes that crisscrossed it.

"I fell, that's all," she snapped, shoving him away with her good arm.

His expression darkened. "This is serious. You need to tell me what happened."

"Why do you care? I'm not important to you, remember?"

He took a step closer. "You know that's not true. Please tell me."

Ella hesitated. Part of her wanted to tell him everything, about what had happened, the strange doorway, and the green-skinned monster. Another part of her just wanted to get back to the citadel, find a way to stop it, then pretend this nightmare had never happened.

A shiver came over her again, and Luc spun around, frowning. "Ella, get back to the ship and stay there."

"But—"

"Go!" Luc barked. "Now! You need to get out of here before the Esrac sees you."

Ella didn't budge. She'd let that thing through, so she'd deal with it.

Esrac? Is that what the creature is called? If so, how does Luc know? Probably another one of his secrets.

A man—or what almost resembled a man—broke through the treeline. He had green skin, long white hair, and teeth that glistened like silver. His dark eyes flashed emerald.

Ella realised this must be the creature that had come through the doorway earlier. It looked almost humanoid, yet not. She hadn't caught more than a glimpse earlier, and it looked even more terrifying now in broad daylight than it had back in the underground room. Her breath caught in her throat as it drew closer.

What is that thing? How does Luc know its name? Wait, how did he even know it was here?

"Go!" Luc shoved her. "Get out of here."

"I'm not leaving you."

She couldn't understand how he expected her to just run away. He couldn't fight the thing by himself, no one could. Luc might be handy with weapons, but she doubted even he could take down one of these strange beasts.

Or could he?

"Avatar," the creature hissed and flew at them.

Luc pushed Ella out of the way, pulling something out from underneath his vest. He gripped a metallic device in his hand, and a beam of light flared to life. It looked like a sword of glowing energy. Ella had never seen anything like it. Weren't swords supposed to be made from metal? That much she'd seen in the ancient scrolls.

The creature hissed the word again, and she froze. *Avatar,* she'd heard that somewhere before.

Luc swung his sword, standing between her and the oncoming attacker. "Back, Esrac," he snarled.

"Valan." The creature grinned. "More blood for me."

Ella stood motionless as she watched Luc and the creature exchanging blows. Bright sparks flared off Luc's glowing sword, and the creature tried to grab him with its barbed hand. In one swift move, the creature knocked Luc's sword from his hand, sending it flying. All of this felt somehow familiar to her, as if she'd seen it before. Purple fire flared between her fingers, and without thinking, she flung it at the creature, sending it crashing to the ground. The Esrac hissed and its eyes flashed emerald again.

What have I done?

She stared at her hand, horrified. She had just revealed her darkest secret. No one was supposed to possess magic, let alone use it. Luc stared at her wide-eyed, as if he couldn't believe what she'd just done, either.

The creature shot back up, lunging at *her* now, not Luc. Even when he was fighting it, Luc seemed nothing more than an inconvenience to it, despite being the one wielding a weapon.

Ella threw another fireball, hitting it in the chest. Damn, why wouldn't the creature just die? Although she had never used her fire on anything living before, she had always thought it would be powerful enough to blow something up.

The Esrac laughed.

"Foolish girl, your power isn't strong enough to kill me."

The scene before her faded, and she stood surrounded by darkness. Fire flashed in the night sky as screams rang out around her.

A horde of Esrac raced toward her, some carrying strange weapons that appeared to be blasters on one end and jagged swords on the other. Ella knew if they didn't stab their victims and bleed them dry, they could carry them off to consume later.

Around her, people lay dead or dying as the Esrac stood over them.

Tears streamed down Ella's face.

They're gone, they're all gone. We are all going to die here...

Ella screamed, suddenly brought back to reality as the creature grabbed her by the throat. Sharp barbs bit into her neck, cutting off her air supply.

"More will come," the Esrac promised. "Soon my queen will walk this world once again and the avatars will—"

Light flashed as Luc's glowing sword swiped the creature's head clean off. The Esrac's eyes widened in surprise as it fell to the ground.

Ella gasped, the creature's barbs still digging into her throat.

"Luc!" She tried to scream, but it came out as a hoarse whisper.

Luc yanked the body away. Both it and the head turned into a messy pile of sludge before their eyes.

"What the bloody hell was that?" Eric demanded as he walked over to them.

Both Ella and Luc looked at each other for a moment. Ella didn't know Luc at all, not really. Everything about their brief relationship had been a lie. She'd had no idea he could fight like that, let alone kill a strange creature that came through a mystical doorway. Neither of them were supposed to even exist.

Ella looked away, unsure of what to say or do as she rubbed her aching throat. She stared at Eric instead, speechless. She had no idea what would happen next, but she did know none of their lives would ever be the same.

CHAPTER 6

Luc flipped his sabre closed, tucking it back into his jacket. Sweat dripped down his face, and he wiped it off with the back of his hand. His heart still pounded in his ears, his breath coming in short gasps.

He'd just fought an Esrac, one of the creatures that had almost wiped out the Arkadians a thousand years earlier.

Eric and Ella stood by him, dumbfounded. Both of them looked just as shocked as he felt. Ella was an avatar, one of the few people in this world who could use and control magic. He had wondered if it might be her when he found out she was in the area, but hadn't thought it possible. Avatars weren't supposed to exist anymore, and even on the rare chance one had been born, most of them were put to death in childhood.

He didn't have time to consider what the revelation meant for her, or them. Too much was at stake. "Ella, how many of those things came through the gate?"

She gaped at him. "What?"

"How many of the Esrac came through the gate? How many of them did you see down in the gate room?" Luc asked. "Think. It's important. I have to find them and before they have the chance to feed on anyone. If they do, I might not be able to stop them."

Eric glared at Luc. "What was that thing? How did you—"

Luc returned his glare. "You stay out of this. Ella, please, you need to tell me what you saw down there."

Eric opened his mouth to speak again, but closed it as Luc shot him a hard look.

"I don't know what I saw down there," she murmured. "I think it was just one."

Luc scanned the area with his mind. He didn't detect any signs of Esrac, but that didn't mean there weren't any there. It had been centuries since they had walked this world, and he might not be able to detect them very easily.

Ella started trembling. He realised she must've been frightened by everything she had just seen and done. It dampened his anger, and part of him wanted to reach out and pull her into his arms. He doubted Ella would welcome his embrace.

He checked her over. Three incisions had been left in her neck by the Esrac's barbs. "Doesn't look like it had enough time to take a lot of blood." She flinched, and he added softly. "How do you feel?"

"Would one of you tell me what the hell that thing was?" Eric demanded. "Where did it come from? Why did it attack you?" He glowered at Luc. "You didn't look surprised to see it, either."

"It's a long story, but it's gone now. You're okay." He touched her cheek, resisting the urge to wrap his arms around her. He had no time for comfort. There was still a job to do.

"Take Ella back to the ship," he told Eric. "I have something else I need to do."

"But what—?" Eric protested.

"Just go!" Luc snapped, cutting him off. "The creature is dead; it's not coming back." He nodded to the pile of sludge that had once been the Esrac. "Ella needs tending to, or would you rather she kept bleeding?" He gave the engineer a hard look, daring him to put up a challenge.

Eric glanced at the pile of sludge, then at Ella, and sighed. "Fine, but you owe me an explanation." He wrapped an arm around Ella, asking if she was alright as he started to lead her away.

Her eyes never left Luc as she let herself be guided back. Luc wanted to stop her, to ask her what she'd seen, what she'd done, but first he had to make sure the gate remained sealed, or more Esrac would come swarming through.

He found the transportation ring where he'd seen it on maps during his Valan training. Carefully, he knelt and pressed the activation rune. Ella and Fidget's footprints were visible in the dust, telling him that must have been how she'd gotten out of the gate room. Three rings shot up and white light enveloped him. His head spun as his energy shot through the underground cavern, reforming back into a body a few seconds later. Luc let out a breath as he reappeared. Darkness greeted him. Only small slivers of light crept down from above. But his magic allowed him to see as if they were in the midday sun.

Luc moved through the chamber and saw the runes surrounding the doorway still glowing dimly.

Ella must have broken the seals.

He sighed and shook his head. Damn her never-ending curiosity! She would have been excited to find a place like this, thinking it an archaeological find rather than a trap containing something better left forgotten. It felt odd being in the place where the knights of the Valan had once worked and died, but he couldn't dwell on the past now. The present emergency called.

Luc headed straight for the gate that acted as the dimensional portal between worlds. The door led to unimaginable wonder, at least until the ancestors had been forced to seal it shut after the Esrac had almost wiped out their entire race.

Despite how final the seal was supposed to be; Luc had always known he might have to fight the very enemy his people had locked away so long ago. Master Griffin had trained him for just this, but part of him had hoped he'd never have to face it and had even prayed to the goddess that this day would never come. Pray as he might, he knew despite his hopes that Queen Esme had vowed vengeance on the ancestors who had banished her and would do everything in her power to return.

The runes that made up the seal around the gate flared to life as he approached. The avatar who'd created the gate had done beautiful work, he noticed. An all-too-familiar symbol—a circle within a wavy line through the centre—still hovered above it. It was their symbol, his and Ella's. A lump rose in his throat. He could remember all their past lives together. Only fragments, but he did remember.

Ella hadn't remembered, and he had hoped it would stay that way, but now he wondered. Had her past life led her back to the gate room? He doubted she would have stumbled on it by chance; the room was too well concealed and sealed shut. Only an avatar could have gotten through it, and even then, only if they desired to get inside.

Luc shook his head, examining the seal further. It had been broken, no doubt, when Ella touched it, but it remained in place, sealing the gate and keeping the creatures on the other side locked in their prison. He traced the runes with his finger, reinforcing the seal so it would hold. He'd been taught about runes, seals, and their power during his training, but had never used them to this extent. The ancient magic would stay in place for now, as only an avatar could truly break it. He'd be sure to keep Ella as far away from the gate as possible from now on.

It could never be opened again, not for anything. Luc ran his hand along the frame, feeling a pang of sadness. He could never step through, never walk between the worlds as he once had so long ago. He had often longed to see what all those places looked like after all these centuries, but he wouldn't dare enter the Esrac prison.

He sighed. It was safer for all the realms this way. If the Esrac were freed, no one would be spared. They'd make the rebels on the other side of the border look like children waving pitchforks.

He had moved without fear in another lifetime. One that had ended centuries ago, he reminded himself, one best forgotten now. He wouldn't let history repeat itself again and would make sure the gate remained sealed. As for Ella, it wasn't up to him to decide her fate.

Heading back to the rings, he transported back above the ground and raised his hands so the platform vanished back within the earth, hidden and forgotten, just like his people.

That's the way it has to be.

Luc headed back toward the Pegasus, wondering what kind of explanation to give Eric and Ella. He didn't know how much she'd remember about being an avatar, or even if she'd want to be one.

As far as his own heritage went, he couldn't tell the truth, not to Eric, at least. Then again, Eric had seen the Esrac, and there was no trying to hide what they were from him now. Luc knew the cocky engineer wouldn't accept any old excuse.

Griffin wouldn't be happy about the news either. Still, Luc had handled the problem. One dead Esrac was a small price to pay when the threat had passed—or so he hoped. If more had managed to come through, he would find them and deal with them alone. Master Griffin was too old to be fighting such creatures, despite being one of the Valan himself.

Eric rubbed ointment on Ella's wounds as Luc headed back inside the Pegasus. Luc's gut twisted at the way Eric smiled at her.

Did he like her?

Luc gritted his teeth, reminding himself it didn't matter. They had broken up a while ago, and she'd been right to end their relationship.

He couldn't be involved with her, not emotionally, at least. After all, he had a duty to the Valan that didn't allow him to have any personal relationships.

Luc wordlessly headed over to the ship's console and set a course back to the citadel. Once they got back, he would have to see Griffin right away about what had happened, including the part about Ella being an avatar. He had no idea how Griffin would react to that, an Esrac escaping had been bad enough. And what would *he* do? He didn't want to think about how he might have to put his duty as one of the Valan before her, not yet.

"Hey, are you trying to fly my ship now too?" Eric demanded.

"Of course not," Luc said, taking a seat by Ella and strapping himself in. "Get us back to the citadel."

"What the hell was that thing that we saw earlier?" Eric pressed, putting down the med kit. "None of the rebels look like that."

"That thing you saw came from another realm. It's dead now, and you can never speak of it to anyone, are we clear?" Luc slumped back in his seat and crossed his arms.

"Where did it come from?"

"That's not important. Just take us back to the citadel. It's not my job to give you all the answers, I'm just following orders." Another lie, but lies were a necessity in his life.

"Fine," Eric muttered, taking his seat as he brought the ship's systems online and took off. The engines whirred to life as the Pegasus took off into the sky and trees blurred past them.

Ella sat still, staring straight ahead. Fidget wrapped his tail around her neck with his eyes closed. Luc doubted the dust bunny was asleep, he'd stay alert for his mistress. They might look cute and fluffy, but he knew them to be hunters, too.

Luc reached out to touch Ella's arm, then hesitated. "Are you okay?"

He didn't know what else to say. There was so much he wanted to tell her, but he knew he couldn't, not in front of Eric. Even when he could, there would be questions he couldn't answer. Griffin was the best person to explain to Ella what would happen next. As for Eric, Luc didn't know what Griffin would do about him. Perhaps he would tell him the truth, or perhaps he would send the engineer away and order him to never speak of what he'd seen, although Luc doubted that would stop Eric looking for answers.

"No," she muttered. "I don't understand what happened, how that thing—" She shuddered then narrowed her eyes at him. "You know, don't you? It's why you were always so secretive, isn't it?"

Luc looked away. He'd always kept secrets from her or avoided questions he didn't want to answer. It had made their relationship difficult best of times, he had hated doing it, but it had been a necessary evil. He had taken a vow to keep the peace and stop the Esrac from trying to destroy their world again, and that meant being apart from everyone else. There was so much he wanted to tell her, so much he hadn't shared with her before.

So much I can never share with her, he thought to himself.

He had to keep his true identity a secret, no matter what. The age-old secret of the knights had already been exposed. He couldn't risk exposing the Valan order and everything they stood for as well.

"You used magic too," he pointed out. "Guess I'm not the only one with secrets."

Eric gave Luc a hard look, and Luc felt a pang of guilt.

"I threw fire. I don't go running around with a glowing sword fighting creepy monsters that appear out of nowhere." Ella's dark brown eyes flashed. "I don't understand what happened. I..."

Luc shook his head. "Ella, I'm not the one you should be talking to about this."

"Luc, you knew that thing was there before it even appeared. That's why you came out there. You weren't looking for me; you were looking for that creature." She gripped the sides of her armrest. "How did you even know it existed?"

Luc's jaw tightened. But he didn't say anything. Couldn't she just wait until they were with Master Griffin again? Griffin would have all the answers, or at least know what their next move was in dealing with an unknown avatar and a potential Esrac threat.

Ella glared at him, annoyed at his silence. "That's why it never worked between us. You kept too many damned secrets from me." She turned away without saying another word.

Luc cursed himself for doing the wrong thing. Again.

He opened his mouth to speak, "I'm...Did you see something when the Esrac attacked?"

Ella ignored him.

Luc sighed, leaned toward her, and hissed, "I see things, too. Battles I've never fought in; people I've never met before."

He couldn't believe he had just admitted the truth out loud, but what other choice did he have? He doubted he could keep it all a secret for much longer. Ella would have questions, and she'd demand answers. He knew her well enough to know that.

"Just stop," Ella snapped. "I'm not your business anymore, remember?"

The rest of the flight passed in uncomfortable silence. Ella hated him even more now. It didn't look like he'd be making friends with Eric, either.

They landed back at the citadel. Luc's mind raced about what might happen next.

"We have to go see Master Griffin." He followed Ella down the ramp.

"Am I required to go too?" Eric asked. "Given that I saw the thing."

Luc shook his head. He didn't doubt Eric wouldn't keep his mouth shut, nor did he want the engineer learning more secrets. He just wanted to be alone with Ella, to have a chance to explain everything to her. Could he get her to listen? Would she ever trust him now?

"I'll get Griffin to brief you later," Luc said.

"Wow, Flynn. You almost sound like you're the one in charge," Eric remarked.

"Don't you have other duties to get on with?" he asked Eric. "Something to go fix? That's what you're here for."

"Nope, they can wait. At least until I know Ella's alright."

Ella glanced between them, frowning. "I'm fine. I'm going to get changed and clean up."

Luc opened his mouth to protest, but she glared at him and stalked off, Fidget trailing behind her. He let her go. He'd have a few moments to clear his head and consider the next course of action once he consulted with Master Griffin.

Eric gave a short, humourless laugh. "Guess she doesn't want to be with you anymore."

Luc's hands clenched into fists. He knew Eric liked Ella, but he didn't think anything romantic had happened between them.

"What makes you think she'd ever choose you either?" Luc scoffed. "Get back to work, engineer."

He knew jealousy was a worthless emotion. He had no right to be jealous, but he still felt its bitter sting. Luc headed to go and see Master Griffin, but hesitated. Maybe he should talk to Ella first and hear her version of events? He didn't know what Griffin would do to Ella once he found out she was an avatar, and part of him still wanted to protect her. He paced up and down the sandstone-walled hallway. Praying to the goddess didn't seem like much of an idea, but he did so anyway, trying to figure out what to do next. If Griffin found out, would Ella meet the same fate as all other avatars did? After unleashing an Esrac on an unsuspecting world?

He glanced down at his link, relieved to find there were no messages from Master Griffin yet, and decided to talk to Ella first. Maybe now she had calmed down he could find out what happened in the gate room.

Luc headed straight for Ella's chamber on the first floor. She could yell at him all she wanted, but he needed a chance to explain everything. He knocked on the door and felt her presence inside.

"Go away, Luc!"

"Ella, we need to talk."

He twisted the handle and opened the door. Ella sat on her bed, now dressed in a clean shirt and trousers, rubbing her long hair dry with a towel. The room had the same sandstone walls as the rest of the citadel, but they were lined with books Ella had brought with her. A small cage sat in one corner, but Fidget perched on a wooden shelf eating honey drops and staring down at Luc. He often wondered what the dust bunny thought. Fidget had always been protective of Ella, so he wouldn't be surprised if the creature tried to bite him.

"What do you want? I said I'd talk to Master Griffin after I clean up." Her dark blue eyes flashed with anger.

"Ella, you need to tell me everything. I need to know how you found the gate room and what you did whilst you were in there," Luc insisted. "It's important. You have no idea how serious this is."

"No idea?" she cried, flinging the towel at him. "I somehow opened a magical doorway that released a creature that looked like something out of a nightmare. Of course, I know how serious this is! If you want me to talk, why don't you tell me how you knew what it was and how to kill it?"

It shook his head. "I can't do that. Not yet," he replied. "Please, just tell me what happened. How did you find the chamber?"

Ella pushed her long hair off her face and crossed her arms. "I was out on an excavation in that area."

"Ella, you can't have found that place unless you were looking for it. The entire chamber had wards around it to stop anyone from finding it. How did you find it?" he asked again.

Ella sighed and threw her hands in the air. "You always did demand your own answers before giving me any," she snapped. "I don't know how I found the chamber, I just knew there was something important there."

"Did you have dreams about it?" He studied her expression, and she bit her lip, something she always did when she hesitated.

Her eyes narrowed. "How did you know? I haven't told anyone about my dreams, not even Fidget. Although, I doubt he could tell anyone even if he wanted to."

I know much more than you think, he thought.

"That's not important. What happened when you got to the chamber? How did you even get down there?"

"I found some rune stones, and Fidget found a gold one, but instead of giving it to me he ran off. I chased him and ended up falling down a cliff face I didn't know was there. I tried to find a way back up again and stumbled upon more runes and a sealed doorway."

"Which you explored even when Fidget tried to warn you away?"

Dust bunnies had excellent instincts. He knew Fidget would have sensed the warning woven into the wards protecting the chamber.

"Again, how do you know that? And why aren't you answering my questions?"

"You didn't listen to Fidget and opened the door, right?"

She gritted her teeth and nodded. "Yes. I explored the room inside. There were drawings depicting the ancestors and green-skinned creatures I didn't recognise. I thought they might be telling a story of some kind...I wish I had known they were a warning." She sighed. "That doorway called to me. I felt drawn to it."

Luc nodded. She would have been compelled, since only her magic could control it. "What happened when you opened the gate?" he persisted.

"The runes glowed, and a blast of energy sent me flying across the room. The door—*gate*—shimmered with light. Like a...portal, I suppose you might call it. It reminded me of something out of the old stories." Ella played with a strand of her hair, then glanced up at Fidget, who was busy stuffing his face full of treats as if he didn't have a care in the world.

"How long was the gate open for?" Luc asked. "Did you see more than one creature come through?"

Ella shook her head. "It was dark. I only saw one Esrac come through. What is an Esrac? Why won't you answer my questions?"

Luc's link started chiming. He glanced down at his wrist and saw it was Master Griffin. "Yes, Master?"

"Luc, where are you?" Griffin asked. "I know you three are back. Come up to my office, we have much to discuss."

Luc looked at Ella. "I should go."

"Wait, what? Don't you mean *we* should go?" She put her hands on her hips. "You said Master Griffin would answer my questions."

"He will, just let me talk to him first." Luc knew his answer would infuriate her even more, but it was better to talk to Griffin first, to convince him that keeping Ella alive would be the best option. He didn't want her finding out what happened to avatars. She might run or do something stupid.

"Luc, I put up with a lot when we were together, but no more lies!" Ella snapped. "I need—"

"Just let me talk to him first. I promise we'll explain everything to you." He turned away before she could say another word.

"What happened?" Griffin asked the second Luc appeared in his chamber. "Is the gate still sealed? Did any Esrac come through?" He pushed a stack of papers and books out of the way as he moved around his makeshift desk.

Luc sighed as he slumped onto one of the wooden chairs they'd discovered a few days earlier. "Yes, I took care of it. I did a sweep of the area and didn't sense any other Esrac. But only Ella knows what happened. She said one came through." Luc prayed that was true.

"Ella? What does she have to do with any of this? She was off excavating in another part of the city. She sent me a message herself. How did they open the gate?" He picked up his teacup and took a sip of tea to calm down. Luc would have chosen to drink something stronger but needed to keep a clear head.

"They didn't. Ella did."

Griffin almost dropped his teacup. "How? That's not possible. Only an avatar..." He shook his head. "No, it's impossible. There have been no signs of one born in over half a century. If Ella were one, she would have been killed long before now. The Senate has tests in place to ensure that going undetected can never happen, and they scan people for magic all the time. Ella was no doubt tested as a child, and she's never shown any signs of magic all the time I've known her."

"When you and I met eight years ago, you took me under your wing and taught me everything you knew about the Valan and how to keep the peace in this realm, even though our people are called rebels," Luc said. "Although avatars are very rare, it does still happen once every few generations. I can sense Ella's one of them. What are we going to do? I know what tradition says, but I can't hurt her, and I don't think you can either. Maybe this is happening for a reason. Maybe it's time to let magic back into the world."

Griffin gulped down his tea and slammed his empty cup on the desk. "We can't! You know the rules. If she is an avatar, she must be put to death. We can't risk the Esrac queen getting her hands on avatar magic again. There are ways she can reach avatars even whilst she's trapped in another realm, and I won't let history repeat itself."

"What are you talking about?" Ella asked from behind them. "What's an avatar? Why would anyone want to kill me?"

Luc turned to see her standing in the doorway and knew he could no longer hide the truth from her.

CHAPTER 7

"What's going on?" Ella demanded. Ever since she'd touched that strange doorway, she kept seeing flashes of people and things that weren't there, and if Luc and Griffin knew why, she wasn't leaving this room until they told her. She put her hands on her hips. "Say something."

Griffin pinched the bridge of his nose, "This is a nightmare." He shook his head and gulped down some of his tea. "I knew doing this excavation was a bad idea. Why did I let you talk me into it?" He gave Ella a hard look.

Ella glanced between them, then glared at Luc. "One of you tell me what this means right now." She needed to know what her strange discoveries meant for her future. If they planned on attacking her, she'd run. Where, she didn't know yet, but she wouldn't sit back and let them try to kill her.

Luc rubbed his temples. "I am a Valan knight, and you are an avatar."

Her eyes widened. She'd never heard of a magic user being referred to as anything other than a rebel. "What is a Valan, and why were the two of you talking about killing me?"

"No one is going to kill you, Ella." Luc got to his feet and reached for her shoulder, but she backed away.

"An avatar is a special kind of magic user," Griffin explained. "Our ancestors—who lived long before the Senate was ever created—were an advanced race. Some even used magic like you and Luc do." He motioned to the vacant chair in front of his desk.

"Please sit down. No one is going to harm you."

Ella shook her head. "I don't believe you. Anyone with magic is put to death or imprisoned if they live within the border." Her heart pounded at the prospect of being exposed. Growing up, only her parents had known. Her father had taught her how to hide the magic, and it had worked well for most of her life. As far as anyone knew, she was normal, and as long as she didn't use her magic, she would be safe.

Until now.

Her mind went to her father's disappearance ten years earlier. People had accused him of using magic, and he'd vanished one night. She'd never seen him again, and never found out what had happened to him. Part of her had wanted to come here in the hope of finding out—as if it knew where all the answers lay.

"The Valan are an ancient order of knights sworn to keep the peace in this land," Master Griffin went on. "We go back to the time of the Arkadians. There were once many of us, but since the Senate came into power and ordered the ban on magic, numbers have dwindled drastically. Most Valan live beyond the border now, forced to live as outcasts, but Luc and I work together in secret."

"Okay, what about me being put to death?"

"Ella, sit down," Master Griffin ordered, using his authoritative teacher's voice. "No one here is going to harm you, you have my word. We have much to discuss."

She lowered herself into the chair, crossing her arms. "What was that doorway I found today?"

Luc leaned forward. "The gate is a dimensional doorway designed to allow people to travel instantaneously. Avatars used to control the gates, but all of them are sealed now."

"What do avatars do?" Her words tumbled out as her mind raced. "Why would you want to kill them? Do they turn into those green skinned creatures?" She bit her lip at the thought. She'd rather die than turn into one of those blood-sucking things.

"That's a long and complicated story," Master Griffin answered with a sigh. "Most of what you have been taught about magic users by the Republic is a lie. They aren't evil, there are good and bad people among them. Avatars come into the world when magic is dying out, as it is here."

"Okay…"

"A thousand years ago, an avatar named Aurelia used magic to create a gate, but she wasn't content to use it as a transportation device to different places within our world alone and enhanced the design so it could be used to travel to other worlds," Luc explained. "The ancestors were enthralled by this new power and sought travel to different realms."

Ella nodded. She'd heard tales of the ancestors travelling across realms, but most people had considered them fairy tales, and she had always agreed. Magic might be real enough, but travelling to different realms seemed beyond anything science or history had ever shown her.

"Aurelia and her Valan protector travelled to the dark realm, where they encountered a race of beings unheard of before, the Esrac. The ancestors were a peace-loving race and sought to be friends with the creatures," Griffin continued. "When Aurelia befriended the Esrac Queen, Esme, she somehow tricked her into sharing the secrets of the gates and learnt to use them, too. They have their own form of magic, and the ability to learn how to use advanced technology quickly. They waged war on other realms, and y came to our world with no interest in peace."

"Many of the ancestors were wiped out in the war with the Esrac, but Aurelia fought by her people's side, and in one final battle tricked Esme to come within the city walls and managed to force the beasts into another realm from which they could never escape. She gave her life to do so."

She thought back to the runes she'd seen carved around the door, and how they'd repelled her after she had opened the gate. "Why were they sealed?" Ella asked. "Why did the Esrac come here?"

"Esrac, feed on blood and are without a conscience," Master Griffin answered. "Our land provided a much-needed feeding ground for them. The humans in their realm were dying out."

"You are the only surviving avatar," said Luc gently. "Your ancestors spent centuries making sure the Esrac never got loose again."

Ella let the information was over her, unsure what to think or feel. "Why did I never know about this?" She gave Luc a pointed look. "Have you always had magic?"

He nodded. "Always."

"No one told you because it's forbidden for avatars to be trained to use their magic," Griffin said. "Your father took a foolish risk by not binding yours."

"How do you know about my father? Do you know what happened to him?"

Master Griffin's expression darkened. "Your father is dead. You need to stop chasing ghosts."

Ella knew him well enough to know when he was hiding something. She wouldn't rest until she found out what had happened to him, but kept pressing for information. "Why are avatars put to death?"

"It's an age-old rule passed down by the ancestors," Griffin said. "An avatar hasn't been born in over half a century but the laws of the Valanl state no avatar shall be allowed to live. The ancestors feared the Esrac would enter our lands again, and they must stay imprisoned."

"So, what happens to me now?" Her head spun, and her eyes darted between them, still half expecting one of them to attack her. She had magic. Magic she wasn't supposed to have, but she would use it to protect herself and stay alive. Even if that meant using it against people she once thought of as friends.

"Luckily, only one Esrac came through today, but it could have been much worse," said Luc, turning his attention to the older man. "The gate has been sealed once again. Master Griffin, we can't kill Ella. She is a valuable member of this team, and we may need her if more Esrac come through."

Griffin nodded. "I propose that once we know the threat is over we should neutralise her powers by binding them."

"What?" Ella shot up from her chair. Magic had always been a part of her, even if she hadn't always used it. She couldn't let them take her magic away from her. It was the only thing she had to protect herself. "You can't do that!"

"Your curiosity today could have cost thousands of lives," Griffin snapped. "I forbade you to excavate that area!"

"I won't let you take my magic away." She glanced at Luc, pleading with him to back her up. Despite their recent breakup, she hoped he still felt something for her.

"Maybe we could teach her..." Luc suggested.

"Rules are rules," Griffin said. "She's too dangerous to go walking around unchecked."

"Train me, then! Like you said, you may need me if more of those things come through. My father always said there's a reason for everything. Maybe I'm meant to help you stop the Esrac once and for all."

Griffin gave her a hard look. "You could be the doom of us all. I say we should strip your powers away and—"

"I'll teach her to control it," Luc blurted. "Please, Master Griffin, we have to at least try it before taking such extreme measures."

Ella glanced at him, surprised. She hadn't expected him to speak up for her, and thought he would insist on taking her magic away.

"Fine, but I warn you," Griffin said, shaking a warning finger at Ella, "You must not even think of those gates."

She huffed a laugh. "Believe me, I don't want to go near a gate ever again."

Once she and Luc were outside Griffin's office, Ella let out a breath she hadn't known she'd been holding and battled her emotional confusion. Was she relieved? Ashamed? Could she also be guilty, perhaps, or a mixture of all those things?

"Can he take my magic away?" she asked. Master Griffin seemed a stranger to her now.

Luc shook his head and took her arm.

"We can't talk here," he hissed, leading her away. "Sara or Eric could overhear us."

She shut the door behind them once they reached her chamber.

"I want answers, Luc." She stepped toward him. "You've always known you had magic too?"

Luc ran a hand through his hair and nodded. "Yes, and like you, I never told anyone."

"How long did you know my father before you met me?" she asked. "Do you know what happened to him? Is he still alive?"

"A few years. He started training me as one of the Valan when I was seven. I don't know what happened to him, and no, I don't think he still alive. Like Griffin said, you should stop chasing ghosts."

Ella glared at him. "I know when you're hiding something from me, I broke up with you because I got sick of all your secrets. You can't keep them from me anymore. Not after everything that happened today."

He sighed. "I don't know what happened to him."

"Why didn't you tell me he trained you?"

"Like Griffin said, we once walked between the worlds. Nowadays, we live in secret and lead normal lives. I never told you about my abilities or being a knight because I watched my family be killed by the Senate's guards for theirs. Keeping it hidden became second nature."

"I get that part, but I don't understand why you wouldn't tell me. I thought we were…" She sighed. "Never mind."

"Now you know why I kept secrets. Ella—"

"This doesn't change anything between us," she insisted. She didn't want to get back together with him just because they had something in common now. He still kept things from her. "I still don't understand why my father never told me about any of this."

"Maybe he knew you'd find out on your own, or that I'd be here for you."

She laughed.

"How could he have known that? He's been gone over ten years." She had so many other questions she wanted to ask, but didn't know where to begin. "What abilities do you have?"

"As well as being able to sense an open gate, I can do this."

Blue light shot from his hand as he spoke.

"It's an illusion. I can also move things with my mind, to an extent."

Ella held up her palm, calling the coloured fire. This time, it appeared purple. "This *isn't* an illusion."

"No, it's called starfire. It's a very powerful ability that will help against the Esrac," Luc told her. "It may not be strong enough to kill them, but it'll slow them down."

Ella snuffed the fire out. "What are we going to do about the Esrac?" she asked.

"Like Griffin said, they almost wiped our ancestors out.

"How did they even defeat them?"

"I remember they sealed the gates and somehow forced the Esrac through by trapping their queen," Luc said. "I only know bits and pieces myself, a lot of our ancestors' knowledge was lost over the centuries, especially when the Senate came into power."

"Wait, there were bodies in the chamber where I found that doorway–I mean, gate. I could examine them, and—"

"I doubt Griffin would like that."

"Why not?" she frowned. "We're here to explore, aren't we?"

"It's safer if you stay away from the gate room all together."

"Are avatars ruled by Griffin?"

He smiled and shook his head. "Not exactly."

"Good, then I'm going back and getting to work on what I do best." Despite the day's events, she still had a job to do. It was studying the ways of the ancestors, and she would do just that. "If it makes you feel better, you can come with me. I swear I won't go near that gate again."

CHAPTER 8

Esme fed on another one of her helmsmen, yet it did little to ease the gnawing pain in her belly. She needed real nourishment, something that would sustain her and fill the void. She despised hunger almost as much as she hated being forced to kill one of her helmsmen. These were *her* men, *her* warriors. They should have been out there gathering blood slaves for her. She shouldn't have to kill them to survive.

Stale blood wasn't enough to give her more than a few hours of strength. She wandered back to the gate, where the wards still held firm. She needed an avatar to bring them down permanently.

Esme raised her hand. The gate glimmered with light, but nothing happened. She needed blood from someone with magic to restore her to her full strength. Maybe then she would have a chance of breaking down the ward herself, but she doubted it.

"Curses!" she growled, storming back to her pod chamber. Rummaging inside the pod, she hoped some of her possessions had stayed with her during her hibernation. She'd been too distracted by the wretched hunger to check earlier. Esme dug through the fleshy skin of the pod, burrowing deep until she finally felt something cold and hard. Yanking it out, she stared at the mirror. The glass held no reflection, and only blackness stared back at her.

Show me the avatar, she commanded.

The glass became illuminated with a swirl of colour.

The woman with long ebony hair appeared, this time dressed in a vest and dark trousers. She looked the spitting image of the bitch who'd sent Esme to this hell realm in the first place, cursing her to a fate worse than death.

Her claws dug into her palms as she thought of Aurelia.

Be calm, she told herself. *Watch.*

"These bodies look human," Ella remarked as she walked into the room containing the gate.

Esme scoffed. Why would the little avatar be interested in a rotting corpse? Bones did nothing, meant nothing. She laughed. *How the mighty avatars have fallen!*

"Maybe they were avatars." A man appeared, dark-haired with dark eyes. Esme froze.

Him? No, it couldn't be. How could the very two people who'd opened the portal to her all those centuries ago be here now? Avatars weren't immortal, they lived and died just like any other scrap of meat.

Yet here they both were, just as they had looked when they'd stepped into her palace millenniums ago.

Her mind wandered back to that fateful day.

Esme reclined, drinking blood from a silver goblet. The contents tasted as good as feeding from the living and sustained her well.

"My queen, human visitors are here asking to speak with you," announced her helmsman, Storm.

She sipped more blood, enjoying the sweet taste of it. She'd have to ask where it had come from. Perhaps the source would still be alive. She'd savour that morsel, perhaps keep them around as a permanent blood slave.

"What visitors?" she asked, stretching out on her divan. "I know of no one coming here today." She played with a strand of her long, blood red hair idly.

"They say they travelled here from another realm."

Esme laughed.

"Such a thing isn't possible," she scoffed.

"They look very different from the inhabitants of any of the lands we have visited, my queen," Storm said. "Should I send them away?"

Esme dipped her hair in the blood then sucked on the end of it. "Let them in. It's not every day food willingly comes to us."

The doors groaned open, and two people came in. They appeared to be a male and a female. Both wore bright colours. Both had dark hair and beautiful faces.

Esme set her goblet down on the table beside her, mouth watering. These two would taste delicious. She could almost hear their blood singing to her.

"I am Esme, Queen of the Esrac. Why have you come here?"

"Greetings, Queen Esme. I am Lucan, and this is Aurelia. We are travellers, peaceful explorers from another realm," the male said. "Thank you for allowing us into your hive."

Esme stared at them, half-bored. "It's not often I have slaves come to join me willingly, if ever."

She cackled.

"Slaves? No, you misunderstand, we're not from your world. We travelled here in hopes of learning about you and your people," said Aurelia. "In return, we are willing to

share the knowledge of our world with you. Perhaps even trade cultural items and—"

Esme rose, her long leather skirt billowing behind her as she cut the male off. "Your words are strange. I do not trade information, or the secrets of my people. Your kind is food, farmed the same way you might farm livestock." She moved toward them. "I don't like talkative food." She reached out to touch the woman's face, the suckers on her palm aching to draw the woman's blood, drain the life from her. This one would be sweet—they both would—and she'd savour them.

Light suddenly flared in Aurelia's hand, burning like fire. "I'd step away if I were you."

Lucan took his wife's arm. "I can see we aren't welcome here. Please excuse us, my lady."

Esme stared at the fire in disbelief. None of the morsels in her lands had even basic magic, let alone real power like this. It wasn't just their blood that called to her, she realised. It was their power. She wanted it for herself.

Both strangers backed away, preparing to leave.

"Wait," Esme growled. "You are truly not from this realm?"

Lucan nodded. "Please accept our apologies. We'll not intrude on you any longer." He bowed his head.

"I want to know how this is possible. None of my people, or the...humankind—" she growled out the word. "—can travel to other worlds."

She'd always believed other worlds existed, had had her best alchemists look into the possibility. They'd dismissed the theory as nonsense, yet these two strangers came from a realm outside of her own. She had to possess this power.

"Good day, Queen Esme," Aurelia said politely as Lucan headed for the door.

Esme blurred in front of them.

"Wait, please." She gave her sweetest smile, fangs glistening. "Forgive me. I did not greet you in a proper manner, and that was wrong of me. I'd be interested in learning more about you and your world. Please, join me."

The two newcomers glanced at each other hesitantly.

"I'll have food and wine brought for you. Sit. We have much to discuss."

The memory faded, and Esme continued to watch the woman examine the bones. She had power, just like Aurelia had. Esme could feel it.

You're the key to getting me out of this hell. When you do, I'll enjoy draining you dry. It won't be a quick death. I'll make you suffer for every century I've spent stuck here, little avatar.

Esme moved away from her pod, setting the mirror down. First, she had to wake the rest of her hive. She'd need a couple of helmsmen to help her enact revenge on the avatar, the Valan and the descendants of the Arkadians. She moved along the row of pods, yanking them open as she went.

"Wake," she commanded. "Rise and greet your queen."

Nothing happened.

"Rise, you fools," she growled, slapping one of them hard.

But none of them awakened. They'd been asleep too long and didn't have enough blood in their veins left to help them rise.

Esme screamed in frustration. One way or another, she would kill that avatar for what she had done.

CHAPTER 9

A few days later, Ella had finally convinced Luc to help her move the bodies back to the citadel, and now set about examining them in her makeshift lab. Master Griffin hadn't been happy when he'd heard what she'd done, but she'd argued the find still had historical significance and might help them learn more about the Esrac. Despite their terrifying nature and appearance, they seemed fascinating. She wondered how they fed on blood, and how different their bodies were to that of a human to allow that.

Sara had been eager to learn more about the gate room and where the bodies had been found after she'd found out about Ella's discovery—albeit with all mention of magic, avatars, gateways and Esrac edited out—but Griffin had made an excuse for her not to go and instructed her to help with the examinations instead. Ella doubted Griffin's excuses would last for long, but knew she'd created the problem by accidentally releasing an Esrac, so she'd fix it.

Sara greeted her as she came in.

"How did your excavation go? I heard you found some bones. Hey, was Master Griffin angry when he heard you did an unsanctioned dig?"

Sara loved it when Ella told her stories about the things she discovered. Ella guessed it was because she rarely left the library back in Celestas. In some ways, Ella envied her friend. Sara never had to hide magic that would potentially get her killed.

"Er—eventful," Ella admitted. "And yes, I found two skeletons, one male, one female, but I haven't got much from them yet." She moved into a smaller room that she'd turned into a makeshift office area with her comp unit and scanners.

"Ooh! Details?" Sara went over to the auto chef and programmed it to dispense tea.

Ella didn't feel like drinking any but poured herself a cup anyway, out of politeness. "It–I..." She struggled to find the right words and wondered if she should tell Sara anything at all.

She wouldn't be hiding everything since Sara knew of her magic. She'd found out when Ella had taken her on a dig. They'd become stuck in a cave. And when she thought Sara had been distracted, Ella had used magic to blast her way out. Unfortunately, Sara had seen the whole thing. It had almost been a relief to finally share her secret with someone; she remembered.

"Come on, spill," Sara encouraged.

Ella hesitated and sighed. "I did something bad, and it could have devastating consequences."

"What did you do? Break off a few bones of a long dead person?" Sara smiled.

Ella didn't return her smile. "Have you heard of avatars before?"

"Sure, but they're just a myth. They were supposed to have lived about a thousand years ago. Why?" Sara leaned forward. "Have you found something to indicate they might have actually existed?"

Ella shook her head and rose, motioning for Sara to follow her into as she retrieved her bag.

"Ella, what's going on?" Sara asked hesitantly. "You're starting to creep me out."

Ella pulled the rune stones from her bag as she described what had happened. Griffin wouldn't be happy, but Eric already knew part of their secret, and she needed to talk to someone who she trusted.

"Let me get this straight. You opened a portal and let a weird creature through who fed on blood, then Luc killed it with a magic sword?" Sara laughed and shook her head in disbelief. "Ella, I know there are a lot of stories about the old city, but even you have to admit that sounds ridiculous. The ancestors used advanced technology! They didn't have *magic*, not like the rebels."

Ella felt a pang of sadness. She'd hoped Sara of all people would have believed her. "Never mind, forget I said anything."

"Wait, you were being serious?" Sara gasped.

"Have you ever known me to make things up?" she asked.

"No, but…Blimey!" Sara breathed.

"Sam, I created this mess. I need you to help me find a way to fix it."

"I'm good with history, not fighting scary monsters. Besides, if your theory about the ancestors having and using magic is true, the Chancellor won't react well to our findings. What does Master Griffin have to say about all this?"

"Not much. He and Luc are being secretive." Ella sighed and took a sip of her tea. "What do you know about avatars?"

"Just rumours. They were apparently powerful beings who travelled to other worlds—your story makes it sound like that could be true." Sara said. "I'll see what I can dig up on them and those Esrac things you mentioned, but I think you should talk to Luc too. Sounds like he has some of the answers you need."

Ella shook her head. "I can't."

She glanced around, wishing Fidget was there, but he'd scurried off for the night on one of his usual hunts.

"Personal feelings aside, he can help you."

Ella shook her head again. Yes, they'd have to start working together if he was going to be training her, but that didn't mean she had to spend more time with him than necessary.

"It still feels strange being around him. I thought it'd be easier by now."

"Now you have magic in common. Maybe he'll start opening up to you. I mean, that's why you broke up with him, right? The secrets?"

"That doesn't mean I want him back. We had major problems, and they won't just disappear because of our gifts." Ella paced up and down, running her hand through her long hair.

"You still love him, don't you?"

She looked away. She didn't want to think of what she felt for Luc, let alone feel it in the first place. He'd broken her heart. There would be no forgiving that.

"He's still a person who can help more than I can."

Ella returned to her chamber that night, changed into a silk nightie, and climbed into bed. It still felt strange without Luc sleeping beside her. She scowled at the thought, turning over and closing her eyes as though she knew sleep would be a long time coming. Images of green skinned Esrac had wandered in and out of her dreams since, and she would often wake up in a sweat, scanning the dark corners of her room for signs one.

She lay still, thinking about the Esrac, the gate, her dreams and what they meant until sleep dragged her under.

Within seconds, Ella found herself standing at the top of the balcony. Gulls cried overhead, and a salty breeze filled her lungs.

Dozens of white stone towers rose up around her, shining like beacons under the burning sun.

This place felt safe, like home in a way the shining towers of Celestus never would.

Strong arms wrapped around her from behind as someone kissed her cheek. This person felt safe, loving, and made her heart soar.

"Time to go, love. Are you ready?" said a familiar voice.

She turned to face Luc and smiled. He took her hand and led her toward a doorway.

A symbol shimmered above the doorframe. It had been carved into solid stone, a circle with a wavy line through the centre. Two halves of a whole.

It's a gate, Ella realised, as she watched Luc touch the arch. Light filled the room as it flared to life.

The image faded, and she found herself in a dark room. She shivered as icy cold seeped through her bones, making her breath visible in the air. This room didn't feel safe or welcoming in the slightest.

"Ella?" a voice called. "Ella, where are you?"

She couldn't make out if the voice was male or female, but it sounded far away. Darkness hung over her like a heavy blanket, making it impossible to distinguish anything around her.

"Ella?" the voice called again.

It sounded familiar, but she couldn't tell who it belonged to.

"Who's there?" she called. "Where are you?"

"Ella? I need your help."

"Who are you?" Ella raised her hand. No magic came to her. "What do you want from me?"

"I'm the one who led you to the gate."

An image of the doorway flashed through her mind. She shuddered. "If you're one of those things that came through, forget about it. I won't help you."

"I'm not an Esrac, I'm trapped. You must help me…" She caught a glimpse of a face in the darkness, but it was too dark and too far away to make out clearly.

Ella jerked awake with sweat running down her face. Her hair was plastered to her forehead and sticking to her arms and neck. She pushed it back, wiping her face with her bed sheet.

"Lights on," she ordered. The crystals overhead flared with orange light, illuminating the room with a warm glow. A movement she spotted out of the corner of her eye made her freeze, but she quickly realised it was just the curtains fluttering where she'd left the window open for Fidget.

She shivered as she rose and went over to it, feeling goose bumps spread down her arms despite the heat.

"Fidget?" she called, hoping his ears or tail would suddenly appear, but there came no sign of him. She would have felt better having him there, even if he did pester her for treats and complain about his cage. Sighing, she closed her window and locked it. Fidget would still find a way in. He always did.

She returned to sit on her bed, now wide-awake. Sleep evaded her, her body fearing more dreams, like the ones that had led her to the strange figure and the gate in the first place. They still made no sense to her, and she hadn't told anyone about them either, not even Sam. Only one person would know what they meant and where they came from. The one person she didn't want to see.

CHAPTER 10

Luc was dragged from the depths of sleep by a quiet, insistent buzzing. He'd had another dream—no, a *memory*—of Ella in one of his past lives. He sat up, rubbing sleep from his eyes, and groaned. They were becoming more frequent than before, almost as if the past was forcing him to relive it. Why, he didn't know. At first, he thought it had been because of the Esrac threat, but most of what he'd seen so far had been glimpses of being with Ella and how happy and in love they'd been.

Ironic, given the state of the relationship he had with her in this life.

He ran a hand through his hair, looking up as the door buzzed again and frowning. He walked down the hall, wondering who'd be calling at this late hour.

He felt her there even before opening the door.

Ella.

Just having her close by felt comforting. Luc hesitated as he reached for the door's control panel. What was she doing here?

He touched the panel, watching as the door slid open to reveal Ella dressed in nothing but a silk nightie. Her feet were bare.

"What's wrong?" Luc asked, brow creasing as he moved aside to let her in.

She walked in, and the door slid shut behind her. "I...I keep having weird dreams."

Luc's eyes widened. "Weird how?"

Telling her he had weird dreams too would mean telling her what had happened then, and he didn't know if he could do that, not yet.

"I see things, people, places I've never seen before. They feel so familiar to me," she said, her hair falling over her face. "I saw something the day that Esrac attacked us. A battle. Hundreds of them were swarming through a city with towers that looked a lot like we have here in the old city." She looked at him. "You were there too. I don't know what any of this means." She shook her head. "Do avatars lose their minds?"

"No, they're just dreams. They don't mean anything."

"They led me to the gate. It's like I was meant to find it."

Luc frowned. Would her past life have been what led her to the gate? They'd vowed never to touch it again. But had something lured her there? He'd heard of the Esrac queen's infamous ability to influence others, but could she really do that from another realm?

He hesitated, wishing he could tell her everything.

"It's been a long day. You should try and get some sleep."

Her eyes flashed with anger. "Why do I feel like you're keeping things from me even now?"

"I'm…We're both tired, and I'm not having this conversation with you right now."

"These things have *happened*. They can't be future events because they feel different, so why the hell won't you explain to me what's going on?" Ella said. "I saw you in the dreams. You looked like you do now, but a little different. I think we were involved then. What aren't you telling me?"

Luc sighed. "I don't know what's going on."

She snorted. "Luc, we both know when you're lying. Why won't you tell me?"

He looked away. She had always known him better than anyone else had. "It wouldn't make any difference if I did."

Ella closed the gap between them and cupped his face, forcing him to look at her. "Yes, it would. If we're going to work together to stop the Esrac threat, we need to trust each other. Right now, I don't trust you, and you're not giving me any reason to either."

Luc pushed her hands away. "I can't. I can't let history repeat itself. I never should have been with you in the first place."

"What is that supposed to mean?" she snapped. "I can't say our breakup was fun, but I thought we at least had some good times together."

"Ella, I'm just trying to keep you safe. Maybe Griffin's right and you should let him bind your talent." He hated saying it, but maybe it'd be safer for all of them if she wasn't faced with the burden of being an avatar and carrying the responsibility that came with it.

Ella's mouth fell open. "There are Esrac wandering loose, and you want to bind the powers that could help stop them?" she cried. "Why?"

"You're the one who let them out in the first place," he pointed out. "It's an avatar's duty to keep the realms safe, and you freed them from centuries of imprisonment. Intentional or not, you're the one who caused this."

"Maybe that wouldn't have happened if you two hadn't kept me in the dark in the first place!" Ella retorted. "If you really cared about me at all, you would have told me the truth. You would have trusted me."

She turned and hit the control panel, storming out before the door fully opened.

Luc watched her go, reminding himself that he had to be done. Duty or not, it didn't do anything to ease his guilt.

Luc went to see Griffin in his office the next morning.

"Have you bound her powers yet?" Griffin asked.

Luc shook his head. "No. I know it's the right thing to do, but it doesn't make it any easier," he said. "And yes, I know if they knew of her magic, the Republic could use Ella as a weapon against the rebels, and the rebels could do the same thing. "

"If an Esrac gets a hold of an avatar again, the realms will be plunged into chaos. I've taught you everything I know about how to keep your own power safe, but we don't have time to teach, Ella. You need to track down the Esrac, kill them, and make sure the other gate stays buried."

That had been Luc's ancestors' way of dealing with the problem, to seal and bury the gates and forbid the use of magic. Hell, his dreams told him he had been the one to come up with the idea—the banning of magic part, at least. It had kept the people of this realm safe from the Esrac, but now he wasn't so sure if it had solved everything. Would taking Ella's powers away really help?

"I need her to agree to the binding for it to effectively work," Luc said. "I can't forcibly take her powers from her,"

Griffin sighed. "I warned you getting involved would only cause you more pain."

Luc looked away. "You didn't know she was an avatar then. Neither of us did."

"It won't stop the curse, will it?"

Luc stared out the window at the white stone towers. His and Ella's past selves had created the gates and brought about the Esrac problem. They would forever be punished for it, but that wouldn't stop Luc from trying to prevent it from happening again now.

Luc found Ella in her lab, examining the bones of the body she had brought back from the gate chamber. He had spent the past few days searching for signs of any other Esrac who may have come through when Ella had opened the gate and had been uneasy ever since the gate first opened. There had to be another Esrac close by, and he had to find it quickly. It hadn't tried attacking Ella yet, which meant it had been watching them instead. No doubt it planned on capturing her and using her to try and open the gate. He couldn't let that happen. He'd show her just how important it was to give up her magic, and how she'd be safe once the Esrac problem was taken care of. If she were no longer an avatar, she wouldn't be able to open the gate, and nor would anyone else. After her magic was bound, he and Griffin would make sure the gate remained sealed, this time using stronger wards to bury it forever. The line of avatars would be extinguished, and perhaps then the Esrac threat would finally be over.

Ella looked up at him as he came in. "What do you want? I'm surprised you'd even have the nerve to show your face here after last night."

"I want you to come with me to find the other Esrac who came through."

Her eyes narrowed as she finally looked to him. "Why? I thought only one came through?"

"Because I want you to understand why they're so dangerous and why I need you to agree to let me bind your powers," Luc said. "And no, another one came through. I wasn't sure at first, but I've been feeling another presence over the past few days. It's waiting, watching us and preparing to use you to try and open the gate. We have to find it and stop it before it has the chance."

"We've been through this. I'm not giving up my powers."

"Fine. Will you come with me or not?"

"I'm beginning to wonder what I ever saw in you," she muttered. "Fine, I'll come."

She rose and pulled off her lab coat.

"Let's get going."

Luc led her out, instructing Eric over his link to have the ship waiting for them. When they arrived outside, Luc punched in the coordinates and Eric arched a brow.

"Off to go look for more of those green-skinned buggers, are we?" Eric winced at Luc's glare and nodded. "Right, I didn't see or hear anything."

Ella gave Luc a pointed look. "What do we do when we find the Esrac?"

"You stay back and let me handle it," he told her. "You're only coming along to observe and help me track them."

"Why do you even need me, then?" she hissed, glowering at him.

Because we're stronger when we're together, he thought.

"Like I said, I'm gonna show you just how dangerous the Esrac can be." He looked her right in the eye. "You have to promise me you won't try to interfere, no matter what happens. You can't let emotions cloud your judgement."

"Fat chance of that happening," Ella muttered. "Fine, I won't get involved even if an Esrac starts tearing you to bits."

She moved away from him, staring out the window.

Luc's felt a sharp pain in the pit of his stomach at her wordless rebuttal. Guilt was eating him alive. He hated the ever-growing distance between them.

This is how it must be. I'll make sure this life is different for both of us.

CHAPTER 11

The trio sat in an uncomfortable silence for the rest of the flight to the gate's location until Luc announced he thought the remaining Esrac would be somewhere close by. At Ella's side, Fidget grumbled about being in his cage. But she wouldn't let him out, no matter how much he protested. It'd be much safer for him in there than anywhere else, and he wouldn't get up to mischief either.

"Eric, stay here," Luc told him, as they got up to disembark. "I don't know how long we'll be, but we might have to make a quick exit."

"Don't let Fidget out of his cage, either," Ella warned. "No matter what he says or does."

Eric stood up as Ella turned away from him. "Wait, what if you get into trouble? What are those monsters, anyway? You and Griffin never did tell me the full story."

Luc's jaw tightened. "We told you what you need to know, leave it at that."

He opened the ship's door. "Ella, let's go."

"Be careful," Eric said.

"I'll be fine," she assured him. "I have Luc."

Eric snorted. "Somehow I doubt your safety is his first priority."

"I can take care of myself." She turned and hurried after Luc, ignoring Fidget's calls to come back.

Luc didn't say anything to her, which she was grateful for. If he had, there was no doubt they'd only end up arguing again. She had so many questions she wanted to ask, about the Esrac, about being an avatar, and about the future, but she stayed quiet, doubting she'd like some of the answers. She knew what Luc was set on, and there was no way she'd let anyone take her magic away without a fight.

Luc stopped when they reached a clearing, and Ella glanced around, half expecting something to jump out at them. Nothing happened.

"Do you feel anything?" Luc asked.

"Oh yeah, tired, irritated…" She pushed her long hair off her face to roll her eyes at him.

"That's not what I meant. Avatars can sense when Esrac are close by," he said. "Close your eyes. Tell me what you feel."

She scowled, but closed her eyes. She heard her heart pounding in her ears and the wind rustling leaves and smelt wet grass and pinecones.

"I don't feel anything," she said after a few moments.

"Concentrate. What did it feel like when you saw that other Esrac?"

Ella shuddered at the memory. "Awful. Cold and empty."

"Good, focus on that."

She closed her eyes again, this time remembering what she felt when the Esrac had attacked her. "I still don't feel anything. I don't understand why you brought me along given how determined you are to take my magic away."

"I already told you why."

Ella's hands clenched into fists, but her eyes stayed shut. "No, you just said it would keep me safe. I know you're still hiding something from me. I get that they're a threat, and I know I screwed up when I opened the gate, but how would you feel if someone tried taking your magic away?"

"That's—"

"Don't you dare tell me it's different. I control my powers just fine! I've kept them a secret for as long as I can remember," she hissed. "Do you just want to be the last Valan knight aside from Griffin?"

"I'm not the last. There are others out there."

Ella's eyes flew open. "What? Where?"

Luc shook his head, his jaw tightening. "I've said too much already."

He turned to go, but Ella grabbed his arm. She'd get answers out of him one way or another, even if it meant pestering him for them.

Energy jolted between them, and the forest faded. Ella lay on the ground in the gate room, feeling her power and her life draining away as it poured into the open gate.

"Aurelia!" Luc appeared at her side, falling to his knees beside her. "Aurelia, what have you done?" He clutched her hand.

"I had to do it." She reached up to touch his face. "I thought I'd lost you."

"You'll never lose me."

"We failed, Lucan. It was our duty to protect the world. If I can stop the Esrac by sealing the gates, I will. I'll give my life if I have to."

"No, you can't die! You can't, I won't let you."

Ella smiled as she felt her life force seeping away.

Another man appeared. He looked so much like Griffin it was eerie.

"The city has fallen, and most of our people are dead," he said. "You did this. An avatar and a knight share a sacred duty to protect the gates between the worlds. You both failed in that duty."

"The Esrac are gone. I sealed them in another realm," Ella rasped.

"We brought the threat here. What's to stop them or another enemy coming through?" the Griffin look-alike demanded. "I warned you both, but you didn't listen. The gates can never be opened again, nor will any other avatar be trained to protect them. I curse you both in this and every future life. You'll never be together. Not until balance has been restored and the threat from the Esrac is finally over."

Ella pulled away, letting go of Luc's arm as she gasped for breath. "What just happened?"

"The truth," Luc said. "Now you know why duty must always come first."

She shook her head. "I don't understand."

"Avatars and knights were sworn to serve the goddess, ensuring the balance between magic being used for life and death was kept between the worlds. In our first lives, we broke our oaths. We not only fell in love, we walked between the realms and found an enemy that almost destroyed the places we were meant to protect. Our people blamed us for the destruction that ensued and cursed us. I've been trying to find a way to stop the Esrac ever since," he said. "Our people decided to ban magic and stop the training of all avatars in the hope the past would never repeat itself, and the bloodline died out. You're the only one because we were cursed to come back over and over again until we fix it."

"And instead of doing that, I started the cycle again." She sighed. "Why didn't you tell me?"

"Because I hoped to keep you away from this. I wanted you to have a life free from the past, for things to be different this time, but I guess I couldn't stop fate from having its way."

"Is that why you pushed me away?"

He avoided her gaze. "It doesn't work between us, Ella. It never has."

"Really? Because something keeps drawing us back together."

"Being together won't change anything. I'll still have to watch you die, and I won't do that again."

"Luc..." An icy feeling washed over her, and she stiffened. "They're here. I feel them."

Luc glanced around, pulling out his sword. "Where?"

"Close." She touched his arm. "Look, I still don't understand what all this means, but whatever happens, I think we're supposed to get through this together. Powers and all."

"Ella, I can't watch you die again. I won't." He touched her cheek. "If that means taking your powers, then—"

He suddenly pulled away, drawing his glowing sabre.

A chill ran over Ella once more. Goose bumps spread over her arms, exactly as they had the day she'd first encountered the Esrac. One of them had arrived.

Something blurred toward them.

Luc shoved her behind him as an Esrac appeared and his sword flared to life.

Ella's scrambled up, sensing a second Esrac. Although an avatar's role was to keep the balance and protect the gate, she hadn't been built to stand back and let someone else fight her battles for her.

Purple fire formed in her hand as the second Esrac came at her.

"Alright, you slimy-faced beast. I'm ready for you this time." She threw the burst of starfire straight at it. The Esrac ducked and the tree behind him exploded.

"Ella?" a voice called, echoing through her ears. "Ella?" It was the same voice she'd heard haunting her dreams.

Who is it? What does it mean?

The Esrac flew at her, but she blasted it again. This time, the starfire burned its arm, making the Esrac howl in pain.

"Ella, you must help me!" the voice called again

Ella clutched her head as the voice grew louder. Seeing its opportunity, the Esrac grabbed her by the throat, its barbs piercing through her neck.

Ella raised both her hands, calling up all the power she could muster, and set the creature aflame. As she caught her breath, she noticed Luc was still battling two of them.

"Ella?" the voice shouted. "Ella, you must come to the gate!"

One of the Esrac knocked Luc to the ground, and the other one fled, heading off in the direction of the gate room.

Without thinking, Ella ran after it. She couldn't allow it to try and open it. With enough blood and force restored to its body, it might be able to weaken the wards that had been placed on it so long ago.

The rings shot up as the Esrac activated the transportation device, and Ella gritted her teeth as the ring platform fell away, disappearing from view. She jumped onto the platform the second it reappeared, ordering the device to take her down into the chamber.

"Ella, no!" Luc called after her.

She ignored him as the rings rose up and light enveloped her.

This time, the chamber was lit by glowing torches that filled the space with an eerie glow, and Ella quickly spotted the Esrac standing in front of the gate.

"Stop!" she cried. "I won't let you open it." Starfire formed in her hand as she prepared to strike.

The Esrac laughed. "You can't stop me, avatar. My queen will walk this world again and destroy everything. Everyone will suffer for what you did to us."

There was a shuffle behind her, and before she could turn around, sharp barbs dug into her neck.

A second Esrac, she realised too late.

The first Esrac bit into its palm, its metallic fangs tearing through flesh as black blood gushed out of the wound. The second Esrac scooped her up, its talons tearing through her palm.

Ella flinched, feeling pain jolt through her. The Esrac were trying to break through the wards! They would weaken and fail if she couldn't stop it. She struggled, trying to break free of the Esrac's grasp, and reached for her magic. Blue fire emanated from her hands, stronger than it had ever been before. She grabbed the arms of the Esrac holding her, and it screamed as its flesh smouldered. She jumped free of its grasp and raised her hands, her eyes flashing with light. The Esrac struggled against nothing as the gate's ancient runes flared to life. For a second, the portal opened, filling with glowing energy as she forced the creatures through. Moments later, the gate fell dormant and went dark.

The rings shot down into the chamber and Luc appeared, his face bloody and bruised. "Ella?"

"I'm fine." She let out a breath. "Did you get all of them?"

He nodded, sheathing his sword. "They're gone. For now, at least."

Ella raised her hand, hurling a ball of starfire at the gate to be sure it was closed.

"I was so worried when you ran off. It's my duty to keep you safe." He pulled her into his arms, no longer caring about the distance he had tried so hard to keep between them. "So that's what I'll do."

"Why don't we just destroy it? Without a gate, no one will ever be able to come through to our realm."

"Don't you think I've tried?" Luc said. "The gates are too powerful to be destroyed."

She clung to him then, glad for the warmth of his embrace. "Come on, let's go back to the citadel."

CHAPTER 12

Ella struggled to sleep, knowing in the morning Griffin would decide her fate and take her powers away. He'd lectured them both the night before for going together to hunt for Esrac. Fidget scurried up the bed as he sensed her nervousness resting against her head. She ruffled his ears, closing her eyes.

She still hadn't figured out who the strange voice was, or why it kept calling to her. She thought about asking Luc, but decided against it. Just because he'd finally revealed some of his many secrets to her didn't mean he'd give her all the answers.

"Ella?" the voice called again, as if it had been waiting for her to think about it. "Ella, please help me."

She covered her head with a pillow. "Go away, leave me alone."

"Ella," the voice called louder this time, stronger somehow. It sounded male and almost familiar. "Ella."

She sat bolt upright as the flickering form of her father appeared at the end of her bed. "Ella, I need your help."

"Dad?" Ella gasped. "What are you doing here?" She climbed out of bed, not believing her eyes. The one person she'd been desperate to see for so long stood in front of her.

Fidget's fur slicked back, and he hissed a warning, but her attention hung on her father.

"Ella, I'm trapped. The avatar I used to protect had to force me through the gates to stop the Esrac," he said. "You must help me come back."

Ella hesitated. Could he still be alive after all these years?

"How do I know you're not some kind of trick?" she asked.

Caspian smiled, as if he had been expecting the question. "You remember the place I used to take you when you were a little girl? The cave with the stars in it?"

Ella's face paled and she nodded. Only her dad would have known about that place.

"Why haven't I seen you before now?"

"Because you weren't strong enough, but your powers have grown now. I'm dying, Ella. I need your help."

"How?" She wanted to believe this was real, but part of her couldn't.

"You know how. You must open the gate."

Ella shook her head. "I can't. I've already caused enough damage." She ran a hand through her hair. "Wait, how are you on the other side of the gate?" she gasped. "I thought only an avatar coul —"

"There's no time to explain how I got here. You must open the gate and bring me through." Caspian reached out as if to touch her. "Ella, I've been trapped in the Esrac prison realm for so long. I want to come home, to be with you and your mother again. Don't you want us to be together again?" He looked at her with longing. "Would you leave me here to die at their hands?"

Fidget growled again, his eyes flashing.

Ella looked down at the dust bunny. He'd warned her to stay away from the gate, and Luc had said the Esrac could trick people…

"I know you're not my father. Go away!" Her hands clenched into fists as the image faded.

That wasn't real, she reminded herself. *It was just a trick.*

Ella shot down the hall, pulling on a shawl as she went. She wouldn't let the Esrac trick her again, and she'd find Luc and Griffin. They'd know what to do.

She turned on her link and tried calling them, but neither answered. She tried Eric and Sara too and bit her lip when static greeted her. Eric always answered his link.

"La," Fidget squeaked. "La, where going?"

Ella ignored him, racing off through the empty corridors to Luc's chamber. She pushed the door open and found the room empty. Where had he disappeared to?

She pressed her link again and hurried toward Eric's chamber, where she banged on the door and waited.

When no reply came, she banged again, called out his name, then flung the door open. Eric's bed appeared just as empty as Luc's had been.

Damn it, where are they?

What if Esme could somehow trick them, too? Had she lured them away?

Ella moved down the hall and into Sam's room, flinging the door open and not bothering to knock. It was empty, too.

Maybe there was a reasonable explanation for them not being in bed. But after what she'd seen, her sense of panic rose as she hurried toward Griffin's office. He spent most of his time there, and often even slept there, so she didn't bother going to his chamber.

She crept to the office, using only the pale light streaming through the window to go by. Inside, she saw nothing but the desk, shelves and neatly stacked paperwork.

"Master?" She moved over to his desk. "Master Griffin, where are you?"

A shadow moved behind her, grabbing her before she had time to react. She struggled against the strength of her attacker's grip and looked up. It was Griffin.

"What are you doing?"

"It's time."

"Time for what? Where the are others?" She tried to wrench her hands free to summon her magic, but he o held her tighter.

"I knew Esme's mind tricks wouldn't work on you for long."

Griffin pulled her across the room and opened a door set into the panelling of the walls that hadn't been there before.

Her heart pounded in her ears and her eyes widened as she spotted a gate on the other side of the room he was dragging her into.

Luc, Sam, and Eric all lay slumped on the floor.

"Master Griffin, what the hell are you doing?" Ella asked.

"You're going to help me open the gate and bring Esme through. I've been waiting almost fifty years for another avatar to be born. Finally, the Valan will rise to power again and destroy the Senate once and for all. Magic users will no longer have to live in fear." He flashed her a maniacal grin.

"We can't do that; you know we can't. The Esrac were banished for good reason. Why would you want to bring them through?"

"Now I have you, I'll also have the power to control Esme. With everyone distracted by war against the Esrac, the Valan can return to the old city, and magic users will be liberated once again. You're more special than you think, Ella. You have been chosen to rid the world of our oppressors. While the rest of the Valan might put you to death because they're too cowardly to see you for what you really are, I know you must do you duty."

Griffin tied her hands behind her back before chaining her to the wall. She twisted her wrists to pry her hands free, and tried to summon her fire, but nothing happened.

Griffin walked over to the gate, touching the different runes around it.

"Master Griffin, we can't do this. The Esrac are too powerful to control. The only way the ancestors could stop them was by sending them to a hell realm, you know that."

She couldn't believe what was happening. Griffin had always been a mentor to her, a friend.

"Nonsense. I organised this expedition because I knew that either you or Sara had the power to be an avatar. Sara is different. I know that from testing her blood, but you? You will be the saviour of our people."

Ella spotted a blur of white shoot across the floor as Griffin touched the different runes. She couldn't let him do this. If he forced her to touch the gate or used her blood as the Esrac had tried to, the gate would open again and there would be nothing stopping the Esrac from coming through. She glanced over at Luc, willing him to wake up, but he lay unmoving, as did the others. They were on their own now.

She looked over at Fidget as he leapt into the air and bit into Griffin's shoulder. Griffin cried out in pain, trying to shove the dust bunny away.

Come on, if I'm so powerful, why can't I break myself out of these wretched chains?

As she pulled against them, she felt it, a spike of heat between her fingers. She caught a flash of silver as Griffin pulled out a knife, ready to use it on Fidget.

Ella felt anger burn through her. No one was going to take Fidget away from her, and she'd be damned if she'd let Griffin unleash a monster into their world.

The chains fell away in a burst of sparks, and she threw out her hand, sending a burst of glowing blue fire straight at Griffin. It hurtled him against the far wall. To her relief, Fidget landed on the floor and scurried toward her, unharmed.

Griffin gripped the knife tighter and slashed it across his palm, then pressed his hand against the gate, making the runes flare to life. She could feel the wards beginning to weaken. An image flashed through her mind, and for a second, there were bodies lying around her as an Esrac woman with long, blood-red hair held onto the gate.

Ella knew what she had to do. She rushed over to touch the wall, watching the runes flare to life as the portal opened.

"I won't let you bring any more Esrac through," she hissed, raising her hand again. Using a finger, she started to trace the runes to seal the gate shut, just as she had done in her first life.

"No!" Griffin tried to grab hold of her, but Ella gripped the sides of the gate and dodged him before he could reach her. He stumbled, falling straight through the glowing portal.

Ella gasped, trying to grab hold of Griffin, but knew it was already too late. A violent burst of energy sent her crashing to the floor as a figure stepped through the glowing light.

A woman with blood red hair stood over her as the light faded there. She gave Ella a fanged smile. "Thanks for your help, Aurelia. I knew I'd convince you to free me." She laughed. "It was so easy. You always were gullible in your need to help people. I see that hasn't changed in this lifetime either."

Ella tried to scramble up and raised her hand again, more fire flaring between her fingers. She aimed it at the Esrac.

"Fool, I will devour everyone in the city before you get a chance to try to take me down again. I am Esme, Queen of the Esrac."

Esme laughed again. "Thanks for your help, little avatar." She grinned. "I'm sure we'll see each other again very soon."

The End

CAPTIVE AVATAR

CHAPTER 1

Ella Noran stared down at Master Griffin. His hair had turned white, his face weathered and more wrinkled than it had been before. His eyes were glassy as they stared up at her, yet their faraway gaze looked almost accusing. Five tiny red incision marks lined his throat where Esme, the Esrac queen, had grabbed him, pierced his skin with her barbs and drained him.

Ella stared down at him, feeling numb.

Luc was the first of her unconscious friends to wake up. "Ella? Ella, what happened?" His eyes darted around the room. He leapt up and rubbed the back of his head.

"He—" She tried to explain what had just happened, how she'd gone in search of them after Esme had tried to lure her into opening the gate again. But no words would come out. She couldn't believe it, Griffin had been her mentor, her friend, yet he'd done *this,* released the age-old enemy of her people that had been locked away in a hell realm.

"Ella?" Luc gripped her shoulders. "You need to tell me what happened. Did you let Esme through?"

She nodded, still unable to speak as she stared at Griffin.

Fidget, her dust bunny, scurried up her arm and wrapped his long, fluffy tail around her neck to comfort her.

"Griffin…" she whispered.

Luc knelt and touched Griffin's neck. "He's dead. Damn it, he caught me off guard and stunned me earlier!"

"He…he opened the gate." Ella finally found her voice and

swallowed hard as bile rose in her throat. Despite her time working with the *bones* of the dead, she'd never seen anyone die before. "He wanted to use Esme. He said with her help, magic could come back into our world and its users wouldn't have to fear persecution anymore."

Luc shook his head. "Griffin was one of the Valan. His sole duty was to make sure this never happened," he said.

Ella moved over to Sara and Eric and huffed a sigh of relief. "They're still breathing."

"Griffin must've stunned them too," Luc said. "How did he force you to open the gate?"

"He didn't. He tied me up and broke through the runes, using his own blood. When he tried to open the portal, I got free. Fidget came to help me and bit him. When they were struggling, he fell into the gate and somehow opened the portal. I tried to reactivate the runes and close the gate before he fell through it, but Esme grabbed him and came through instead." She glanced over at the darkened symbols that had once held the power to keep the gate shut. "Griffin said he could use me to control the Esrac." She straightened. "What are we going to do, Luc?"

The one thing she and Luc had to prevent in their past lives happened while they were helpless. The queen of a vampiric race had been unleashed into their world once again.

Ella felt tears prickle her eyes at the thought. But now wasn't the time. They would do nothing to cast Esme back into the other realm or ease the sting of Griffin's betrayal.

Luc ran a hand through his hair and sighed. "We're going to have to contact the Senate and report what's happened."

"How are we going to explain this?" she said. "If we tell them the truth, we'll have to admit I have magic." Ella left the death sentence that would come as a result unmentioned. Magic was forbidden, and anyone suspected of having it was burned alive.

"We don't have a choice. We can't hide this."

"Do you want to watch me burn?" Ella cried, her hands clenching into fists.

She couldn't believe he was even entertaining the idea! Despite their recent breakup, she had hoped he still cared about her on some level, at the very least as a teammate on the same expedition.

"Of course not!" Luc snapped. "I'll contact the Valan. If we could get you across the border—"

"Why should I trust the Valan? I trusted *him*." She motioned to Griffin. "Look what happened. How do I know the Valan won't try to kill me, or worse, try to use me like he did? Even Griffin said they fear avatars."

Someone groaned, and seconds later Eric scrambled up. "What the hell happened?" He glanced between them, then down at Griffin. "What...?"

"It's a long story," Luc said.

He turned back to Ella. "We need to work out what we're going to tell the chancellor."

Sara woke up next, letting out a horrified gasp when she spotted Griffin.

"Griffin attacked us. He tried to use me to open the gate...and Esme, the Esrac Queen, came through," Ella explained what had happened.

"*Griffin* did this?" Sara asked in disbelief. "But he..."

Ella watched as puzzlement overtook her features and felt a pang of sympathy for the other girl. She knew Sara had idolised Griffin.

"What are we going to tell the Chancellor?" Eric asked. "Ella has magic but couldn't fight off the thing that got Griffin? That's a one-way ticket to a death sentence."

Ella released a breath in relief when they moved into what had been Griffin's makeshift office, which still had papers stacked up in neat piles on the desk. She tried to ignore the fact he would never leaf through them again. At least here she wouldn't have his glassy eyes staring up at her.

"We need a cover story," Ella said as she watched Luc pace up and down. It was something he always did when he got anxious. "To explain to the chancellor what happened without exposing our magic."

"Wait, you have magic too, Luc?" Sara remarked.

"Yes, but not in the way Ella does. She's an avatar, I'm a Valan knight," Luc replied. "There's a big difference."

"Why can't we just dump Griffin's body somewhere?" Eric suggested. "That'd solve all our problems."

Sara glared at him. "That's a terrible thing to say!"

"Why? It's no more than he deserves. He released the queen of those green skinned freaks!"

Luc shook his head. "No, it would only create more problems. Griffin is too well-known to go missing, they'll have people searching everywhere for him."

"We should be as truthful as possible," Ella suggested. "Lies always unravel." She gave Luc a pointed look.

"Why not just say we found a strange device, the green thing came through it and killed Griffin?" said Eric.

"I suppose that could work," Luc mused, as he ran a hand through his hair. "I still think Ella should leave, though. It'd be safer—"

Ella took hold of his arm, glancing at Eric and Sara. "Excuse us for a minute." She dragged him out into the hallway before he had a chance to protest and let go of his arm as she frowned at him. "I know what you're trying to do," she said. "You think me leaving will protect me from the curse that will strike us down if we fail to stop the Esrac this time."

Luc looked away, and she knew she had been right. "You'd be safer."

"How? Even if the curse and the Senate don't get me, Esme *will* come after me," she pointed out. "I'm the last avatar, she still wants revenge for what I did to her a thousand years ago."

Luc sighed. "I don't want to watch you die."

"This time is different. *We* are different," she said. "We know we can find a way to stop Esme, we just have to work together to do it."

He ran a hand through his hair again, something he always did when he got anxious. "I can't believe Griffin betrayed us. He was my mentor, he trained me to be one of the Valan knights."

"You're not the only one he betrayed, but we can't think about that now. We have to come up with a believable cover story, one that won't give the chancellor or the Senate any reason to doubt us."

Luc pulled back. "It's not just that. Esme is free and I'm afraid they'll either ignore the problem or hold us responsible for it, even if they can't prove it. Either way, we need to tread carefully."

"We will, but I'm not leaving. I'm the one who found the gate, the one who first created it. One way or another, we'll find a way to stop the Esrac."

"I need to contact the Senate. We can't leave Griffin's death unreported for too long without it raising more unwanted questions."

After some further discussion to finalise the plan, they moved back into the office.

"Okay, our story is Griffin called us all in to show us an area of interest he found, and there was an accident," Luc said.

"How do we explain why none of us are hurt?" Eric folded his arms.

"We should say Master Griffin stumbled upon a device and accidentally triggered it," Sara suggested, then bit her lip. "Although he'd record the finding and make notes first."

"He'd also have you or I there with him." Ella pushed her long black hair off her face. "Can we really get away with this?"

"We can, and we will. We'll say Griffin stumbled upon the gate and must have used forbidden magic to bring something through," said Luc. "Upon hearing his screams, we all ran up and found him dead. I'll be the one who found him first."

"You want to tell them *Griffin* used magic?" Sara gasped. "That would make him a heretic."

"He *did* use magic to open the gate," Ella pointed out. "Just not his own. We wouldn't be lying."

"We have to keep the suspicion off us," said Eric. "So we're clear. We heard Griffin scream, and rushed here. Luc found him, and we arrived soon after."

"We have to tell them about the Esrac," Ella insisted.

"That insinuates we have some knowledge of the gate, and magic," Sara remarked, playing with a strand of her long blonde hair.

"No, not if we're careful. I'm the only one who saw Esme come through," Ella replied. "We'll say I came in next. I saw a glimpse of Esme as Luc tended to Griffin. Then she vanished. That sounds reasonable enough."

The sound of heavy footsteps cut off their conversation as they echoed down the hall.

"Master Griffin?" a voice called.

"What's that?" Ella gasped, glancing at Luc. "I thought you hadn't called anyone yet."

"I haven't!" he hissed back.

The footsteps stopped and seconds later a man dressed in white armour came in, alerted by their whispering. "I'm Commander Ronin of the Celestus troopers. We received a distress call from Master Griffin's link. What's going on here?"

Ella's heart started pounding in her ears, and she swallowed hard.

Luc stepped forward. "Griffin is dead. He triggered an ancient device and a strange creature inside it killed him."

The trooper glanced between the four of them, then walked into the next room where Griffin's body still lay. When he returned, his expression hardened. "You are all to be taken back to Celestus for questioning," he told them. "If any of you are responsible for this, I will find out."

CHAPTER 2

Luc forced himself to remain calm during the flight back to Celestus after he noticed how anxious Ella seemed. He was the one who had to handle things now Griffin was gone—he was the only Valan left, and the Commander had already made it clear the Senate wouldn't be their ally.

Sara sat across the aisle crying to herself, and beside her, Eric looked tense.

Luc hated the fact they'd been dragged into this mess. Why hadn't he tried harder to convince Griffin that doing an excavation in the old city would lead to nothing but trouble?

He recalled how eager Griffin had been to go there, and how he thought it'd been to find historical artefacts. Now he guessed he'd been wrong about that. Ella chewed her lip and Luc reached out to take her hand, but she pushed him away and turned to gaze out of the window.

Great, even more distance between us.

But he supposed that was for the best. Just because she knew who and what he was now didn't change anything. She had broken up with him for a reason, and with Esme on the loose, he didn't have time to think of any romantic notions to win her over again.

Better they stayed apart. Falling in love was what had got them into this mess in the first place. Because he loved her, he'd supported her love for invention and exploration in their first lives, which had led her to create the gate that had taken them to the Esrac home world. That had started everything all those years ago.

Luc hissed out a breath, pushing away thoughts of their past. He needed to focus on the situation at hand. He knew he'd keep Ella safe no matter what happened, but he couldn't afford to let his concern for her cloud his judgement now, and focused on his alibi, silently willing the others to do the same. They couldn't go over the cover story anymore, not with a ship full of troopers to overhear them.

He still couldn't believe what Griffin had done, though he didn't doubt Ella's word. Griffin had, after all, stunned him.

Damn it, I should have done something! I should've seen Griffin as a threat.

His hands clenched into fists, but he forced himself to remain silent and take deep breaths for the rest of the flight. Anger wouldn't change anything.

The flight from the old city of Arkadia where the team had been excavating to the shining towers of Celestus lasted only half an hour, but to Luc, it felt like an eternity. The Chancellor and leader of the Senate had no tolerance for anyone suspected of using magic, but Luc didn't have to worry about his own. He'd been trained from an early age to hide his abilities as one of the Valan, an ancient order of knights sworn to keep the peace in their land. They'd been forced into obscurity when the Senate had come to power and anyone who seemed to have magic was either killed or forced to live on the other side of the border as a so-called rebel.

The airship landed at the dock, and Commander Ronin approached them outside.

"You're all to be taken into custody and questioned."

The smell of fumes and raw of airships made Luc miss the peace of the old city. He wondered if any of them would ever see it again.

"Questioned about what?" Eric demanded. "Griffin used magic, and some—"

"Silence," Ronin snapped. "You're all involved in Griffin's death until I say otherwise."

Another trooper prodded Luc in the back with his stunner, and he glanced over at Ella.

Be careful, he said, hoping she'd hear him.

Ronin marched Luc off to the city's security tower. A huge shining building, surrounded by cold hard steel and meant to intimidate anyone who saw it. It didn't bother Luc. He worked there as a trooper himself, overseeing security in the city. For the past couple of years, he'd been stationed at the university's campus, where he'd met Ella a few months earlier.

On the way in, the troopers scanned him for magic, which he passed. He only hoped Ella had passed as well. Satisfied with the result, Ronin herded him into a small room with once-whitewashed walls that had turned almost black with age. It contained nothing but a metal table and two rickety metal chairs. Ronin hooked Luc up to a monitor that would read his vital signs and indicate if he lied or not.

He sat down and pulled out a recorder crystal.

"This is Dex Ronin with Luc Flynn, a captain in the Celestus security division," Ronin began. "Today at 0200 hours, Master Rhys Griffin, head of Celestus University, sent a distress call," he continued. "Upon my arrival in the old city of Arkadia, I found Master Griffin dead and Flynn present at the crime scene. How do you explain that, Flynn?"

Luc shifted in his own seat and kept his expression neutral. He'd been trained for years to hide his secrets in plain sight. One thing Griffin had taught him was to tell as much truth as possible, to make lies more convincing.

"I was awoken by the sound of someone calling for help, so I proceeded to Griffin's office by myself, where I found Master Griffin dead and an unknown monster standing over him." Luc knew he couldn't hide the fact Esme had come through the gate and was now on the loose, so made no attempt to.

"What kind of monster?" Ronin arched a brow.

"It appeared to be female with long red hair, green skinned with metallic fangs," Luc said.

Ronin's lips quivered into a smile, and he bit back a laugh before responding. "Where were you when Griffin sent out the call for help?"

"In my chamber, sleeping." Luc still had no idea why Griffin would have sent out a distress call after he summoned Esme. The nearest troopers would have been over half an hour's flight away. Griffin wouldn't have done it by accident, either.

"Did you hear the call?"

Luc hadn't had the chance to check his link before Ronan had removed all their gear and weapons back in the old city, so the call would show as unnoticed on it.

"No, but the signals were unreliable in the citadel thanks to its thick stone walls and interference." Again, the truth, their links *had* been unreliable. Eric had been working on a way to boost the signal, but never had the chance to test anything.

"How did you hear Griffin calling for help, then?" Ronin asked.

"He screamed. It was hard not to hear."

"Why were you in the old city? Griffin went there with a small team leading an archaeological expedition. Were you part of it?"

"I went along as security. Given how close the old city is to the border, Griffin was concerned the team might be attacked."

"What was Griffin doing when you found him?"

"As I said, he was already on the floor, dead, with a monster standing over him." Luc watched the lines of the monitor he'd been hooked up to smoothly zigzag across the screen. Good, it showed he spoke the truth.

"Where did this so-called monster come from?"

"I imagine through whatever device Griffin discovered in the room he died in."

"And why weren't you with him?" Ronin's gaze hardened.

"It was the middle of the night. The whole team had gone to bed hours before."

"When did you last see Griffin before he died?"

Before he called me into his office and stunned me. Luc noticed the lines on the monitor increase as his heart rate picked up.

"Around ten. We had tea together and discussed what we'd be doing the next day. Then I headed up to my chamber. I last saw my teammates at dinner around seven. Ella was the next person I saw. She came in not long after me, having heard the commotion."

Ronin glanced over at the monitor, but Luc's life signs stayed smooth. "What was the monster you saw?"

"Female, with red hair and green skin."

Again, smooth lines showed.

"How did she kill Griffin?"

"I don't know."

The lines didn't waver, much to his relief.

"Did you see her kill him?" Ronin asked. "Where were Sara Morgan and Eric McGee when this attack took place?"

Already unconscious when Griffin called me. Thank goodness he knocked on the door and didn't send a link call.

Griffin had roused Luc from sleep, insisting he needed help.

Luc hadn't bothered to question Griffin either. Another failure on his part.

"No, I didn't see what she did. The others were sleeping their chambers."

"Was Ella Noran with you when the attack happened?"

Luc frowned, surprised by the sudden change of direction in questions. "No, why would she be?"

"We are aware of the fact you two were romantically involved, and you went away on an expedition together," Ronin said. "If you were distracted—"

"I wasn't. My relationship with Ella ended months ago." His hands clenched into fists underneath the table.

"Your duty was to make sure Griffin, and the team stayed safe. That hasn't happened," Ronin said bluntly. "You're to be held in custody until we get to the bottom of what happened to Griffin."

Ronin had him taken to a holding cell and left him there. Luc slumped onto the metal bunk and sighed. He'd been so worried about protecting Ella from the curse and stopping any more Esrac from coming through the gate. He hadn't been prepared for anything else. Or what Griffin's betrayal and the fallout from it would entail.

Why hadn't he called the Valan the moment he'd found Griffin's body? Almost as soon as he asked himself the question, he knew the answer.

Because I was too shocked and let emotion blind me. I won't make that mistake again.

CHAPTER 3

Esme raised her hand as bright sunlight blinded her. Her throat felt raw, and her stomach gnawed with hunger. All the renewed strength she'd received by killing the old man had worn off after running through the night.

The sunlight stung her skin, making it prickle with pain, and she ducked underneath a large tree, using its canopy to shield her from the sun's rays. Everything here looked so green, smelled so fresh and clean. How she missed the darkness and cold of her own world. The sun wouldn't kill her, but it would burn her if she exposed herself to it for too long.

She hated this world. The humans and their ways were alien to her, but it was still a rich feeding ground, the likes of which her people hadn't had in centuries.

Esme heard the distinctive thump of a heartbeat, and her fangs glistened as she grinned. *Good.* She needed energy, blood. Her kind required blood the way humans needed food to survive.

She'd run all night to put some distance between itself and the city of Arkadia. Not because she feared the avatar or the Valan—she'd kill them both soon enough—but they wouldn't have quick deaths. She'd make them suffer tenfold what she had suffered during the long centuries she'd spent trapped in the hell realm with no sustenance.

With no food source, her people had gone into a long hibernation in pods that kept their bodies alive. Esme herself had been forced to feed from her own men when she'd woken a few days ago, but now here she was, free in a rich feeding ground that could sustain her and her people for centuries to come. She finally had a chance to rule over this pitiful world, and neither the Arkadians nor the Valan would stop her this time.

Feeding on the blood of humans allowed her to access the memories of people she fed on, and she saw now that the one she had just killed, Griffin, had been a Valan too. The old fool had thought he could use the avatar to control her, and the rest of the Esrac. The thought made her laugh, but she had learnt valuable information from him.

The Arkadians' descendants relied on technology and had abolished magic. The Valan was almost extinct. There would be no one left to oppose her, since the avatar was an untrained girl.

The Arkadians failed to stop her once before and would again.

Esme leant back against a tree, wincing as her hands and face still stung. *Damned sunlight.* She'd blast that golden orb from the sky if she could. Hunger gnawed at her stomach anew as the heartbeat grew louder. She let out a low growl of excitement as a young man dressed in a white shirt and black trousers approached.

Esme ducked behind the tree as she spotted a weapon in his hand. It had a sharp edge and a wooden handle.

An axe, Esme realised. *A useless human creation used for cutting wood.*

She gripped the tree trunk as the man came closer. The pulse in his neck throbbed, making her fangs and barbed hands ache to drain the blood from him. Despite her need, she waited, urging him to come nearer with her thoughts so she wouldn't have to endure the sun's blistering rays again.

Come to me, she ordered.

The man looked up, surprised, as the voice entered his head. "Is someone there?"

Unable to wait any longer, Esme flew at him. The barbs on her hand dug deep into his chest, and she bit into his neck, lapping at the blood that flowed into her mouth. Images flashed through her mind as his memories came to her.

She saw her image reflected back in his eyes as they glazed over. He struggled, and his blonde hair whitened. Esme let go, wiping blood from her lips with the back of her hand as his dried-out husk fell to the ground.

Body sated at last, her skin stopped stinging and the hunger eased. Esme slumped back against the tree. She needed somewhere to get out of the sun, somewhere to create a new base. She'd need more warriors to succeed in taking control of this world later, but she still felt too weak from hibernation. She moved through the forest, using the canopy of trees to shield her from the worst of the sun's rays, and let memory take her.

Aurelia and Lucan, the strange visitors who claimed to come from another world, had come to visit her again. The feel of the magic pulsing from them made her barbs ache, but she had to pretend to be hospitable, for now at least.

"Greetings, Queen Esme." Aurelia gave her a warm smile. "I hope you're well."

Aurelia, with her waist-length black hair, ice-blue eyes, and pale skin, looked skinny for a human. Her companion Lucan had a lean, muscular body, short black hair, and dark eyes. Not that Esme cared what her food looked like. She only cared what they tasted like and knew these two would be tasty morsels indeed.

Esme wished she could feast on both of them, yet she waited. They amused her with their strange customs and polite small talk.

"I am." Esme gave what she hoped appeared to be an inviting smile. "Tell me, how did you come to my realm? I'd like to know more. We've never had visitors from another world before."

"We came through a portal," Lucan replied.

"Does this portal exist here?" She gripped the sides of her throne in an effort to hide her eagerness for the response.

"No, it only appears in our world," Aurelia replied, sharing a glance with her companion. "We're eager to learn more about you. This is the first land we've travelled to outside of our own world." Esme noticed Lucan grip Aurelia's hand as she continued speaking. "We're here to exchange information and customs with other realms."

"Is it true you feed on humans?" Lucan asked.

"Yes. My people require blood to survive," Esme admitted. "Like your people require sustenance."

His lip curled. "Do you kill people for blood?"

"No, we only take what we need from them," Esme said. "Though some do volunteer to have their lives ended."

Lucan's frown deepened. "Why would anyone do such a thing?"

"Those who are sick or unable to care for their families know they are doing a noble thing," Esme replied, playing with a long strand of her hair. "In exchange for their lives, we provide food and land for their families. We are not monsters. If we were, humans would have become extinct centuries ago."

Aurelia paled, and steered the conversation to Esrac customs, droning on until Lucas said it was time for them to leave.

Esme tried asking more questions about them and their world, but they didn't provide the kind of answers she needed.

"Good day to you, Queen Esme." Aurelia bowed her head. "Thank you for allowing us to visit you again."

Esme rose from her throne. "A pleasure. You will come back, won't you? I'd be happy to allow you to meet some of my…humans next time. Then you can see for yourself how well cared for they are."

"We must be going." Without answering her, Lucan gripped Aurelia's arm and pulled her toward the door.

"We would like that," Aurelia added. "Good day to you," she called as Lucan led her away and out the door.

Esme waved her hand and summoned one of her helmsmen, Storm. "I want to learn more about our visitors. You captured the slaves who escaped?"

"No, my queen. We found them dead," Storm replied.

"Curse it! Our human numbers are dwindling. We'll never be able to sustain the hive unless we find a better feeding ground." She clenched her teeth together with a clank.

"Would you like me to follow the visitors?" Storm asked.

"No, I'll do it myself."

Esme's long leather skirt billowed behind her as she stalked out to watch Aurelia and Lucan walk away from the hive. By keeping to the shadows, Esme knew they wouldn't see her. Her eyes flashed as she cloaked herself with an illusion. She'd blend in with the background, and they would be none the wiser.

"I don't think we should come back here again," Lucan said.

"Why not? This place is fascinating." Aurelia grinned. "Doesn't it excite you to visit a new world?"

"It's dark and disturbing. That queen isn't what she appears to be. We can't associate with monsters." Lucan's jaw tightened. "We'd be doing more harm than good if we came back here. What if she doesn't let us go next time?"

Monsters. Esme almost laughed at the notion. How were her people any more like monsters than humans themselves? She'd seen what humans were capable of doing to each other. The Esrac were no crueller than they were.

"This is the first place the gate brought us. Our invention has proved more incredible than I could ever have imagined," she said. "It's a way to travel to different lands, not only in our world but others too."

"If the high council finds out about the gate, there's no telling what they might do. An avatar is meant to teach and ensure the balance of magic. But this?" He motioned to the husks of trees that were long since dead. "This isn't the way."

Aurelia frowned at him. "I'm not giving up on the gate. The high council will eventually see what a wonder it really is."

"My love, I know you want to share your love of creation with others, but this will only lead to more danger." Lucan gripped her hand. "Please, Lia, let's not come back here. The Esrac see us as nothing more than food."

"You're wrong. We could learn from them, they can learn from us," she insisted. "The Esrac only feed on blood to survive. What if we could find a way to help them so they wouldn't need to anymore?" She gripped both his hands and stared into his eyes. "I want to run tests to see how closely humans and Esrac are related."

Tests? Esme's lip curled in a snarl as they moved further down the trail to the ruins of an old human settlement the Esrac had destroyed when they had first come to create a new hive. Comparing her people to humans was unthinkable. The Esrac were faster and superior to any humans in any world.

She stalked after them and crouched by a broken wall. Peering over it, a glowing doorway of golden light appeared. *Could this be the portal they'd spoken of?*

"Please consider what I've said." Lucan gave Aurelia a quick kiss. "I couldn't live with myself if anything happened to you."

Aurelia hugged him. "At least here we can be together without fear of anyone seeing us."

Esme watched them vanish through the portal. When she rushed over to the wall, the portal had gone. Regardless, she had learnt something valuable. Human emotion was a weakness that could easily be exploited. She would use them both to get what she wanted, and one way or another she would possess the portal's power and find her people a new food source.

CHAPTER 4

Ella's heart pounded so hard she thought it would burst out of her chest as two troopers led her into the security tower. The great steel building reached toward the heavens, joined by much taller towers. A few months ago, when she'd arrived in the city to start her scholarship, she'd been in awe of them. This place had been a new world to her compared to the tiny village she'd grown up in. Antaria was in the middle of nowhere, and they had little in the way of tech there.

Ella had loved coming to live here. She'd felt so stifled back home, and no one there understood her passionate fascination with the past. Once she met Griffin and Sara and found they shared her passion, she'd felt at home at the university.

She was about to be asked questions about Griffin's death. A lump formed in her throat. Griffin had welcomed her, told her stories about her missing father, but he had also opened the gate and let out the enemy she'd been fated to stop.

Part of her couldn't understand why he'd do it.

I guess I didn't know him at all. He must have known I had magic or suspected it, she thought. *He admitted as much before he died.*

One of the troopers, a man with dark hair and watery blue eyes, ran a scanner over her.

Fidget, who still sat perched on her shoulder, hissed and the scanner wailed in warning.

"What is that thing?" the trooper demanded.

"It's a dust bunny." She stared at the man, surprised by the fear in his eyes. *It's just Fidget, for goodness' sake. He looks like a ball of fluff.*

"You can't bring that thing in here," he snapped, making a grab for Fidget.

Fidget's white fur slicked back, and his blue eyes flashed as he let out a low growl.

"He's not a *thing*." Ella gritted her teeth. "I wouldn't touch him if I were you. Dust bunnies have very sharp teeth." She ran a hand through her hair. She just wanted to get these questions over with and then talk to Luc. They needed to discuss what to do next.

"Whatever. You can't have a rat in here."

Fidget flashed his teeth this time. "No rat," he growled.

"It talks!" the other trooper gasped, pulling his stunner out.

Ella felt heat flare between her fingers, but caught herself. *No, not now!* She couldn't risk her magic coming to life here. Still, why couldn't these idiots learn about indigenous animals that came from across the border?

Ella rolled her eyes. "Why? He won't hurt anyone." The lie tasted bitter in her mouth as her mind flashed back to how Fidget had fought when Griffin tried to break the seal on the second gate.

Fidget had tried to protect her and would again. His weight felt comforting on her shoulder. She didn't want him to leave her, but knew they wouldn't let him stay. They didn't understand him the way she did.

Ella's eyes widened when the first trooper raised his stunner. "Put your weapons down," she hissed. "All of this fuss over a dust bunny, honestly. And they call you the city's finest." She rolled her eyes and stroked Fidget's soft head, ruffling his ears. "It's okay, Fidge. Go outside."

Fidget gave his best imitation of a glare, which under other circumstances would have made her laugh. "No," he squeaked.

"Go, I'll be alright. They just want to ask me some questions."

"Bad." Dust bunnies only had a limited vocabulary. So bad could mean a lot of things, but Ella knew he could sense her fear. He'd seen what had happened to Griffin.

"Maybe we should question the rat too," the second trooper suggested.

"He can barely speak more than five words. I won't have you upsetting him," she said. "It's not like he could have hurt Master Griffin." Ella put her hands on her hips. "Fidget was out hunting, like all dust bunnies do during the night." She picked Fidget up and set him on the floor. "Go, Fidge. It's okay."

"Bad, bad, bad," Fidget repeated.

"Go!" She made a shooing motion, and to her relief, he scurried away.

The troopers took her into a droning lift that went up several floors. Ella's stomach twisted as the doors pinged open. She prayed her emotions wouldn't get the best of her or give her away.

Keep cool, you did nothing wrong. Griffin opened the gate, and you tried to stop him. An image of Esme feeding on Griffin flashed through her mind, and she shuddered. *Why couldn't I have been quicker? If I could have sealed the gate again...*

"What's wrong with you?" The first trooper gave her a shove, pulling her out of her thoughts.

"I'm...It's been a long night," she said. "My mentor just died."

A tear dripped down her cheek, and this time she let it fall.

The second trooper shoved her with his stunner. "Keep moving."

Ella felt a flash of anger at his callous response. Hadn't they heard of the whole innocent until proven guilty thing?

She reluctantly kept on walking as they led her into another room. She barely noticed the green walls and shiny oak floor, and for a moment she wished Luc, Fidget, or any of her team members were with her. She felt stronger with them by her side. As she thought about her team and how they had been endangered, she was surprised to find that pain gave way to anger at Griffin for his actions. One way or another, she would find a way to reverse what he'd done and stop Esme and the Esrac.

"Hello, Ella," said a female voice.

Ella looked up to see a redheaded woman sitting on the other side of the desk and gasped. It was Ezmeralda Aren, the Chancellor and leader of the Senate.

Ella felt her throat go dry. She expected to be questioned by the troopers, not by the Chancellor herself. Why would she be here? They'd already scanned her for magic, and she'd passed. Her father, who she had recently discovered had been one of the Valan, had taught her how to control it so it wouldn't be detected. It was all a matter of keeping her breathing under control and staying calm.

"Madam Chancellor." Ella blinked, surprised by how calm her voice sounded. "I...Master Griffin is gone." She slumped into a chair and buried her head in her hands in an honest show of devastation. Better to be grief-stricken than afraid. Fear would imply a guilty conscience.

"Yes, I know." The chancellor reached across the table to squeeze Ella's hand. "You poor dear. I can't imagine what you and your team must have gone through."

Ella sniffed and wiped her eyes. "I can't believe he's gone," she whispered, looking down at her lap.

"Ella, I know you've been through a terrible ordeal, but you must tell me what happened."

Ella looked into the other woman's eyes. There was a coldness there despite the concern in her voice. Ella knew she couldn't trust her.

"I-I woke up when I heard the screams. When I got to the office, someone—some*thing* came out. A woman with green skin." She shuddered. "The woman ran when I screamed. I ran over, but Master Griffin was already dead." She wrapped her arms around herself.

"Did Master Griffin tell you he was investigating a potential artefact?"

She shook her head. "No. Everything seemed fine when I went to bed."

Aside from seeing my dad in my room when I woke up. Good thing she'd seen through Esme's mind tricks.

"Have you seen Griffin do anything strange before now?" the chancellor prompted.

"Strange how?" Ella frowned. Griffin had never done anything to make her suspect him before they'd gone to the old city.

"Any unusual things that defied explanation?"

"No, Master Griffin is—*was* like a father to me. He knew my father Caspian and helped me get the scholarship here." She gave a weak half smile at the memory of how happy she'd been then. "I don't know what Griffin did, but he let a monster out and she's running free. You have to do something. The monster has to be stopped."

"Tell me, Ella, how much do you know about your father's disappearance?"

Ella's frown returned at the question. Why would the chancellor bring that up? Her father had vanished over ten years ago. That had nothing to do with Griffin being killed by the Esrac Queen.

"Not much, it's all classified," she admitted. "He went on a mission near the old city, and no one ever saw him again. Why? Do you know what happened?" She leaned back and crossed her arms, watching for a reaction, but the chancellor's face remained impassive.

One of her main reasons for coming to Celestus in the first place had been to get answers about what had happened to her dad. Everyone always said Caspian was dead, but Ella continued to hope he might still be out there somewhere.

Ezmeralda nodded, her eyes now hard as flint. "Yes. He tried to help a rebel across the border, but our troopers stopped them. He was caught using magic. A battle ensued, and he got killed in the crossfire."

All the blood drained from Ella's face. "You killed him," she whispered.

Of all the things she'd imagined, being killed by the very people he worked for hadn't crossed her mind.

"I know your father had magic, Ella, and that you do too."

Ella gripped the edge of the desk. Part of her wanted nothing more than to throw her starfire at the woman responsible for killing her father, but it wouldn't bring him back.

"Listen to me, chancellor. Master Griffin used magic to release a creature that almost destroyed our world," she snapped. "Magic shouldn't be your concern. That monster will kill millions and destroy the Republic unless you find a way to stop her."

"The only threat to the Republic is people like you."

The Chancellor snapped her fingers, and two troopers grabbed Ella's arms and pulled her to her feet.

"You're to be placed under house arrest until I decide what to do with you. Judging by the magic we found you using on Griffin's keyno, you must be something special indeed." The chancellor's lips curved into a malevolent smile.

Ella's heart sank. Griffin had recorded her when she opened the gate?

She struggled as one of the troopers slapped a metal cuff onto her wrist. "You can't do this!" she cried. "I'm the only one who can help you!"

The chancellor waved her hand and motioned for them to take Ella away, her cries for help fading as they dragged her behind them.

CHAPTER 5

Ella stared out of the window as the sun rose over the city's shining silver towers. Celestus looked like something out of a fairytale, but her life here was far from being one. For the past month, she'd been locked in her apartment, but no one could decide what to do with her. Today would be another day of trying to amuse herself whilst fighting off the madness that threatened from being locked up for so long.

Why haven't they done anything to me yet? Ella paced the length of her sitting room. Though she had been put before them after Griffin's death and they had issued an order, the Senate hadn't removed her powers yet, just placed a metal band on her wrist that was supposed to block all magic. The thought of when the day would finally arrive made her stomach turn with dread, but she was still amazed they hadn't killed her, especially when her warnings about the presence of Esme had been dismissed. They killed those suspected of magic for less. She wanted to escape, to try and save her world from the horrific threat the Senate had simply ignored, but they kept guards outside her apartment, and had devices watching her too. No move would go unnoticed.

She'd petitioned the Senate to let her retain her powers to protect them more than once, but her pleas had fallen on deaf ears. It was only a matter of time before the chancellor had someone remove her magic for good, or they decided she was too much of a threat to them and killed her.

Ella knew she couldn't let that happen.

As for Luc, he hadn't come to see her once during her month-long imprisonment. The Chancellor had appointed him to take on Griffin's duties, and he'd become an unofficial member of the Senate. Part of her still resented him for not telling her the truth about them or his magic long before now, but despite having broken up with him, Ella knew they had to work together to stop the Esrac and restore the balance of power once and for all.

Her tiny apartment consisted of nothing but a sparsely furnished bedroom and bathroom, a sitting area with a black leather sofa and a small wooden table complete with two chairs, a kitchenette with an auto cooker, and whitewashed walls. Ella never had the time or money to furnish the place. It only served as a place to sleep and eat when she wasn't busy working at the university alongside Master Griffin.

She loved the views of the city outside when she first arrived here, but after being stuck inside for so long, she hated the shining towers. The city that had once filled her with so much wonder now felt like a prison.

The door buzzed, and Ella rose, hurrying down the hall. She pressed the control panel to open the front door and shielded her eyes before a familiar light flashed in front of her. A force field had been placed on the door and windows to prevent her from leaving her apartment.

Her heart sank as she saw Sara holding a basket full of food on the other side. "Oh, hey." Ella forced a smile.

"I thought you'd be happy to see me," Sara said, dropping the basket on the table as she walked in. "You must be bored." Sara's long blue university robe accentuated her long blonde hair and bright blue eyes. The sight of the robe made Ella's heart twist. She hadn't been able to set foot on the campus since she'd been placed under house arrest.

"Bored would be an understatement." Ella had tried filling her time by scouring the records written by Griffin that Sara managed to smuggle to her in the hope of finding answers about the Esrac threat and her own uncertain future. She'd spent most of the time holed up inside her bathroom to avoid the camera's prying eyes. No doubt whoever'd had been watching her had thought she'd been in there crying—which she had for the first day. But the bathroom was the only place to get any real work done. So far, she hadn't found anything that could be useful in solving either problem.

"Eric's not here, is he?" Sara glanced around.

"No, he doesn't come until late evening when he's finished his shift."

Eric worked as an engineer for the city's fleet of airships and had been a good friend to Ella. He came to see her and have dinner with her almost every night. Thankfully, both he and Sara had been cleared of any suspicion in connection to Griffin's death.

"Have you seen Luc?"

Sara shook her head. "No, he's been so busy since he started serving as Griffin's replacement."

Ella winced. Every time she thought of Master Griffin, she saw Esme draining the life out of him and remembered how he'd wanted to use her to become powerful and bring magic back.

"How's Fidget?" she asked instead. Since her imprisonment, her dust bunny had gone to stay with Sara. He'd gone half mad being forced to stay inside so much, but Ella missed having him around. He still popped through the window to come and see her, but it felt too quiet without him.

"Fine. I haven't seen much of him in the past few days. I think he's been off hunting. Have the dreams stopped?" Sara settled on the sofa.

Ella shook her head. "No. I've been seeing bits and pieces of my first life, but nothing helpful."

Sara shook her head. "I can't imagine ever having lived before. What was it like?" she said. "Do you remember much?"

"I remember being with Luc. He was so different then."

Past Luc had actually enjoyed spending time with her, had made her laugh. They'd been open and honest with each other, having no secrets, unlike present Luc, who seemed withdrawn and convinced it'd never work between them. The two short months they'd spent as a couple seemed a distant memory now.

"Sara, I've got to get out of here. I need to go home. My father was a Valan knight too. He may have known way more than Griffin. I can't find out unless I get out of here." She'd been too afraid to talk about her possible escape for fear the Senate might have planted listening devices in her apartment. But after being cooped up so long, Ella didn't care.

"How? There are guards everywhere."

"I'll figure something out, but I've got to see Luc. Can you get a message to him for me?"

"I'll try." Sara hesitated, glancing around the room, then fumbled in her basket for a moment. "I found this in the vault at the university." She pulled out a small crystal ball.

"I'll get into big trouble if anyone finds out I took it, so we'll have to be quick." She put it down on the table. "It's supposed to show glimpses of the past. I thought it might help you with your memories."

"I'm not sure the past can give me any answers," Ella admitted. Her dreams had been nothing but fragments of a jumbled-up jigsaw puzzle that made no sense to her.

"What has it shown you so far?"

"That Luc and I were happy, for a while at least. Then it all turned to crap, and the rest is history." She tugged a lock of dark hair behind her ear and sighed. "What do I have to do?"

"In truth, I don't know how it works, but Master Griffin gave strict instructions never to touch it, especially not with their bare hands. Try it." Sara leaned forward.

Ella picked up the orb, half expecting it to burn her or for guards to come swarming in, but nothing happened. "I've only seen glimpses of my first life once whilst being awake." Sure enough, she closed her eyes and felt the orb grow warm in her hand.

"Do you see anything?" Sara's voice drifted away as she spoke, as though carried off in the wind.

Ella opened her eyes and looked down, surprised to see she was wearing a low-cut long red dress that had no back. The fabric felt soft and silky against her skin.

"Ella?" Luc appeared in the doorway, frowning at her. "What are you doing?"

Ella? She had been expecting to hear him call her Aurelia, her past name.

"Luc? How are you here too?" Before the question had left her lips, she knew the answer had to be their connection. Whether he liked it or not, they were bound together by more than just their past mistakes.

He gave her a hard look. "I was hoping you'd answer that."

This was present Luc, the one who wouldn't even come to see her, not the past Luc who'd rushed into her arms whenever they met.

"I'm trying to see the past so I can learn from it," she said, folding her arms. "Go. You don't have to be here."

Luc grabbed her arm. "Haven't you learnt anything from our past mistakes? I don't need to revisit them to know what we did was wrong."

"Falling in love wasn't a mistake," she snapped. "Not then, at least. In our present lives, it might have been." Her fists clenched as she felt the familiar unwanted ache in her chest. He had hurt her in a way no one else could, and she hated that she still loved him. "Look, I'm sorry about Griffin. I never meant for it to happen." She sighed. "I made mistakes, I know that, but we—"

Luc raised a hand, cutting her off. "The chancellor wants me to strip your powers away. Maybe that would be for the best."

"Esme is still on the loose. You need an avatar to help stop her, and like it or not, I'm the only one you've got. Go. I didn't come here to see you."

Ella turned to walk away, but before she could, Luc caught hold of her and gave her a passionate kiss. A whirl of thoughts and pictures flashed through her mind until something yanked her away.

As she slumped back on the sofa, the crystal fell from her hands and clattered to the floor.

Sara gave a cry of alarm, dropping to her knees to grab the crystal with sleeve-covered hands. "Oh, thank goodness it's not broken!" She glanced over at Ella. "What did you see?"

Ella sat still, a whirl of colours flashing past her eyes. "I'm not sure."

Her lips tingled from Luc's kiss. It had felt so real.

Sara slipped the crystal back into her basket and touched Ella's forehead. "Are you sure you're okay? You look a bit weird."

Ella blinked, shaking her head to clear it. "I'm fine, but you should go." She needed time to process what Luc had just shown her.

Sara frowned. "Really? Did you see anything?"

"Maybe. Go. Don't forget to feed Fidget or he'll get grumpy."

Sara picked up her basket, leaving a bag of food on the table. "I'll talk to Luc for you, but maybe you should move on. You said yourself that it didn't work between you, and there's always Eric."

"I have more important things to worry about right now. See you later."

CHAPTER 6

Luc leaned back in his chair. He sat surrounded by the rest of the Senate as the Chancellor droned on and on. He didn't take in half of what she said, nor did he care about any of it. Just because he was a trooper who had served under Master Griffin, it didn't make him a politician, yet the chancellor had insisted he take over Griffin's duties. He sighed, missing Ella's presence at the edge of his mind, where she had been a few moments ago. He hated not feeling her there anymore.

Get a grip, he told himself. *You know why you can't see her, why you can't be near her.*

Finally, the meeting ended.

"Luc, can I have a word before you leave?" the chancellor asked.

"Of course, madam. What is it?" He gave her a smile that didn't meet his eyes.

"How goes the organisation of the guard?"

One of the chancellor's first orders of business had been to reorganise the city's troopers. Griffin hadn't overseen them, but he seemed to have had some authority. Luc was rapidly discovering the magnitude of Griffin's role in the Republic and wondered if he'd really known the man at all.

"Er…I'll discuss it with Commander Ronin," he said, wishing he could just get out of there. He hated these meetings and everything that went with them. This hadn't been what Griffin had trained him to do, even if Griffin had been a traitor.

"I expect results, Luc. Griffin spoke highly of you. I'd hate for that to have been false," she said, shuffling her papers into a neat pile. "I need people who get the job done."

Then why did you pick me? I'm no good at this job, it's not what I trained for. I'm a Valan knight, not a bloody Senator.

"Will do, madam." He rubbed his temples and turned to leave, but stopped with his hand on the doorknob. "Have you decided what should be done about Ella Noran yet?"

The one thing he wanted the answer to was the one thing he dreaded hearing. Although he'd been cleared of any wrongdoing, Luc wondered if the Chancellor had given him Griffin's duties, so she could keep a close eye on him. *It has to be done,* he reminded himself. *I have to keep her safe. It's the only way.*

The chancellor's lips thinned as she turned toward him. "Ah yes, that girl," she said with a scowl. "We saw on Griffin's keyno she used magic and opened a door of some kind. If it were anyone else, I would have had her put to death by now, but out of respect for Griffin I haven't yet."

Luc's eyes widened. He guessed she was lying. They hadn't killed Ella yet because they knew there was something different about her. She wasn't just any ordinary magic user. He had no idea how deep the chancellor's knowledge went. Did she even know what an avatar really was? Did she suspect Ella was the key to bringing magic back into the world?

"We can't keep her under house arrest forever. Something must be done."

"I'll make a decision when I'm ready, Luc." She frowned. "Why so eager to have Ella dealt with?"

"Because magic is a threat."

Because it's the only way I can think of averting the curse and saving her life.

"Magic will *always* be a threat. That's why we have such strict laws."

She waved a hand in dismissal.

Luc headed out, moving through the halls until cool air hit his face. It felt good just to be outside. Being inside those great stone walls felt suffocating, and the outside world took some weight off his shoulders for a while. He wished Griffin were still here to guide him.

He'd never thought he'd be leader of anything, much less an unofficial Master.

He moved through the city, staying out of sight of any troopers as airships droned overhead and lights flashed. In the distance stood the glowing white towers of the old city of Arkadia, home to the ancestors and once the seat of power for magic throughout their world. So much had changed in the last thousand years, and the unforgiving steel and constant surveillance of the Republic now replaced those towers.

Luc headed into the ruins of an old tower that had been an old lookout point. The roof had long since fallen away, and trees now grew through the walls. He settled on a pile of rubble, glancing at the time on his link. Eric should have been there by now—not that Eric enjoyed helping him, but Luc didn't have any other allies within the city, as Sara couldn't get the kind of information he needed.

While he waited, Luc pulled out a crystal. One that he'd used during his first life, but its counterparts were still used by the Valan knights. Ella's father had given it to him when he'd first started mentoring Luc as a boy.

"This is Luc, the last Valan knight left in Celestus. If anyone can hear me, please answer," he said. "If there are any other knights out there, be warned. There is an Esrac on the loose."

He tried contacting the Valan Order numerous times over the past month Ella had been imprisoned, but so far hadn't received any kind of reply, even though Eric had checked the crystal and insisted it still worked fine. Griffin had always told Luc to use the crystal if something happened to him. Luc needed to contact the others, and even now, he kept his word.

"Master Griffin is dead, and the gate system is at risk. Does anyone hear me?"

The crystal remained dormant, and no one replied.

Luc sighed and tucked the crystal back into his pack.

"Hey." Eric appeared in the doorway. With his long blonde hair, multiple piercings and tattooed arms, he looked nothing like an engineer, but he had a brilliant mind and was good at finding out things that Luc couldn't risk getting information on himself.

Luc looked up, relieved. "Were you followed?"

"Hell, if I know." Eric shrugged. "What's with all the secrecy? Afraid someone might see us together?"

Yes. I can't risk the chancellor finding out I'm digging around.
"I can't be too careful right now."

"You're a *senator*," Eric scoffed. "Shady dealings come with the territory. I'm only helping you because you said you'd help Ella, who is still locked up and being accused of murder, in case you'd forgotten."

"I'm not a senator. We are helping Ella. Have you had any reports or not?" Luc didn't have time for yet another of these fights, he had to get back before someone noticed he was missing. The chancellor probably had people following him too.

Eric handed him a data crystal. "There have been five unusual deaths in the past week alone. All five victims had identical marks on their necks." He paused. "How does this help, Ella? Are you trying to prove to the Senate those freaky green skinned monsters exist? I'll testify to seeing one if need be."

"No, proving it to the Senate won't achieve anything. They'll still deny the Esrac exist," Luc said, pressing the crystal so the details appeared on a holo.

"Then what are you trying to do?" Eric asked. "Why haven't you gone after the bitch who killed Griffin?"

"I can't. I've tried to leave the city more than once. Troopers have stopped me every time. At least this way, I can track her. Thanks for this." He pocketed the crystal. "I appreciate your help."

Eric's lip curled. "I'm only doing it for Ella. Remember her? The one you haven't even bothered to visit?"

Luc shook his head. "It wouldn't change anything even if I did."

"You know, you don't deserve her. I get that you two were supposedly punished for mistakes you made a million years ago, but you did a pretty good job of screwing up your relationship with her all by yourself."

Luc's fists clenched. "Don't pretend you know anything about me and Ella. Everything I'm doing is to keep her safe."

"Right, never mind breaking her heart in the process."

Luc tried to remain calm, telling himself what Eric thought didn't matter. "Just go."

"No. I want to know why you're not doing a damn thing to get her out of there."

"I'm doing everything I can."

"Yeah, right! If you were, Ella wouldn't still be locked up while you're walking around with your new senator mates. Bet you were really happy to take over from Griffin, weren't you?" Eric snapped. "I don't see you using that newfound power to help Ella though."

"You think I actually *enjoy* being the Chancellor's lackey now?" Luc retorted.

"Yeah, and you like watching Ella suffer too."

Luc punched Eric in the face, feeling the crunch of bone under his fist. "Don't pretend you know anything about me," he growled.

Eric blinked, surprised, then took a swing at Luc. Easily dodging the blow, Luc pulled out his sword, the blade flaring with light.

Eric backed away, raising his hands in surrender. "Who the hell are you?"

"I am a Valan knight. Now get out of here!"

Eric took off without saying another word.

After calming himself down, Luc headed back to the citadel and his apartment. Paperwork and crystals littered his desk, but he ignored the memos and messages left by people expecting him to carry out Griffin's duties.

He had only one true duty, to keep peace and balance between the realms. To do it, he needed to find that Esrac before she managed to create more of her own kind, or worse, open the gate between realms. The task seemed impossible, since he couldn't get out of the city. The chancellor had people watching his every move, and even seeing Eric had been a huge risk.

He felt a stab of shame for hitting the other man. Valan knights were taught to always be in control of their emotions. But when it came to Ella, he couldn't always think straight.

He sat down, scanning the reports and marking various discovery sites on a map as he tried to narrow down the area the killings were happening in. He hoped he'd be able to track Esme and find out where she was hiding.

The apartment door buzzed, and Luc muttered a curse, closing the door to his study as he walked out. He glanced at the screen to see Sara standing there.

The door slid open as he pressed the control panel and rubbed his aching eyes. Glancing over at the window, he saw bright lights cutting through the black sky. He hadn't realised night had fallen already.

"Evening." Sara smiled as she walked in. "I brought you some dinner."

"I'm not hungry, but thanks. I have a ton of work to be getting on with."

Sara frowned. "When did you last eat?"

He rubbed his temples. "Breakfast. Maybe. Look, I appreciate you—"

"Sit," she ordered, pointing to a chair. "I'll warm this up in the auto cooker."

Luc reluctantly sat. Sara had been stopping by every couple of nights to bring him meals and stock up his auto cooker with food, and he still hadn't found a way to tell her no.

"How's Ella?"

"Frustrated, as you can imagine." Sara sighed as she pressed buttons on the cooker. "Has the Chancellor decided what to do with her yet?"

"Not yet, I have a feeling she's terrified of what might happen whatever she does."

"She can't keep Ella locked up forever," Sara said. "Ella wants to go home to her village. She thinks there might be answers there to help deal with the Esrac and everything that has happened."

Luc frowned. "I need to find the Esrac queen myself and stop her," he said. "I have to convince Ella to give up her powers. The longer she has them, the longer she's in danger, and not just because of the Esrac." He pulled a bottle of wine out of Sara's basket and gulped some of it down. Normally, Valan knights were forbidden to consume alcohol, but after the month he'd had, he couldn't bring himself to care.

The timer on the auto cooker beeped, and Sara pulled out a bowl of stew out. It smelled good and had thick pieces of meat mixed in with the fresh vegetables. As she set it down in front of him, he dug in, realising just how hungry he felt.

"I've been reading through Griffin's records and doing some of my own research." Sara said, as she sat down opposite him. "I found a story. It talks about an avatar and a Valan knight who worked together to keep the peace between lands. They fell in love and used a gate to explore other realms that didn't fall under their protection.

On one such trip, they caught the attention of a deadly enemy, who learnt how to use the gates from them. A lot of the people they were supposed to protect died because of it."

Luc sat there in silence, gulping down the stew in big mouthfuls now.

"The survivors blamed the two of them for it. A Valan Master decided to punish the pair by cursing them, not just in that life, but in all their lives after it. The curse says the perpetrator is doomed to die every twenty years, and that it will continue until they somehow restore the balance of magic being used for life and death between realms. From what I can tell, according to the curse, only the avatar must die. The knight lives on. Ella turns twenty soon. Do you want to remove her powers so you don't have to watch her die again?"

Luc put down the wine bottle. He had no idea how Sara could have found out. He thought the order had kept that secret, erasing the curse, its details, and his and Ella's past selves from all their records.

"It's the only way to keep her safe," he murmured. "We never enough time, no matter what happens. I won't let history repeat itself again."

CHAPTER 7

Ella cowered on the floor; her hands held by invisible bonds. She couldn't move, couldn't get away. *How could this have happened? I haven't done anything wrong!*

"You have failed in your sacred duty to keep the balance between the realms. For this, you will be punished," a man's voice called, echoing around her.

She couldn't see any individual faces, but knew there were people there watching her, judging her. She felt the heat of their gazes as their accusing eyes stared at her.

"The Esrac destroyed our city," said another voice. "Hundreds are dead. You brought them here…"

Next came the screams. A blur of faces all condemned her for the evil she had brought to their world. She tried to open her mouth, to apologise and tell them she had never meant this to happen and had only created the gate as a way of exploring other realms, teaching others magic, and giving them the knowledge that had been passed down and through the generations as was an avatar's duty. Instead, her device had only brought death and suffering to their world. Lucan's warning rang through her mind. He had told her they should never go back to the Esrac home world. Oh, how she wished she'd listened to him now!

She tried to move, to get up, but her limbs refused to comply. As if the weight of all the victims' emotions held her in place. Was this it? Would she be forced to suffer for this for the rest of eternity to pay for all the lives Esme and her people had taken?

She screamed, trying to summon her magic, but nothing came to her, not even the deep-seated power she had used to create the gate. She was alone, trapped, and the darkness around her threatened to swallow her up.

Ella gasped as something tightened around her throat, choking her and leaving her lungs screaming for air.

"I curse you both in this and every future life…"

Ella woke up gasping for breath, taking in huge gulps of air. Sweat plastered her hair to her face, arms and neck. Her nightgown felt wet all the way through, and her heart pounded in her ears.

"La?" Fidget appeared beside her and scurried over to her lap, worried.

She sat up, still choking, and touched her throat, half expecting to find something there. The first rays of dawn were creeping in, bathing the room in a cool glow.

She might have been cursed for her failure then, but she didn't know why she had to suffer for it now. "Just a stupid dream," she muttered. "Not real…" She shook her head to clear it.

Was it all because of the Esrac coming through? Had she let them through the gate back then, just as unintentionally as she had done recently?

She still had so many questions and very few answers.

Ella stroked Fidget's head as he stared up at her with wide, blue eyes.

"Damn it, I need to get out of here," she muttered, picking the dust bunny up and clutching him to her chest. As well as wanting to end her entrapment, she worried for the innocent thousands who remained unaware there was an Esrac on the loose.

Were Luc or the Senate even doing *anything* to find Esme? It didn't sound like it, but how could she help fix the problem by being stuck in here?

The front door buzzed, and Fidget wriggled out of her arms to sit up, nose twitching. "Food?"

"Later." Ella pulled on a robe and hurried to the door, wondering who'd be calling by so early. As she headed for the front door, she hesitated.

What if they had come to punish her? If the chancellor had made her mind up, Ella knew she would either lose her powers or be put to death. She turned to stare through the huge glass windows. Could she somehow get past the force field they had put there to prevent her from escaping? It was a three-storey drop, but even that would be better than what the Senate had in store for her. Fidget somehow managed to get in and out through her windows when they were open. Could she do the same?

She headed over to the window and pressed the panel to open it. The glass slid aside, and static flashed when she reached out, signalling the force field still held in place.

"Fidget?" Ella whispered, and motioned for him to come over.

The dust bunny scurried across the wooden floor and leapt up onto the windowsill, staring up at her. "Food?" he squeaked again.

"Fidge, I need you to go outside for me. Can you do that?" She glanced back over at the door as insistent knocking replaced the buzzing.

If the troopers had come for her, the front door wouldn't slow them down for more than a second. She needed to hurry.

Fidget's pointed ears drooped as he realised he wouldn't be getting any treats, but he scurried out onto the ledge beyond the shield's parameters. The force field had no effect, apart from making some of his long fur stand up in places.

So that's how he sneaks in and out.

Another burst of knocks echoed down the hall, this one louder than before.

Ella took a deep breath and climbed onto the windowsill. She had no idea where she would go or even how to get out of the city, but she'd worry about that later. She just had to get away from this place before they came in.

"Ella?"

She froze, recognising the sound of the muffled voice. *Luc. What's he doing here?*

Ella moved away from the ledge and turned on the video screen, gasping when she saw Luc standing there. She thought about letting him in, but hesitated. Part of her wanted to see him, but another part dreaded it. She let out the breath she'd been holding. At least it wasn't the troopers. But why had he come now, after all this time?

Ella moved down the hall, pressing the control panel to let him in. "What are you doing here?"

Luc looked paler than usual and had dark smudges under his eyes. He looked as though he'd aged ten years. "I'm leaving soon. I came to—" His shoulders slumped, and she knew why he'd come.

"No! You can't take my powers away. You can't! I won't let you." Ella backed away. How could he do this to her after all they'd been through together? Hadn't he cared for her at all?

"Ella, it's the only way I can keep you safe." Luc's jaw tightened. "Without your powers, you'll be free. You won't have to stay locked up, and you'll be safe from the Esrac."

"How do you know that?" Ella demanded, her fists clenching. "What's to stop more of them from coming after me? This isn't because of them, is it? I know there's more you're not telling me." She shook an accusing finger at him. "You said we were cursed because we failed in our duty, and that we're doomed to keep paying for it until we restore the balance between the realms. Taking my powers away makes no sense if we ever have a chance to break it! How can I fix my mistakes without magic?"

Luc's eyes flashed, and he took her hand. "Because this way you'll be safe from the Esrac and the curse."

"You might as well be killing me anyway," she snarled. She tried pulling away, but his grip on her wrist tightened.

Before she had a chance to react, Luc muttered words of power, and Ella felt something inside her snap. She raised her hand to try and summon her magic, but nothing happened. She panicked, clinging onto the thought she still wore the band the troopers had put on her a month ago, so maybe it hadn't really left her.

Was that it? Was that all it took to take away part of her soul?

She'd expected something more, flashing lights or the agony of something ripping through her chest, yet she felt nothing but a cold emptiness.

"It's done," Luc said, unclasping the shackle and letting go of her hand. "How do you feel?"

"How can you even ask me that?" Ella turned away, tears filling her eyes. "How could you do this? Don't I mean anything to you?" She covered her face with her hands as tears dripped down her cheeks.

"I'm sorry," he murmured. "I—"

"Get out! I'll never forgive you for this," she snarled. Grabbing a candle off the table, she threw at him. Luc ducked. She heard the tinkle of broken glass as it hit the wall behind him.

"The force field is down, you're free. The Chancellor has said you can go back to working at the University."

Right, just what she needed, to spend time stuck in a lab cataloguing dusty artefacts belonging to the civilisation she had helped wipe out. It'd be another prison, just in a different part of the city. She'd been praying for the chance to go back to her old life, but deep down, she knew that would not be possible now. Too much had happened for her to go back to that. Now she wanted to get away from the city, away from Luc, away from everything.

"Why would she let me do that? They say I killed Griffin!" She wiped her eyes with the back of her hand.

"I convinced them of your innocence. Now you don't have magic, the Chancellor no longer views you as a threat. There'll be restrictions and conditions on what you can do in the city, but at least you won't be locked up anymore." He reached for her, but she shoved his hand away.

"Don't touch me."

"Ella..."

"Get out!"

This time, Luc left without saying another word.

Ella crumpled to the floor, feeling tears that would no longer fall prickle at her eyelids. She felt numb inside now. Even when she had been forced to hide her magic, it had always been part of her, another limb. Now that it was gone, she didn't know what to do.

What even was she now? Human or an avatar without power?

Fidget jumped onto her shoulder, wrapping his long tail around her neck. "La, no cry," he mumbled.

She stroked his head and stood up. "Thanks, Fidget."

Now she was a free woman, she'd be damned if she just sat around and cried. Magic or no magic, she wouldn't feel sorry for herself. She had made mistakes, she'd find a way to fix both her past and present ones.

Ella took a quick shower, dressed, and threw supplies in her pack. She didn't care how she got out of the city, she'd walk if she had to.

"Come, Fidget. We're out of here." Ella hesitated when she reached the front door, half expecting guards to appear. To her relief, she saw no one.

Taking a deep breath, she took a cautious step into the hallway. Then another.

Nothing repelled her. Luc had been telling the truth there. At least, the force field had been lifted.

Ella took off down the hall and ventured outside, breathing in the familiar smells of the greenery and flowers that lined the street. The

Chancellor would no doubt summon her for a lecture soon, but Ella didn't plan on sticking around that long.

She ran through the cobblestone streets with Fidget at her heels, racing toward the great library. Within minutes, she burst through the double doors, her eyes scanning the counter for Sara. To her disappointment, someone else stood behind it.

Ella hurried on through endless rows of books, wishing she could call out for her friend. She didn't want to draw any more unwanted attention to herself. People were already staring.

Instead, she headed into the vault. "Sara?" she yelled as she made her way down the spiral steps.

Sara gasped as she scrambled up from the floor. "Ella, you're here." She bit her lip. "How?"

"Luc let me out. I'm free!" she cried, twirling. "I just came to say goodbye."

Sara's eyes widened and her mouth fell open. "What? You can't leave! Don't you have to get permission for that?"

Ella waved a hand dismissively. "I don't care, I'm going home."

"What happened?" Sara asked, searching her friend's face. "What did Luc do to get you out?"

The familiar ache in her chest returned. "He stripped my powers," she spat. "I can't believe it, but I'm not letting that get in my way."

"Maybe he's just trying to protect you." Sara put down the pile of books she'd been holding.

"Protect me? Ha!" Light shot from her hand as her anger flared, making a vase behind them explode. Ella stared at her hand in disbelief.

How could this be? Luc had stripped her powers…hadn't he?

She laughed despite her confusion, relief washing over her.

"You still have magic! I thought you said Luc—"

"Maybe it didn't work." She frowned. "Or maybe he didn't really do it." She ran her fingers through her long hair in exasperation. "He's so confusing!"

"What will you do now?"

Ella hesitated. Her first instinct had been to get out of the city as fast as she could, yet part of her wondered why Luc would convince her her powers were gone without taking them. "I…I don't know," she muttered. "I need to figure out why Luc would do that."

"Maybe you should talk to him," Sara suggested.

"Maybe."

Just as she expected, Ella was summoned to the chancellor's office later that day and given a list of all the things she could and couldn't do now. When the chancellor seemed satisfied, someone performed a scan that showed whether she had magic or not. To Ella's relief, the scan came back with a negative reading.

For the next hour, Ella searched everywhere for Luc, and even resorted to trying to call him on the link. He didn't answer, and she could find no sign of him.

Eric came to visit her that night for dinner, bringing a bottle of wine. "How does freedom feel?" he asked as he rooted through her drawers for a corkscrew.

"Pretty good, but it has restrictions."

Restrictions I don't intend to stick around to put up with.

She'd find Luc, even if it meant going to his apartment and waiting for him there. She'd wanted to do just that earlier, but the chancellor insisted she go back to work at the University, albeit in the archives, cataloguing everything. She would no longer have access to the lab or any of its equipment, and the Chancellor had revoked both her scholarship and archaeology apprenticeship. She'd been demoted to nothing more than a file keeper with no hope of career progression or escape—her record meant she could never secure a job anywhere else.

"Let's have a drink anyway," Eric said, popping the cork. "How about we go out and celebrate?"

"Go out? No thanks, I'm pretty tired." Ella glanced at her link, hoping Luc had answered her messages. No such luck.

Where was he? Why wouldn't he answer her calls? Deep down, she suspected he knew she still had her powers, but if he didn't, what would he do?

She wouldn't let him try to take them again, not without a fight.

"Fine, I'll make us dinner." Oblivious to her inner turmoil, Eric headed over to the kitchen area and turned on the auto cooker.

Ella laughed. "You've *never* been able to cook!"

"Hey, I'm a man of many talents." Eric pressed a few buttons on the auto cooker to bring up the list of ready-made meals stocked in it and the cooking times for each one. "I must admit, I thought you'd want to see the back of this place."

Believe me, I do, she thought, fiddling with her link again. A dial tone echoed in her ear, then ended. *Why won't he answer?*

"It's probably best we stay inside anyway," Eric continued. "At least until Luc's found that thing."

Panic rose like bile in Ella's throat. He was hunting the Esrac Queen *alone*?

"Eric, I've got to go." She shot up from her seat, swinging her pack over her shoulder. "Sorry, I can't do dinner tonight."

"Why?" He frowned. "Is it because of Luc? Please don't tell me you're still into him. The guy dumped you."

"I dumped *him*," she corrected.

Eric crossed his arms. "I can't believe you still love him after everything he's done."

"I didn't say that," Ella said.

She turned to go, but he grabbed her wrist and tried to kiss her.

"What are you doing?" Ella cried, shoving him away.

"I am...I—"

"I'm leaving. Let yourself out." Ella turned and stormed off without another word.

CHAPTER 8

As the rings of the transport platform fell away, Luc reappeared in Griffin's old office. He'd spent most of the afternoon and evening hunting for Esrac in the villages close to the gate Esme had come through, but hadn't had any luck. He hadn't been able to find much info on the string of recent deaths, either. The troopers seemed to be keeping everything quiet. They wouldn't want any deaths associated with magic getting out.

He sighed. As a Valan knight, he didn't need much sleep—he could get all the benefits in half the time thanks to meditation—but today he felt exhausted, both physically and mentally. As he arrived back at his apartment, his link flashed with a dozen messages from the Chancellor and Ella, but he ignored them. He keyed in his code, frowning when he saw the lights were on.

Luc pulled out his sword as he crept down the hall.

Why would anyone have broken in? He didn't have anything worth stealing. Had the Chancellor sent someone to spy on him?

"Fidget, come here!"

Luc lowered his sword at the familiar hiss, which was followed by the sound of something breaking. "Ella, what are you doing here?" He tucked the sword away as he moved into the sitting room containing bare whitewashed walls, a tattered sofa, and a chipped coffee table.

Fidget ran across his feet, a piece of fruit between his paws. He paused and waved, then scurried away, vanishing from sight.

"Eric told me you went hunting the Esrac Queen." From her seat on the sofa, Ella crossed her arms.

He arched a brow. "Did he?"

"Not in so many words, but I knew. Did you find her?"

He rubbed his aching eyes. "No. You're not a part of this anymore."

Ella raised her chin. "Yes, I am. I still have my powers, and I think you know that."

Luc slumped into a chair. "It doesn't change anything." He pulled out the wine Sara had left the night before and took a deep swig straight from the bottle.

"We need to work together. When are you going to realise that?" Ella snapped. "We created this mess, we should fix it."

She put her hands on her hips and glared at him.

"You've got to stop shutting me out. I know you think you can protect me from the curse the ancestors placed on us, but we're never going to find a way to end it unless we put our differences aside and team up."

Luc shot to his feet. "Don't you think we've tried that thousands of times over the centuries?" he cried. "You can't see every life we've lived yet, but they always end the same. I have to watch you die, but I won't do that this time. I love you too much to lose you again."

Ella's eyes widened. "You love me?"

"Of course I do. I'll always love you, no matter what lifetime we're in," he said. "I tried to take your powers to protect you, not for what happened to Griffin."

"Then when are you going to accept we need to work together?" Ella asked. "One way or another, we'll fix this."

She'd said that more than once, and in every lifetime, he'd wanted to believe it. If only things could be that simple, and they could find a way to stop the Esrac once and for all.

He sighed. "I hope so."

"I know so." She wrapped her arms around him.

Luc held her close, breathing in her sweet scent.

"Maybe we can track down the Esrac," he mused, "but you should know we've never been able to figure out how to completely destroy them. They breed fast, and—"

She shushed him. "We'll figure it out."

"Will you stay with me tonight?" Luc asked. "I'm tired, and I just want to hold you."

Ella nodded. "Okay. We'll get started in the morning."

When he woke early the next morning, Luc felt refreshed, surprised he'd slept through the night without being plagued by dreams filled with memories that were best left forgotten.

Ella lay snuggled against him, and he smiled at the sight. He'd forgotten how much he enjoyed waking up next to her.

She glanced up at him. "I wonder how long it's been since we did this," she said.

"Too long." Luc kissed her forehead.

"I keep having dreams about us in the past." She stared up at him, resting her chin on her arm. "You've been having them too, haven't you?"

"Yes, I have." He wrapped an arm around her shoulders. "I think we're cursed to remember everything that happened to us back then."

"Do I let the Esrac through in every life?"

Luc shook his head. "No, but one way or another they always seem to find a way back."

"I want to go home today. If my father was a Valan too, he may have known more than even Griffin did," Ella said. "Besides, we can't work here and fix this mess. It's not safe to have so many eyes watching us."

"I know. In truth I'm tired of being here too, I'm not part of the Senate, and I never will be." He gave her a quick kiss. "I'll make us breakfast."

"How did you get out the city yesterday?" Ella asked, as she scrambled out of bed.

"I bribed one of the troopers to let me out. No doubt the Chancellor will give me crap for it, but I had to go." He ran a hand through his tousled hair. "I scoured the area close to a village where an unnatural death was reported a few days ago, but it turned out not to be an Esrac attack. The person just died from poisoning."

"There has to be another way out, one we can both use."

Luc nodded. "We'll find one, don't worry, but we need to be careful. The Chancellor will still have people watching you. In all honesty, you shouldn't have come here, but I'm glad you did. I've missed you."

He set about programming the auto cooker when the front door buzzed.

Ella came out of the bedroom and smiled as she leaned against the doorframe. "I'll get it. Who'd be calling this early?"

"No, you sit. I'll get it."

Still clad in nothing but trousers, Luc headed out to answer the front door. Eric's image filled the house screen. Luc was surprised to see him after their altercation the day before, and hoped Eric hadn't come seeking retribution. He didn't have his sword nearby, but he could call it with his mind if he had to.

He pressed the panel, and the door slid open.

"Hey, I think I found—" Eric's eyes widened when he saw Ella in the hallway. "Oh, I didn't realise you were here."

"What were you saying?" Luc asked. He wrapped a protective arm around Ella's shoulders.

"There's been an attack close to Ella's village."

Luc and Ella glanced at each other, and all colour drained from Ella's face. "Are you saying Esme is in my village?" she gasped.

"No, but she might be close by," Luc said, squeezing her shoulder.

"How could she even have known about where I come from?" Ella asked. "She doesn't know anything about me except that I'm an avatar. Aurelia never lived in Antaria, she came from Arkadia." She moved away from Luc and motioned for Fidget to come to her. "Forget breakfast, we need to leave as soon as possible." She turned to Eric. "Can you fly us to my village?"

Eric nodded. "I'll get the ship ready, but what about the troopers? Are you even *allowed* to leave the city?"

"We'll worry about that later." Ella pulled on her shoes and took off out the front door.

Luc quickly got his things together, putting everything he might need into one pack. There wasn't much—mainly supplies and a couple of changes of clothing. All his books and other data were stored on crystals, which were already inside. Once finished, he followed Ella to her apartment, where she had already packed her clothes the night before. She stuffed more books and food into her bag and pulled on a cloak. "Do you think that's enough?"

Luc nodded, and she swung the bag over her shoulder.

"The flight to my village shouldn't take more than a few hours."

She picked Fidget up, who started struggling when he saw the cage. "Cage bad! Cage bad!"

Ella caught hold of the scruff of his neck and pushed him inside. The cage door closed with a snap. "Sorry, Fidget, but we're gonna fly for a while. You can't go wandering around an airship."

Hand-in-hand, Luc and Ella made their way down to the dock. As they approached, Luc came to an abrupt halt and pulled Ella behind one of the buildings.

"There are troopers waiting down there. They must know we're planning on leaving. Damn it! We'll never get out of the city undetected now."

"It must be the chancellor's doing. Maybe she didn't believe you really stripped my powers away," Ella said. "Wait, they built Celestus over some parts of Arkadia. Do you think there's a ring platform we could use?"

"Good idea, there's one inside Griffin's old office." Luc pulled up the hood of her coat. "Try to keep your face covered. Let's go."

"What about Eric?"

"We'll have to leave without him. Come on, let's get to the university before anyone sees us."

Luc headed toward Griffin's office. He insisted on going first to see if the way was clear. Three troopers armed with guns stood there, waiting for them. *Damn! The Chancellor must have watched me more closely than I thought!*

As he turned to leave, he found his way was blocked by two more troopers standing behind him.

"Luc, you're to come with us," said the one on the left. "By order of the Chancellor."

Luc thought fast. He and Ella had to get out of the city before the Esrac did any more damage. If they were taken into custody, they might not be able to find Esme before she started breeding more of her kind.

Luc's hand went to the hilt of his sword. "No can do, boys!"

He narrowed his eyes, causing all five men to rise into the air, their weapons falling from their hands, then flung all five of them against the far wall and took off in the opposite direction.

"Going into Griffin's office isn't an option," he said when he caught up with Ella in a small courtyard filled with trees and a fountain. They wouldn't be seen here. Griffin had used it as his private area and kept the location quiet.

"How can we get out of the city?" Ella glanced around to see if anyone was watching them.

"There might be another way, but we need somewhere safe to hide first."

"I know somewhere." Ella gripped his hand. "Let's go."

Ella led him through the back entrance to the city archives, then down to the vault. They passed several rows of shelves filled with old books and dusty manuscripts, as well as dozens of boxes that had yet to be catalogued.

"We'll be safe down here. Are there no other ring platforms anywhere in the city?" she asked. Crystal torches flickered as they made their way down the stone spiral steps.

"The only unguarded one exists in Griffin's quarters. He kept it there concealed," Luc said, following her into what appeared to be an underground bunker.

Below, Luc was surprised to see Eric and Sara. The two of them were arguing about something, and they both looked up as Luc and Ella walked in.

"Fine bloody mess you've got me into," Eric grumbled, crossed his arms. "They seized my ship. I had to make a run for it before anyone spotted me. Would you please tell me what's going on?"

"The chancellor wants to arrest us," Ella answered. "She must suspect that Luc and I are both using magic, or she overheard our plan. It doesn't matter how she found out, but she knows we're planning to leave."

"I knew she didn't trust me, not really," Luc said. "Either way, Ella and I need to get out of the city. Fast."

"How can we go anywhere? They have the air dock locked down." Eric scowled. "I knew helping you would get me into trouble, and I *still* don't know what you're planning."

"The Senate doesn't believe the Esrac are a threat, but we know better," said Ella, putting her pack and Fidget's cage down on the floor. "Eric, you saw what those things are capable of. We have to stop them."

"I'm sorry for dragging you into this, but we need your help." Luc said.

"What if I could help?" Sara cut in. "There's an old tunnel that leads out of the city somewhere down here. Griffin told me about it."

Luc shook his head. "That's too risky. It would take too long."

"Cage bad!" Fidget screeched, gnawing at the metal bars.

"Hush, Fidget," Ella scolded, "we're in trouble." She handed him some honey drops through the bars and looked at Luc. "What's the other way you mentioned earlier?"

"You are. I want you to try and open the gate," he said.

Ella's mouth fell open. "Are you serious? Opening the gate got us into this mess. I'm never touching one again."

"The gate is our only means of escape, and you're the only one with the power to control it." He'd been reluctant to bring up the option before now, but with the city on lockdown and Esme free, they didn't have a choice.

"You're nowhere near a gate," Sara pointed out. "It's in Griffin's old quarters, right?"

"Ella can open the gates and use them no matter how far away they are from her." Luc explained, putting his hands on Ella's shoulders. "You have to try."

"What if I let more Esrac through?" Ella said, hesitating. "Then we'll have even more of them on the loose."

"Esme would have to be here to bring them through. You'll be fine. I'll be right here with you. Just close your eyes and clear your mind," Luc told her.

"Easier said than done," Ella muttered as she closed her eyes.

Luc glanced over at the others. "Thanks for your help, but you should go now. I don't want you two getting into any more trouble than you already have," he told them. "When they question you, tell them the truth. You saw us, but have no idea where we were going, and you had nothing to do with helping us escape."

"I'm coming with you. My knowledge of history might come in handy," Sara said, pulling a packed bag from behind a nearby shelf.

"Me too." Eric cut in, picking up his own pack. "I'm in trouble already just for helping you, and I need to make sure you don't get anyone killed."

"I can't and won't let you put yourselves at risk—" Luc protested, falling silent at the sound of banging against the vault's outer door.

"I feel the gate," Ella smiled. "It's calling to me."

Luc turned to her, grabbing her shoulders. "That's good. Now picture it opening. Remember what it felt like when you opened it the first time."

Seconds later, a glowing doorway appeared on the wall behind them, radiating with gold light as a portal opened within it.

"Time to go," Luc said, picking up their packs and Fidget's cage and taking Ella's hand, before glancing at the others and sighing.

"Oh, come on then."

As the four joined hands, he pulled them through the portal and into the unknown.

CHAPTER 9

Ella let out a breath as they reappeared inside the chamber she'd accidentally uncovered weeks earlier. This place had set her on the path to finding out who and what she really was and everything it entailed. It felt odd being back here and to have actually used the gate, but it had felt as natural as breathing.

Small slivers of light seeped down from the world above. The chamber had been buried fifty feet underground after the fall of the old city. Ella had stumbled across it during an excavation.

She raised her hand, causing purple flames to crackle between her fingers, and then threw the fire up into the air so it hovered above them, bathing the chamber in an ethereal glow. Runes covered the stone walls, outer door, and on the other side of the room along one wall were depictions of a battle between the Arkadians and the Esrac. Ella remembered being fascinated when she'd first seen the drawings and wondering what they had meant, but she wished she had realised they had been warning her not to go anywhere near the gate.

Ella glanced at Sara and Eric. "You two should go back," she said. "Luc's right. It isn't fair for us to drag you into this."

"We're already part of this, Ella." Sara crossed her arms. "I'm not going anywhere."

"Me either," Eric added.

Ella glanced to Luc, but he just shrugged. "It's up to them."

"We're the ones who are cursed, not you," Ella said, looking between them. "You shouldn't put your lives at risk for us."

"We're your friends," said Sara. "We go where you go. Besides, we're involved now. We can't go back, or they'll arrest us."

"What she said," Eric muttered, glancing back at the gate. "Too bad this thing can't take us back to your village. Maybe we could hide out here in the old city? I'm sure there are a lot of places we could hide."

Luc shook his head. "No, the chancellor will suspect we'd come here. She'll send troopers looking for us."

Ella looked back at the glowing portal. "*Can* the gate take us to Antaria? I only thought of this place because it contained the only other gate I knew of."

"Just as you can summon the gate, you can direct it to where you want to go, but we'll need to be careful. Esme can no doubt sense the use of the gates too," Luc warned, "but it would take too long to get there on foot. The gate is our only option."

Ella hesitated, feeling the wards engraved on the gate as she ran her fingers over the runes. They were another reminder of her failure in her first life. She raised her hand again and red light flared between her fingers as she thought of her mother's home.

The gate fell dormant, its golden light fading.

Ella frowned. "It's not working."

"Maybe your dad warded the house. He was a pretty skilled knight," Luc said. "Think of somewhere close by where we can come through without being seen instead."

Her brow creased as she thought back to all the places she remembered in the remote village she'd grown up in.

"I know somewhere." Light flared again as the gate reopened.

"That's incredible," Sara breathed.

"Impressive," Eric agreed.

"Imagine the places we could travel to," Sara said, wonder filling her eyes.

Ella and Luc glanced at each other before Luc leapt through, vanishing into the golden light. Sara and Eric followed suit, but Ella stood there for a moment, remembering how much she'd loved stepping through the portal and travelling to different places. She should be in awe of the gate too, but she felt only dread. The invention that had once seemed so wondrous now, possibly doomed her and Luc forever.

Taking a deep breath, Ella joined the others outside the old stone temple. Its window columns were empty of glass and the roof had long since fallen away, but the tall spire still remained intact. This place felt sacred and safe, the ideal spot to travel to.

"My house isn't far," Ella said, bending to pick up Fidget's cage from where Luc had rested it on the ground.

"Out, out!" Fidget screeched, gnawing at the bars again.

Sighing, Ella opened the cage. Fidget shot out, running around their feet happily.

"The last possible Esrac attack wasn't far from here," Eric noted.

Luc bristled. "I should go."

"No, not until we make sure my mother is safe," Ella insisted. "The Chancellor will probably send troopers to the house. We can hide out here if we need to."

Ella led the way. Fidget running ahead of her to sniff different plants excitedly. It felt strange being back here. A few months earlier, she was desperate to live in the shining city where she'd met Luc, but her life had changed so much in that short time. She was no longer a girl with a strange gift she had to hide, but she still didn't know what she was. An avatar with an uncertain future ahead of her, she guessed.

"This is where you lived?" Sara took in the tiny shops and people scurrying about. With its cobblestone streets and grey stone buildings, it looked a world away from Celestus. Even airships were a rarity. Most people either used cars or old-fashioned horse-drawn wagons. "It's so…"

"Uncivilised?" Ella said. "Basic?" She had spent most of her life wanting to get away from it, but it felt good to be home again. She'd always been safe here and now hoped she would for a while longer. She hadn't talked about Antaria much and knew it would take the troopers a while to here in search of her.

"I was going to say remote." Sara jumped as a man pulling a cart almost bumped into her.

"People here live a simple life. It's a far cry from Celestus," Luc said. "We should get off the street. Four visitors will draw unwanted attention."

"What if they've got troopers already stationed at the house?" Eric said, glancing around as people scurried by them.

"I'll sense them if there are, but I need to be closer to the house first," Luc replied, taking Ella's hand and giving it a squeeze.

She gave him a grateful look. She didn't know where they stood, and doubted he did either, but it felt good to be working together instead of pushing each other away.

People glanced over as they made their way through the village, but no one stopped them, much to Ella's relief.

"So what's the plan when we get there?" Eric wanted to know.

"We'll make sure the house is secure. I'm going to scout the area for the Esrac Queen whilst Ella searches through her father's things," Luc answered. "Once we find Esme, we'll have to figure out a way of killing her."

Something we've never been able to do, despite a thousand years of trying.

She searched through her scattered memories for help, but she had no idea if Esme could even be killed. The queen herself had proved much stronger and more powerful than the Esrac they'd faced before.

"We're all on the run from the Senate now. I say we need to worry about our own safety too," Eric pointed out, glancing behind them to see if anyone was following. "They won't stop looking for us, especially not you two."

"I'm working on a plan for that," Luc said. "Last chance. Ella can send you both back now, and you can go back to your normal lives."

Without pause, Sara and Eric both shook their heads.

"I think our normal lives ended when we became part of this," Sara said, playing with a strand of loose hair. "Or at least when Master Griffin betrayed us. We can't go back, not now."

"I've been part of it since that creepy green thing attacked us." Eric shuddered. "Plus, you need us. Maybe we can help you figure out a way to stop the green skinned bitch once and for all."

Luc moved ahead of them, and Ella felt him using his mental powers. She'd always been able to feel things, but hadn't given it much thought. Maybe she could finally start learning more about her own abilities. She quickened her pace to keep up with Luc and took his hand in hers.

"They shouldn't have come with us," he said.

"They're our friends. I don't want to risk it either, but I'd miss them if we had to leave them behind."

"They're your friends maybe, but they don't like me much—or at least Eric doesn't."

"You don't need to worry about him." She squeezed his hand.

"One way or another, we can break this curse. I believe that, and you should too."

Luc nodded, and they kept on moving.

Ella felt the pit in her stomach deepen the nearer they got to her former home. She and her mother hadn't parted on good terms when she had left for Celestus, and they hadn't spoken to each other since. She had no idea how her mum would react to her coming back, and wondered if she would even want to see Ella again. They had always clashed over the years, and Ella had always been closer to her father than her mother.

You don't have to stay long, she told herself. *Just look through Dad's things, then we can leave…to wherever we're going.*

Neither she nor Luc had planned that far ahead. Their only goal had been to get out of the city and track Esme before she had the chance to do any more damage, but now she could use the gate more freely, they could go anywhere they chose. It would certainly come in handy for escaping from the pursuing troopers.

"If we see any Esrac, be careful. They can try to deceive you and are good at illusions," Luc told the group. "Don't believe your eyes. I'll show you some ways of seeing past any illusions once we know the house is safe."

"Any tips on killing them?" Eric asked.

"The best way to kill them is by cutting off their heads, but that won't work on a queen. They're strong, and almost impossible to kill. The Valan knights have been killing her warriors for centuries, but none of us have been able to kill Esme herself."

"You'd think after a thousand years you would have figured out a way," Eric muttered.

"You and Ella both have magic," Sara said. "Why won't your joint powers work?"

"Esrac are strong, fast and can regenerate pretty quickly, especially if they manage to feed on someone after they are injured," Ella said. "Blood gives them the ability to live for centuries. The only way we stopped them was by sealing the gates. We tricked them into a hell realm, and I forced Esme through the gate." She shook her head. "But it wasn't enough. I won't let the past repeat itself again." After being forced to endure failure in so many lifetimes, she'd make sure make sure this one turned out differently.

"Why will this time be any different?" Eric wanted to know. "Doesn't the same thing always happen?"

Luc and Ella looked at each other, both wondering the same thing.

"This is different," Luc said. "Esme hasn't escaped until now. She's only sent drones when past avatars have tried using the gates. Now is our chance to stop her."

Ella took a deep breath as she approached the front door and knocked. Her house looked just as she remembered it, with grey stone walls and a tiled roof. Dozens of flowers lined the front garden. They were something her mum always insisted on having outside. A couple of outbuildings stood off to the side of the farm that had once stood here. Everything had fallen into disuse after her father, Caspian, had disappeared. Her mum hadn't been able to keep up with the work.

"I only sense one presence inside the house," said Luc as his brow furrowed. "It's your mother."

Ella waited, feeling her heart pounding. Fidget climbed up onto her shoulder and she ruffled his ears. Glancing round, she noticed weeds growing in patches across the grass, which was overgrown. That seemed odd. Her mum loved her garden and would never have abided it being neglected like this.

She bit her lip. What if something had happened? Ella hadn't tried to contact her since she'd gone to Celestus, she'd been too stubborn after their argument.

Oh, why didn't I call her before now?

The door clicked open, revealing the surprised face of her mother, Mary, who wore one of her usual floral dresses.

"Hi, Mum. Can we come in?" Ella wanted nothing more than to throw her arms around her mother and tell her how sorry she felt at how they had parted, yet something held her back. Something didn't seem right.

"You're home." Mary threw her arms around her, hugging Ella so tight she couldn't breathe. "Come in, come in. It's good to see you."

Ella glanced back at Luc, half expecting him to warn her of impending danger, but he only nodded.

She let out a breath and walked inside.

CHAPTER 10

Luc glanced around the small sitting room with its flagstone floor covered in a makeshift quilt rug, two wooden sofas with handmade cushions, and a large empty stone fireplace. Ella had never spoken much about her home, other than to say her family had never had much.

"What are you doing home?" Ella's mother asked with a smile that didn't quite reach her eyes.

Luc frowned, surprised by her behaviour. From what he had heard from Ella, she had been a loving mother, despite often clashing with her daughter. It seemed strange she wasn't happier to see Ella.

"Mum, these are friends of mine, Luc, Sara, and Eric," Ella said. "I had some free time, and I thought I'd come home for a visit. How are you? How have things been?" She glanced around the room nervously until Luc could feel the waves of unease radiating off her.

Fidget scurried in after them, sniffed the air, and stared at Mary. Luc noticed how the dust bunny seemed the edge.

"Same as usual," Mary said. She looked around, smiling at the other three of them. "Good to meet you. Would you all like some tea?"

"I'll get it," Sara offered. "You two catch up." She dropped her pack on the floor and left the room. Fidget scurried after her, no doubt going in search of food.

"Right, Eric and I will give you some time alone. Nice to finally meet you, Mary."

Luc took Eric's arm and pulled him into the hall, leaving the door behind them slightly ajar.

"Hey!" Eric snapped.

"Shush!" Luc put a finger to his lips, then opened and closed the front door before sneaking back to stare through the crack in the kitchen door.

Eric opened his mouth to speak.

"Something isn't right," Luc mouthed at him.

Eric frowned. "What?" he mouthed back. He shrugged, peering through the door as Ella tucked a lock of hair behind her ear.

"Mum, I'm sorry."

"For what?" Mary's smile didn't waver.

"For our argument before I left."

Ella, something is not right. Luc directed his thoughts at her. *Be careful.*

In their past lives, they had been able to communicate with each other in thought, but he didn't know if it would work. Ella hadn't been fully trained yet. Even if Caspian had taught her to hide her magic, she still didn't know its full potential. Without Master Griffin around, Luc might be the one of the few people who could teach her the ways of being an avatar.

"Oh, nonsense. That's ancient history." Mary waved a hand in dismissal. "It was a long time ago. I'm just glad to have you back. Will you and your friends be staying long?"

"But you wanted me to go to Celestus, and I didn't, remember?"

Luc grinned, knowing that wasn't true. Ella had been desperate to go to Celestus, but Mary had been dead set against it. She had tried to convince Ella to postpone the scholarship for another year, yet Ella had gone anyway.

"Let's just forget about it. I'm happy to have you here," Mary said.

Luc frowned, resting his hand on the hilt of his sword. He couldn't sense if she was an Esrac drone or not, but if it was a drone, they had got much better at disguising themselves over the centuries. No doubt Esme would have started creating them since her arrival in this world, but he hoped she didn't have a whole army of them yet.

Sara came in, carrying a tray of tea. The tray slipped from her hands as she screamed, sending the cups and the pot crashing to the floor. "You're one of those things!" Her hand shook as she pointed at Mary.

Mary frowned, and glanced from Sara to Ella, then back at Sara. "Ella, what is your friend talking about?"

"You've got green skin and fangs!" Sara screamed.

Luc pushed at the door, but a wall of energy now blocked his way. *Esrac!*

Mary flew at Ella, making a grab for her.

Ella raised her hand and hit her with a blast of starfire. Mary stumbled, and the illusion dissolved, revealing the long blood red hair, metallic fangs, and green skin of Esme.

The Esrac Queen snarled, glaring at Sara. "How can you see me?" she hissed. "What are you, girl?"

"Never mind that. Where's my mother?" Ella demanded, as more fire flared between her fingers.

Luc continued thrashing at the door. Eric grabbed a small crowbar out of his pack to help wedge it open.

"Where did you get that from?" Luc asked.

"I'm an engineer. I always come prepared," Eric replied. "Can't you use your glowing sword thing to break through?"

Luc pulled out his sword. He tried slicing through the door, but sparks glanced off the glowing blade.

"Your mother is dead. Such a tasty morsel," Esme sneered, raising her hand as she prepared to strike Ella again.

Purple fire flared in Ella's hand. She hurled it at the Esrac, who ducked. The wall behind her exploded, sending dust and shards of wood flying.

Esme turned and seized Sara by the throat, her barbs digging into Sara's neck. Sara yelped, and Esme screamed as her hand sizzled like she'd been burned by fire.

Luc thrust his sword through the door again, and the wood finally gave way, splintering into pieces. Sparks continued to fly from his sword as he tried to break through the force field.

Sara ducked out of the way, hiding behind Ella as she hit Esme with another burst of starfire.

Esme fell to the floor, clutching her burning hand. "You can't kill me, avatar. You never could. You've always been too weak to kill me."

"Doesn't mean I won't try." In response, more fire flared in Ella's hand. This burst hotter and more powerful than it had been before.

Esme cackled. "You're too weak to defeat me, girl." She grabbed hold of Sara's arm, hissing with pain as Sara's skin burned her, but picked her up and flung her across the room. Sara landed a few feet away with a grunt.

"Ha, you forget I'm the one who banished you into the hell realm!"

Ella threw another burst of starfire at Esme, exploding the cabinet behind her.

"Is anything else we can do?" Eric demanded, digging into his pack and pulling out a stunner. He held up the weapon. "Will this work?"

"I don't know, but it's worth a try."

Eric aimed the stunner and fired. A burst of blue-tinged white light shot out. It bounced against the glowing wall of energy and headed straight back toward them.

Luc yanked Eric out of the way before the blast had a chance to hit. "Don't do that again!"

"What about the walls? Does the shield extend that far?" Eric slipped his stunner into his belt.

Luc paused, then sliced his sword through the nearest wall. The glowing blade slide sliced through the wood and plaster like butter.

Ella and Esme continued to battle it out. Windows and pieces of furniture exploded around them as Ella continued to hurl bursts of starfire and Esme avoided them.

Guess she remembers a lot more than I imagined, Luc thought, feeling a fleeting sense of pride. Breaking through a big enough portion of the wall, he kicked away the rest of the wood and moved through into the sitting room.

Esme dodged another blast of fire and grabbed Ella in a headlock, looking directly at Luc. "Move and I'll kill her."

Ella cried out as Esme's barbs dug into her neck and thin trails of blood seeped down her throat, staining the top of her shirt. She gritted her teeth.

"Not if I kill you first," she snarled.

"Ella, don't!" Luc hissed. *Don't antagonise her. She could kill you.*

Sara scrambled up from where Esme had thrown her. Rushing forward, she grabbed onto Esme's arm, making the Esrac howl as her flesh began to smoulder.

"Whatever this burning power is, I like it. Now get your hands off my friend," Sara growled.

Esme's barbs dug deeper into Ella, draining more of her blood. She needed to withstand the burning, but after a few seconds, it was too much. As Esme's arm burned white hot, she released Ella with a strangled scream.

Luc grabbed Ella, yanking her free from Esme's grasp, and shoved her toward Eric.

"Sara, don't let go of her," Luc called.

He thought fast, trying to figure out a way to contain the Esrac.

Eric threw him a crystal. "Here, throw at her!"

He caught it and threw the crystal at the Esrac. It landed at her feet, and white light exploded as the crystal shattered. The light expanded, wrapping around Esme like a cocoon as it held her in place.

Sara yelped as the force of it sent her crashing to the floor.

Esme clutched her burned arm, fangs glistening. "Fools, this won't hold me for long," she snarled. "I'll devour all of you." Her eyes flicked to Ella. "You, I'll save for last."

Luc moved over to Ella's side, checking the bleeding gashes on her throat. They didn't appear to be deep. At least Esme didn't seem to have taken too much blood. He wrapped an arm around her shoulders and held her close for a moment.

She clung to him and rested her head against his chest. "I'm alright," she whispered.

Esme let out a hiss.

Ignoring her, Eric helped Sara up. "You okay?"

She nodded. "Now what do we do with her?"

"Nothing. I need to find my mum," Ella said, glaring at Esme. "If you hurt her—"

"You'll what? Kill me?" Esme snorted. "You never could, Aurelia. You were weak then, just as you are now. It's only a matter of time before the seal on the gate breaks and my people walk freely between the realms once more."

Ella disappeared for a few moments, returning with a healing wand that she used on her neck. At Luc's insistence, she and the others left the room to start searching the house for the real Mary.

When they were gone, Luc glanced at the Esrac Queen. It felt strange standing face-to-face with her after all these centuries.

"Hello, Lucas. Bet you thought you would never see me again." Esme gave him what he guessed was supposed to be a sweet smile.

"I hoped I wouldn't," he snapped, clenching his fists.

Part of him wanted to rip into her. She was the reason why he and Ella had been cursed, why they'd never had a chance of a real future together.

"Right, can't have your love finding out what you did, can you?" Esme sneered. "I wonder how she'd feel she knew the truth."

Luc looked away and shook his head. "The past doesn't matter anymore, Esme. You won't win this time."

He had to stay calm. He couldn't let Esme's taunts get to him. Besides, that was all in the past now. It had nothing to do with his present life.

She laughed so harshly it sounded like a growl. "We'll see. I've used the gate before, I'll do it again. Ella is the last of her kind. She doesn't have the power to seal it again. Pity, you were both strong and powerful once," Esme said, fangs glistening. "Now you're just clueless children who haven't known what to do since I killed your precious Master Griffin."

Luc paced, trying to figure out the best way of dealing with her. Cutting off her head wouldn't be enough, he'd tried that before and it hadn't worked.

Ella stormed back into the room, eyes blazing. "Where's my mum?"

"Dead, cast off like the worthless meat bag she is," Esme scoffed.

White light flared in Ella's hand as more fire formed in her hand.

Luc grabbed her wrist. "Torturing her won't make her talk."

"No, and you'd know that, wouldn't you, Lucas?" Esme snorted.

"You wouldn't kill my mother, she's more valuable to you alive. Where is she?"

"As if I'm going to tell."

"Maybe I'll just have my friend come over and touch you again," Ella threatened, snuffing out the flames.

Esme snarled, fangs glistening. "It doesn't matter what you do. I will win and finally get my revenge on the pair who sentenced me and my people to a fate worse than death. There's one thing you should know, Aurelia. You weren't the one who showed me how to use the gate. Your knowledge helped, but *he's* the one who taught me." She pointed a barbed hand at Luc.

Luc flinched, praying Esme wouldn't say anything further.

Ella glanced at Luc, then back at Esme. "Did you torture him?"

"Oh no, I got out of him the easy way—by pretending to you." She cackled again, thrashed against the weakening crystal cage, and bolted headfirst out of the window.

Luc made a move to go after her, but Esme had already vanished.

CHAPTER 11

Ella paced up and down the living room, her mind reeling from everything that just happened. She'd scaled every part of the house, but so far hadn't found any trace of her mother. She wanted to believe Esme would keep Mary alive, even if just to use as leverage against her, but she couldn't be sure. Luc and Eric had gone off to search the outbuildings and surrounding area for any sign of her or Esme, but didn't seem to share Ella's hope.

She's got to have kept mum alive. She would have needed someone to feed from regularly, and no doubt tried to pump her for information, Ella thought determinedly.

"Your neck is still bleeding," Sara said, picking up the healing wand Ella had abandoned on the floor to confront Esme.

Ella fumbled in the med kit she'd retrieved from the kitchen earlier and slapped a plaster over her neck, continuing to pace as she did so. Master Griffin had died instantly from Esme's touch, but from what Ella remembered, the Esrac didn't have to kill their victims, and could control the amount of blood they absorbed from them. But where would Esme have taken her?

"I'm sure your mum is okay," Sara said, as she wiped up spilt tea from the floor.

Ella snorted. "This is Esme we're talking about. She's an evil, manipulative bitch who sees people as nothing more than food." She resumed pacing again, trying not to glance around her. It made her heart ache to see the shattered ruins of what had been one of her favourite rooms in the house.

She closed her eyes and stood still, concentrating. If Luc could sense things, maybe she could too, beyond just sensing the gate. She tried to calm her mind and feel something, anything, but thoughts continued to race by. Fear twisted in her stomach like a knife.

The front door creaked open as Luc came in, and Ella's eyes flew open.

"Did you find anything?"

Luc shook his head. "No sign of Esme or your mum." He slipped his sword back into his belt in defeat.

Ella's fists clenched. "Damn it, why didn't I come home sooner? Why didn't you tell me I could use the gate? I could have escaped!"

"Because I..." Luc's voice trailed off, and he shook his head again. "I'm sorry."

As she stared Luc down, Eric came in, his expression just as downcast as Luc's had been. "I talked to a farmer down the road. He says he hasn't seen your mum in over a week."

Dread filled Ella's chest. That didn't sound like her mum at all. Mary worked as a librarian and taught in the village. She was always on the move.

"If Esme was here for several days, she would have needed someone to feed on. There have been no disappearances reported here, right?" she said, not waiting for an answer. "So my mum must have been kept alive."

"Ella..." Luc said.

"No, don't say she's dead. I lost my father, I can't lose her too. Not like this."

She wouldn't be able to live with herself if her mum had died because she had released Esme.

"Why did me touching that creature make her burn like that?" Sara asked as she picked up broken pieces of crockery and put them in a bin she'd brought in with her. "I've never done that to anyone before, it looked like I'd burned her with acid."

"I honestly don't know. You don't have any magic. I'd sense if you did," Luc replied. "but whatever it is might come in handy in our fight against them."

As the others spoke about Esme's possible whereabouts, Ella moved into the kitchen and opened the door to the cellar. Her father's former workspace. She never liked going down there as a child because it always seemed so dark and scary. But it would be the perfect place to hide someone you didn't want to be found. The door sat at the far end of the utility room, so no one would find it unless they were looking for it.

"We've already looked down here." Luc said from behind her.

"Let's look again." Ella conjured an orb of light, and it rose into the air, chasing away the shadows as they climbed down.

The cellar had boxes everywhere, and old furniture scattered across the floor. Shelves filled with jars, bottles and other junk lined one wall. Ella scanned every inch of the cellar, moving boxes and other rubbish aside as she went. She coughed, then sneezed as dust hit her face.

Luc sighed and helped clear the way. Eric and Sara joined in, their attention caught by the commotion. They moved boxes, furniture and a heavy cabinet out of the way, but still no sign of Mary anywhere.

Ella pushed away the idea of Mary being dead. She wouldn't consider that, not unless they found Mary's body.

"Luc, can you track Esme?" she asked. "If we capture her again, maybe we could—"

Luc shook his head, making her fall silent. "Esme isn't like her drones; she can shield herself from my senses."

She sighed and opened the door to a cabinet filled with old pots and pans. "She has to be here somewhere!"

An hour later, they still hadn't found a trace of Mary.

"Ella, maybe..." Luc put a hand on her shoulder.

"No, she's not dead. She's not!" She wiped sweat off her face, shoving him away. She couldn't have let her mum die without apologising her first. She had to make things right between them. She rounded on Luc. "What did Esme mean earlier? She said I wasn't the one who showed her how to use the gate, you were. How is that possible?" She stared at him, seeing a flash of fear flicker in his eyes.

"Ella, she was—"

"I know when you're hiding things from me. I can feel it." She put her hands on her hips.

Luc turned to the others. "Can you give us a minute alone?"

Sara and Eric nodded and headed back up the cellar steps.

"I didn't die first in our first lives. Esme captured me and got the knowledge from me," he admitted. "I spent weeks as her blood slave."

"She tortured you?"

Luc shook his head. "She somehow made me think you were her and got it that way. I don't remember much of that time, but I know *I'm* the real reason she learnt to use the gates and managed to invade other realms. I'm the reason we're cursed."

When he reached for her in apology, Ella backed away.

"You let me think I was to blame for everything this whole time!"

"Ella—"

"No. I don't care what happened, it's *your* fault my mum is gone," she snapped. "If we hadn't fallen in love in the first place, none of this would have ever happened."

Light shot from her hand, exploding the wall next to them.

Ella blinked, coughing as dust flew everywhere. When she could see again, she looked down to see someone lying slumped on the floor, a woman wearing a tattered dress smudged with blood.

"Mum!" Ella fell to her knees beside her.

Mary had been bound and gagged. Dust now covered her from head to toe.

Luc knelt beside them, touching Mary's throat. "She's still alive."

He cut away the ropes with a knife and pulled off the gag. Ella felt a flood of relief wash over her and called for Sara to bring down the med kit.

When Sara appeared with it, Ella grabbed the healing wand and got to work. Her mum had numerous bite marks and incisions covering her neck and wrists.

"I'll kill Esme for this," she murmured.

Mary's eyes fluttered open, and she groaned as she finally came to.

"Mum, it's me. I'm here."

Mary looked up, wide-eyed. "Ella? Is it really you?"

"Yes, Mum. I'm here." She smiled.

"How are you feeling, Mary?" Luc asked.

"I-I don't know." Mary sat up, glancing around. "How did I get here? Who are you?"

"Let's go upstairs," Luc said, as he helped her up. "We can talk more up there. I'm Luc, by the way, Ella's boyfriend."

Ella arched an eyebrow at him. *Boyfriend, huh? You and I really need to have a chat later.*

Once upstairs, Mary settled onto an armchair, frowning at the shattered remains of her living room "Goodness, what happened?"

"It's a long story," Ella replied. "Mum, what's the last thing you remember?"

"A woman came to visit. She was interested in... something." She put her hand to her face. "Everything is such a blur."

"It's okay. All that matters is you're safe now." Luc squeezed her hand.

Mary stared up at him, then at Eric and Sara. "Why are you all here?"

Ella glanced at Luc, wondering how much she should tell her mother. "I came home for a visit and brought my friends with me," she said. "These are my friends, Eric, Sara and Luc. There must have been a big storm. I think you fell when you went down into the cellar to get the candles."

It surprised her how easily the lie came. If Mary couldn't remember what Esme had done to her, Ella wanted to keep it that way. Why make her suffer with terrible, traumatising memories?

"I'll make some more tea," Sara offered.

"Good idea. Eric and I will head into the village to see if we can get a new window and some boards to cover up the wall." Luc turned to Ella. "Will you be okay here for a while?"

Ella nodded. "We'll be fine. Go."

She didn't want to talk to him right now, but nor did she want to worry her mum either.

"I'm so happy to have you home." Mary squeezed her hand. "It's been lonely here without you."

"Mum, I'm sorry for everything I said before I left."

"I'm sorry too. I know how much you longed to go to the big city. I should have been more supportive. I felt terrible after you left but couldn't bring myself to call in case you wouldn't answer. You and I are as stubborn as each other." She smiled.

Ella hugged her mum tight, feeling her worries melt away. "All that matters is I'm home now."

Mary returned her embrace. "I missed you, but I'm happy you came by for a visit. Are you staying for long?"

Ella shrugged. "I'm not sure yet. Is it okay for my friends to stay here too?" She tucked a lock of hair behind her ear. She couldn't tell Mary the real reason why she had come home. Better to pretend this was just a normal visit.

"Of course, they're welcome to stay. I'll…" Mary made a move to get up, but Ella stopped her.

"No, you rest. Sara and I can take care of everything, you just relax."

Mary laughed. "Being in the city has changed you. You hate doing any kind of chores."

"Thanks for helping to clean up." Ella walked into the kitchen and moved over to the stove, where Sara had started brewing a fresh pot of tea.

"No problem. What did you tell your mum?" Sara pulled down some fresh mugs from the cabinet and placed them on the counter.

"Not much, it's better she doesn't know anything. I don't want to leave her. Esme might come back, but I know we can't stay here for long either." She glanced out of the window, half expecting troopers or a band of Esrac to come swarming in. "We'll stay here tonight, just to make sure my mum is alright, but we'll leave at first light. Be careful what you say to her though."

She grabbed the teapot and poured some tea into each of the mugs. She had no idea how her mum would react if she found out Ella and her friends were fugitives on the run from the Senate.

Sara nodded. "Are you sure are staying here is a good idea, though?" she whispered. "What about the troopers? And Esme?" She grabbed a pot of honey from the counter and handed it to Ella. "Here, the sweetness will help your mum. It's good for trauma."

Ella took it gratefully and poured some into her mother's mug. "You and Eric can leave. I'm sure Luc will get you somewhere safe. I'm not leaving my mum alone."

"We'll stay. If Esme comes back you might need me," Sara said, shaking her head. "I'd still like to know why I burned her the way I did. I took Griffin's data crystal from the university. I'll look through the archives for anything that might help us."

Ella's eyes widened. "You took Griffin's data crystal? Wow. Usually you're such a goody two shoes."

"I had to. It wasn't stealing, anyway. It's safer with me than in the hands of the Senate. They would only misuse Griffin's knowledge." Sara raised her chin. "Can't you ask your mum about your dad's stuff?"

That was the reason why she'd come home in the first place, but it had been pushed to the back of Ella's mind. It seemed wrong to ask after everything Mary had been through.

"Mum, do you remember where dad kept all of his journals?" Ella asked, as she walked back into the lounge. She handed her mother a mug of tea from the tray she'd set down on a nearby table. "The ones he didn't want me to find, I mean."

She knew he'd written everything down, but she'd never seen anything other than tame diary entries and notes on how to control her powers.

"You've come home because of the magic, haven't you?" Mary said, as Ella handed her a cup of tea. "I knew you wouldn't have come back unless it was important."

"Mum, I..." Ella's stomach twisted with guilt. In truth, she wouldn't have come home if Esme hadn't been released.

"It's alright. We both knew this would happen one day." Mary stood up. "Your father told me to give you something, but only when I knew the time was right." She went over to the sideboard and pulled out a small wooden chest. She held it out to Ella. "Here. I may not have understood his work, but I knew how important it was."

"Thanks." Ella set it down on the table and tugged to open it, but it wouldn't budge.

"I've had enough rest." Mary sipped her tea and set the mug down. "Time for me to get to work on straightening this place out again."

CHAPTER 12

After Luc and Eric had boarded up the broken window, Luc spent time warding the house with magical barriers to protect them from any unwanted visitors.

Mary seemed to accept the story about a bad storm and being knocked unconscious, but Ella suspected deep down she knew the truth and didn't want to acknowledge it.

She sat in her old room trying to pry the box open, but nothing she did would break the lock, not even magic. Exasperated, she sighed and dropped it on the mattress next to her. It felt strange being back in her old room. She had changed so much since she'd last been here. Yet the room looked the same with purple walls and canopy over her small four-poster bed. A large mahogany chest of drawers took up one wall next to a built-in wardrobe, but the rest of the room was covered in shelves. Books and paperwork covered every available surface, including the small desk that sat under the window.

Heading over to the window, Ella spotted Luc outside, standing with his back to her. Grabbing the box again, she snuck out of the room and downstairs. The air felt cool against her skin and stars sparkled in the blanket of darkness overhead.

Luc turned around in surprise as she walked out. "I thought you were asleep," he remarked.

"It's kind of hard to sleep given everything that happened." She set the box down on an old rocking chair. "I still can't open this thing."

"Listen, about earlier. I'm—"

She held up her hand to silence him. "I'm getting tired of our past lives dictating everything we do now. Things happened in the past, but that's not who are who we are now," she said, taking his hand. "Promise you'll be honest with me from now on. No more secrets."

"No more secrets," he agreed.

"Be wary of my mum. I've never brought any boys home before. You probably shouldn't have introduced yourself as my boyfriend." Her lips curved into a smile.

"Am I your boyfriend?" He kissed the back of her hand and smiled back at her.

She arched an eyebrow. "Do you want to be? Despite all we've been through, I think it's pretty obvious we're meant to be together."

"Ella, I love you. I always have." Luc wrapped his arms around her. "I only kept you at arm's length before because I wanted to keep you safe, but I see now that was a mistake. I know we can see this through together. We'll find a way to break the curse, and things will be different in this lifetime."

Ella returned his embrace and rested her head against his chest. It felt good to be back in his arms again. She glanced over at the box. "Maybe you should try opening that stupid thing."

Luc pulled away from her to narrow his eyes at the box, but nothing happened.

"Mum says my dad didn't leave the key, but I don't know how else to unlock it." Fire flared in her hand as she threw at the box. The magic crackled as it hit the lock, then fizzled out.

"Maybe you're not meant to open it yet. Perhaps it will only open when the time is right."

"Now you sound like my dad."

"He was a wise man."

"I still half expect him to come walking through the door sometimes," she admitted, staring off into the distance. "He just vanished." Her heart twisted as she remembered the Chancellor's words about how he'd died.

Luc hesitated, and Ella frowned. "Do you know?"

"Not much. The report said was he went to investigate a possible Esrac attack. After that, no one knows what happened."

"When we arrived back in Celestus after Griffin died, the Chancellor told me my dad was killed trying to help someone cross the border." She sighed and shook her head. "Deep down, I always knew he was gone. I just thought—*hoped*—I'd see him again. What happens now? We can't do this on our own."

"You should go to see your grandmother," said another voice.

Ella and Luc both turned to see Mary standing in the doorway.

"Mum, how much did you have you heard?" Ella pulled away from Luc, heart pounding. How could they have been so careless? Why hadn't Luc sensed Mary approach?

"It doesn't matter. Your dad said if you ever needed help with magic, I should tell you to go and see your grandmother, Adria Noran."

"Adria Noran? She's still alive?" Luc asked, eyes widening.

"I believe so," Mary answered. "Caspian said I would know when to tell you. Now is that time."

Ella scowled. "She's ignored us for the past twenty years."

She'd never given her grandmother much thought. Adria hadn't even come to visit after Ella's father disappeared.

"You need her. She knows about magic, and I suspect a lot more."

Ella felt Luc tense beside her. "Someone's coming," he hissed in her ear.

"Mum, take this inside and stay there." Ella picked up the box and shoved it into Mary's arms. "Go."

"Ella, what's—"

"Please, just go."

Nodding, Mary hurried inside.

"What is it? Esrac or troopers?"

Luc pointed to the glowing lights in the sky. "I'd say troopers. We need to get out of here." They hurried back inside the house.

"I'm not leaving my mum behind." Ella said as she slammed and bolted the door shut behind them. She ran into the living room, where Mary stood at the window. "Mum, go…"

"I'm not hiding away," Mary insisted. She fumbled inside a drawer and pulled out a stunner.

Ella's eyes widened. "Mum, troopers are coming after us. I have no time to explain why."

"They know about your magic, don't they?"

"It's a lot more complicated than that," Luc replied, "but Ella's right, you should stay out of this."

Ella looked out of the window, seeing the lights of the ships getting ever closer.

"Mary, go and seal up the windows," Luc told her.

Mary obediently disappeared.

"They're never going to stop looking for us, are they?" Ella said.

"We're known magic users outside the Chancellor's control. Short of us dying, no, they won't stop looking," Luc said. "You should open the gate. We can all get out of here, including your mum."

"I won't make her become a fugitive too." Ella turned and ran upstairs to warn the others.

"Are we using that gate thing to get us out of here?" Eric asked as he followed Ella back down the stairs moments later, carrying a sleepy-looking Fidget.

"If we keep running, we'll always be looking over our shoulder," Ella said. "You and Sara—"

"I'm not leaving," Eric snapped, pulling out his own stunner. "So forget that."

"I can't leave either. I'm the best defence you have against the Esrac," Sara pointed out.

"This is Commander Ronin of the city troopers," a voice yelled. "By order of the Republic, you are to vacate the building and come out with your hands up."

"Ella, you need to go," Mary said. "Go to Adria's. I'll stay here, don't worry about me."

"No, Mum, I'm not leaving you," Ella protested.

"They won't hurt me. I'll tell them you weren't even here."

Ella glanced at Luc, who nodded. "Your mum doesn't have magic. They won't view her as a threat. If we leave now, we can avoid anyone getting hurt in the crossfire." Luc pulled out his sabre.

"Go but be safe." Mary hugged her daughter. "I love you."

"I promise we'll see each other again soon." Ella squeezed her back. "I love you too." She quickly grabbed her bag and tucked the box under her arm as Luc and the others gathered their things.

When they were ready, Ella turned to the wall, closing her eyes as she envisioned a gate opening. Golden light flashed as a doorway appeared and the portal opened.

Mary gasped. "That's…"

"You mustn't tell anyone about this," Luc warned.

She nodded. "Go, be safe all of you."

Eric and Sara headed through first, followed by Luc vanished.

Ella glanced back at her mum, then grabbed Fidget from the floor and vanished through the gate.

Ella blinked as she reappeared with the others.

"Where are we?" Eric asked. They now stood in the middle of an open field near the remains of a building that had long since fallen away.

"I was supposed to bring us to my grandmother's house," Ella said. "but I only remember going there once, ten years ago. She and my dad didn't see eye to eye."

"Mary said she still lived in the same place," Luc said.

"Maybe that gate thing didn't work very well this time," said Eric. "It has hardly been used in a thousand years, right?"

"Avatars control the gates, it should have worked," Luc replied. "Unless Adria did something to prevent us from gating directly to her."

"How?" Ella asked.

"Adria Noran is the only other avatar born in the last century," Luc explained. "She could have placed wards around her home to stop any gate activity."

"So I'm not the last avatar?" That should've felt comforting, but Ella couldn't say she was looking forward to seeing the grandmother who'd ignored her all her life. "We should get moving." She tucked the box under her arm, suddenly feeling the lack of another weighty object. "Damn, I left Fidget's cage behind."

"Cage bad," Fidget grumbled.

They all laughed, grateful for the small relief of tension.

Eric tapped his link, bringing up a map. "The first house looks to be about a mile from here," he said. "We should check it out."

"Adria's wards would only divert any gate travel, so there's a good chance that's her house," Luc agreed.

Ella nodded and followed after them.

The first rays of dawn crept through a blanket of heavy clouds as Adria's tiny cottage came into view. It looked just as Ella remembered. She tried to decide the best way to approach her estranged grandmother. She only remembered meeting her once, as a child, and Adria hadn't been very welcoming. Ella had never known why. She had loving parents, and that had been all that mattered to her.

She had no idea how Adria would react to seeing her after all these years, but they didn't have much of a choice other than to visit her. With Griffin gone, there was no one else left to help them.

"Wow, I thought your mum's house seemed remote, but this is..." Eric trailed off.

"In the middle of nowhere," Ella finished. "Yeah, she's somewhat of a recluse from what my dad told me. Luc, are you sure she's an avatar?"

"I learnt the names of all the avatars when I trained to become a knight, but I thought she was dead," he said. "Avatars being born became such a rarity the Order just told new knights they all died out."

"Do you think she'll help us?" Sara asked.

Ella shrugged. "I have no idea."

She approached the door, heart pounding. She hadn't even been this nervous when she'd gone to Celestus to start her apprenticeship, she noted.

She knocked on the wood of the door a couple of times and waited, taking a deep breath and letting it out again as she tried to calm her nerves.

The door creaked open, revealing an old woman with a creased face, grey hair, and sharp green eyes.

Ella stared at her, trying to see a resemblance between the woman and her dad.

"What do you want?" Adria demanded.

"I'm—I'm Ella Noran, your granddaughter," she started. "These are..."

"Lucas Flynn, you're Valan," Adria finished for her, spitting the last word. "Why have you come here?"

"Esme is on the loose."

Adria muttered a curse. "You let her out, didn't you?" She shifted her gaze to Luc. "Did that useless Griffin teach you nothing?"

"Listen, we're on the run from the Senate and the Esrac queen is on the loose," Luc said. "Griffin is dead because Esme killed him, and we—"

"Are running around like lost sheep not knowing what to do." Adria laughed. "Why come to me?"

"Because like it or not, you're our last hope," Ella said.

CHAPTER 13

Esme stumbled and hissed in pain. Her flesh still burned, and some of it looked like it had been melted away. She needed blood fast, but so far hadn't found any potential food sources while tracking the avatar from her mother's house. If they thought they could harm her and get away with it, they were dead wrong. She'd make them pay, especially the girl who burned her.

Night still darkened the sky as she stalked over to a small cottage with a tiled roof and weathered old stone walls.

What an odd little place.

Didn't most humans prefer big cities like Celestus that she'd seen in Griffin's memories?

She crouched down by a small open window voices drifted out of.

Esme caught the sound of six heartbeats inside, though one was fainter than the others. No doubt it came from that furball who followed Ella around. She quickly spared a glance through the window. The four of them crowded around a tiny kitchen table and the rat creature settled on Ella's shoulder, his teeth chattering nervously.

"The Esrac has been a plague to all the realms for over a thousand years. What makes you think I can help?" An old woman Esme had never seen before moved over to the stove and filled a teapot with water as she spoke.

"You're still an avatar and one of the few surviving people left who can help," Luc said. "You have a duty—"

Esme's fangs gleamed. Another avatar? So Ella wasn't alone. No doubt they had come here to seek this other avatar's help in destroying her people. Esme bit back a laugh. Whether it was one or two avatars, they didn't matter. Both would die at her hand.

"Don't talk to me about duty, boy. I gave my life to working with the Valan knights, and it cost me everything. My husband, my son..." She shook her head and set the teapot down to boil. "If Esme is free, you should warn the Senate and get them to help you."

"We already tried. The Chancellor wouldn't believe us," Ella said, and crossed her arms. "Is it true they killed my dad?"

Adria's eyes flashed. "Of course they did. The Senate doesn't tolerate anyone who goes against them."

"The Chancellor believes the ban on magic will protect the people," Luc said. "Even after Griffin's death she refused to accept the Esrac could have returned."

Adria fixed her gaze on Ella. "How could you let that bitch through? Your father always said he'd raise you as a human. How did you even access a gate? There are only two left in this realm."

"He taught me to control my magic about a year before he disappeared. I guess my powers were too strong for him to ignore," Ella said. "I read some of his journals too, but I had no idea about avatars or the Valan knights until I moved to Celestus and met Luc."

"You know about the curse then?" Adria asked. "On the two of you?"

They both nodded.

"And you're still together?"

"We created this mess. We'll try to fix it together." Luc reached across the table and squeezed Ella's hand.

"You honestly think the Esrac can be stopped? As long as their Queen lives, they can breed and produce dozens of drones."

"Then we have to stop Esme. Will you help or not?" Ella demanded. "I've never asked you for anything else. Just teach us what you know. That's all we want."

Adria glanced over at Eric and Sara. "Why are the humans here? They have no business in this mess."

"I kind of fell into it," Eric said.

"I can burn an Esrac with my bare hands," Sara added.

Esme's ears perked up at that last comment. She wanted to kill that strange blonde girl more than anything, perhaps even more than Lucan or Aurelia. How dare she burn her!

Adria's eyes narrowed, and she touched Sara's forehead briefly. "You're ungifted."

"Excuse me? I happen to be the youngest ever archivist in Celestus' history!" Sara said.

"An ungifted is someone who magic cannot harm. You possess a kind of anti-magic. Your touch will be harmful to anyone who possesses magic. Your gift I triggered by your emotions, especially fear or anger." Adria shook her head. "Esme won't like that." She poured the tea. "You're all barely more than children. What makes you think any of you can fight someone as strong as Esme?"

"We've managed so far, despite a few mishaps," Ella said. "Will you help us not?"

Adria blew out a breath. "I can't do everything. I'm too old. Our best bet would be to travel to the Valan compound at Arkadia."

Luc's eyes widened. "It still exists?"

"Of course. The Senate haven't destroyed the old ways yet," Adria said. "But you should know Esme won't stop hunting you. She'll want to bring her brethren through the gate."

She looked at Eric. "You shouldn't be part of this. You're just a powerless human."

"We're friends," he insisted and folded his arms. "Anyway, if the bookworm goes, I'm going too."

"Arkadia is a thousand miles from here. I'll have to arrange some type of transport," Adria said.

"Didn't I see an old airship outside?" Eric asked. "Looks like an old Pegasus model."

"Oh, that thing hasn't run in years." Adria waved a hand dismissively. "No, give me a few days and I'll find a transpo, but we'll have to be discreet about it. They're already circulating your pictures around."

"You get screen service out here?" Eric asked in surprise.

"No, I have a link."

Adria held up a square shaped link that looked like a brick.

Esme stayed outside as they continued to chat, listening to everything she could. The one called Eric had wandered off to work on the ship, and Luc went with him. Esme crept closer to them. If she took down Luc first, the avatars and the strange ungifted girl would be left unprotected.

"You think you can get it going?" Luc asked Eric.

"Maybe. It's not in bad condition, just doesn't have any power," Eric replied.

Luc frowned as Esme made a move to lunge at him. She smiled as she sensed one of her drones nearby.

"Esrac."

Luc's sword flared with power.

A drone lunged at him, making a grab for him. Luc lashed out with his sword, the glowing blade slicing off the Esrac's hand at the wrist.

Eric looked up, grabbed a laser knife, and flung it at the other drone as it advanced toward him. It hit the creature in the eye, making it howl with pain.

Luc swung his sword, but missed, and leapt into the air, slicing the drone's head off before his feet hit the ground. Seconds later, the other drone grabbed Eric by the throat.

Luc grabbed the drone's shirt, yanking the beast backward and slicing off its head.

Eric let out a breath, looking at the blood and bodies that surrounded him. "Well, that was easy."

"Too easy, they're newborn drones. Esme is the still real threat."

Luc hurried back inside, dragging Eric with him. The wall behind him exploded as blasts from a stunner hurtled toward him.

Adria appeared, also holding a glowing sword, and swung it at Esme.

"You're not welcome here, demon."

Esme laughed. "Fool, I'm not here for you. Get out of my way!"

Ella raised her hand, sending Esme stumbling backward with a burst of starfire.

Sara grabbed Esme's arm, making the queen howl in agony as her flesh started to burn.

"Hurry, Ella, open the gate!" Luc yelled.

Ella raised her hands again, and light shimmered as a glowing doorway appeared on the wall behind them.

"No, I won't go back!" Esme screamed as the glowing gate tried to suck her backwards and pull her through.

Sara shoved Esme toward the gate, but Esme's claws dug into the side of the gate. The portal started dragging her through, its light enveloping her body.

Ella moved forward, touching the runes on the gate.

Esme grabbed her arm. "If I go back, I'm not going alone."

Luc dropped his sword in panic, grabbing Ella's other arm as the portal tried sucking them all into it.

Adria raised her hand, throwing a fireball at Esme. As she did, Luc and Ella collapsed to the floor in a tangle of limbs.

When they scrambled up, Esme had vanished from sight.

She screamed as darkness enveloped her. When she opened her eyes again, she found herself outside. She didn't know where she was, but one thing was for certain.

This world would soon be hers. One way or another.

FALLEN AVATAR

CHAPTER 1

"Are you sure this thing isn't going to fall out of the sky?" Ella asked Eric, motioning to the old Pegasus airship.

"It's flying, isn't it?" Eric replied.

"Yeah, but it's so old you couldn't even find new parts for it," she pointed out.

"The current parts work just fine."

Ella wasn't convinced. She didn't like flying at the best of times, and being in this old bucket of bolts did little to ease her fear. The fact it could even carry five people and a small dust bunny amazed her. Eric's confidence in the age-old vessel didn't inspire her much, either.

Ella glanced over at Luc, who seemed lost in thought. Behind her, Adria, her estranged grandmother, had her head slumped against her chest as she slept, whilst Sara sat trying to keep Fidget, Ella's dust bunny, out of the food supplies.

"Are you sure you can't magic another cage into existence?" Sara grumbled. "We'll have no food left by the time we get to the border."

"Fidget, leave," Ella ordered. "You can't have any more." Her tone was firm but not angry. She knew the dust bunny got antsy whenever he wasn't on the ground. "No, I can't conjure a cage. Believe me, I would have done it already if I could." Her magical talents didn't extend as far as creating objects out of thin air.

She leaned over and rested her head against Luc's shoulder.

He smiled and wrapped an arm around her shoulders, but said nothing.

"Do you think the Valan can really help us?" she asked.

"They are our best shot and our last hope."

Luc himself was a Valan apprentice who had been trained by the ancient order of knights to protect and keep the peace throughout the realm.

Luc had trained under Master Griffin until the Esrac Queen, Esme, had killed him. The Esrac were a vampiric species that fed on blood to survive, and Ella had accidentally released Esme when she'd opened one of the gates that served as a portal between realms.

Ella was an avatar – someone who could control the gates. She and Adria were the only surviving avatars left because of the Republic's ban on magic and determination to rid their realm of all magic users.

Since then, Esme and her drones had hunted her. A thousand years ago, the gates had been sealed during the first war, after Aurelia, Ella's past self, had trapped Esme and dozens of her kind in a hell realm. Esme had learnt to use the gates after she'd befriended and tricked Luc and Ella's past selves into sharing their knowledge of the system. Locking her away had been all Aurelia could do to stop Esme from killing humans in droves. No avatar or Valan knight had been able to kill Esme so far, as the Esrac had regenerative abilities, and she was the strongest of them all.

It still amazed Ella just how much her life had changed in such a short time. A few weeks ago, she'd been a normal young woman studying archaeology at the prestigious Celestus University. Although she had possessed magic all her life, she kept it secret, determined to prove that the Republic's version of the realm's history was wrong. It went back a lot further than they said. Only she'd found a lot more than she'd bargained for.

Neither she, nor any of her friends, had expected to have to go on the run from the Senate. Being a Valan and her boyfriend, Luc became part of the mess too. The Valan knights and avatars worked together to keep their realm safe. However, she still felt a little guilty for dragging Sara and Eric into it. They'd only come because they were her friends—friends she'd pulled into her messy life without even meaning to.

"I hope the Valan don't react the same way to our relationship as Griffin did," Ella remarked.

"It doesn't matter what they think. We're not gonna be defined by our past lives or some stupid archaic rules." Luc kissed the top of her forehead.

She smiled. Their relationship had never been easy due to them both keeping secrets from each other. One good thing to come from all this was it brought them closer together. As long as she had him by her side, she knew they'd get through anything. Even living as fugitives and being hunted by green-skinned psychos.

"How long before we reach Arkadia?" Sara asked, running a hand through her hair.

"We've got several hundred miles to cover," Eric replied. "I thought you were happy to get out of the stuffy old archives, bookworm?"

Sara scowled at him. "The archives were a damn sight safer than your flying."

"Hey, I'm a first-class pilot."

"Stop bickering, children," Adria grumbled.

"We're not children," Ella retorted.

"You're barely more than teenagers, that makes you children." Adria sat up to pour some tea out of a flask. "It will take at least a couple of days to reach the border."

"Er, we've got company," Eric announced. "An entire fleet of Republic cruisers is heading straight for us."

Ella leaned forward to see tiny glowing dots on the screen. "I thought this thing was too old to show up on scanners?"

"I thought it was too," Eric muttered. "I checked—"

"Never mind that, just try to lose them," said Luc.

The ship fell into complete darkness as Eric turned off all the lights and switched to minimal power. "Hold tight. I'm gonna try and lose them by going into that tree line. There's enough cover so they shouldn't be able to see us down there."

"Fidget," Ella called. "Come here."

The dust bunny jumped up into a small storage compartment where he'd taken to sleeping and huddled inside it.

Ella stifled a cry of alarm as the ship nosedived, plummeting toward the tree line. The engines groaned, and branches batted against the sides of their craft.

"Does this bucket have any weapons?" Sara called.

"It's a cruiser, not a military vessel," Eric replied, guiding the ship down to a safe landing spot. He disengaged almost all the systems, leaving only the tracking system online.

The fleet of aircraft whirred over them, filling the air with the faint drone of engines. None of them said or did anything for several minutes and even Fidget remained unusually silent. All eyes stayed riveted on the screen until the fleet moved off into the distance.

"Phew, that was close." Ella let out a breath she hadn't known she'd been holding. "You think they'll come back?"

"I think we should find somewhere to camp out for the night. We could all use some rest, and it'll stop any other ships in the area from detecting us," Eric said, settling back into his seat and turning the radar system offline.

Ella gripped her armrests as the airship bucked and swerved to take off again, clutching Fidget to her chest.

"Bad," Fidget squeaked, and his body trembled against her.

Luc reached over and squeezed her hand to try and reassure her, but Ella didn't find it very comforting. Alarms started wailing throughout the ship.

"We've got two airships right behind us. They must have cut off from the fleet," Luc said. "Eric, you need to lose them!"

"I'm trying!" Eric snapped, causing the Pegasus to veer to the left.

Fidget screamed, digging his claws into Ella's arms. She clutched him tighter and glanced out of the tiny window. So far, their plan to leave Adria's cottage and fly across the border in search of the Valan didn't seem to be going to plan. After spending the past couple days getting ready for the trip and preparing the ancient Pegasus for flight, Ella couldn't believe the Senate's airships had found them already and wondered how they'd managed to track the ship so quickly. After all, she and the others had used the gate to reach Adria's cottage.

"Eric, there are some woods close by," Adria said. "We can leave the ship and lose them in there."

"We can't just ditch the ship," Sara protested. "It's the best way of us getting across the border!"

Eric glanced back at Luc, who nodded. "Do it."

Ella wondered when they'd started looking to Luc as their unofficial leader, but he was a Valan knight himself.

Eric gripped the controls and sent the ship into a sharp nosedive. Ella's teeth clenched as the g-force ripped through the ship, and the Pegasus' engines roared and groaned.

Light flashed past the window, and Ella's heart went to her throat. "There's a torpedo!" she cried. "Eric—"

The ship banked sharply and trees flashed past.

Before Ella had the chance to catch her breath, Eric shut down the engines, leapt up, and pushed the bay door open. "Everyone out, quick!" He grabbed his pack and jumped from the ship without unfolding the ramp.

Luc helped Sara up. "Go!"

"My things!" Sara protested, but Luc pushed her out before she could argue any further.

Adria scrambled up and jumped. Ella clutched Fidget and went next, with Luc right behind her.

Seconds later, the ship exploded behind them as the torpedo struck.

Luc covered Ella's body with his, but she still felt the heat of the explosion ripple across her skin. She gasped for breath as Luc rolled away from her, and scrambled into a sitting position to watch the burning inferno where the ship had once been. "Damn, we didn't have a chance to grab our supplies," she groaned. "That was the last of our ration packs."

They hadn't had much, just a couple days' worth of food they would've had to ration, but now all of it was gone.

Now what are we gonna do? Ella wondered. Adria's old airship had been their last hope of getting safely to the border undetected by the Senate's troopers, who were hunting Luc and Ella for being magic users.

Luc gave her a hand up. "Everyone alright?" he asked.

The others appeared unharmed, though their clothes were rumpled and dirtier than they had been before. Adria stood to one side coughing and seemed to be struggling for breath.

"Are you alright?" Ella asked her grandmother.

Adria took a few deep breaths and waved her hand in dismissal. "I'm fine. We need to get moving." She leaned heavily on her walking stick, taking rasping breaths. "Have a look through the rubble and see if there's anything we can salvage, but don't take too long. Those ships will still be circling the area for us."

Sara ran a hand through her long blonde hair, her blue eyes dark in the low light. She rubbed her hands down the torn university robe that she'd worn since they'd left Celestus. "What do we do now?"

"We'll have to continue on foot," Luc replied, looking at Adria. "Will you be okay to do that?"

Adria coughed again, but nodded. "Of course I will. There's still life in this old girl yet."

Ella still didn't know how to react around her grandmother. Up until a few days ago, Ella had only ever met her once, and now Adria was the only one who could help them find the Valan.

"Our packs were fireproof. Maybe we can still salvage some of the contents," Eric suggested. His earrings jangled as he pushed his long blonde hair off his face.

Adria folded her arms. "This place will soon be swarming with troopers. We don't have time to search through a pile of rubble!"

"But we need our supplies," Sara said. "How else will we manage without food?"

Ella raised her hands, trying to channel her power. She'd moved small things before and knew Luc could move things, too. She'd seen him send a group of men flying.

More flames sparked among the burning remains of the ship, growing hotter and brighter.

"One of you really needs to teach me how to use my magic," she grumbled. She pushed her long black hair off her face, wishing she'd taken the time to tie it back before they'd left Adria's cottage.

"You have the ability to find what you want." Luc squeezed her hand, and a black object flew into his arms as his own pack appeared.

Show off! Why does he have to make it look so easy?

"Concentrate," Luc said. "Picture your pack in your mind."

She closed her eyes and thought of her leather satchel. Something slammed against her chest, knocking the air from her lungs as she stumbled, then fell backward. Her pack slid to the ground with a thud alongside Sara and Adria's.

"It's a start," Luc said. "Come on, let's move."

Ella grabbed her pack and swung it over her shoulder.

The five of them hurried away, moving deeper into the forest as they went.

Ella's feet were killing her by the time they reached the clearing and moved out of the dense foliage. Night enveloped the sky like a heavy blanket, a scattering of tiny stars flickering overhead. Ella slumped down onto a log, relieved they wouldn't have to walk any further.

Adria groaned and sat down beside her, breathing heavily. Ella noticed how out of breath she'd been all day and knew the walking must have taken its toll. Still, Adria wouldn't let anyone fuss over her and insisted she was fine whenever they asked.

"Food!" Fidget chirped and scurried off. He'd no doubt be gone for the night, hunting or doing whatever he did on his nightly excursions.

"Don't go far," she called after him.

Luc and Eric appeared, carrying sleeping bags for all of them, and prepared to make camp for the night.

"Don't light any torches," Adria told them. "We'll eat the cold food from our ration packs to keep the light to a minimum. There could still be scouts in the area that might be able to see us if we're not careful."

Ella sat and ate from her ration pack. The food inside was meant to be chicken and vegetables but looked like a sludgy mess and tasted like rubber. She ate it anyway since food would be hard to come by now.

Sara and Eric bickered as usual whilst Luc and Adria discussed that the land. Ella half listened as she gulped down rest of her dinner. Rising, she said, "I'm going for a walk."

"I'll come." Sara shot to her feet.

Ella gave Luc a quick kiss and headed off, with Sara trailing behind her.

They moved through the tree line, but Ella wasn't nervous. She knew Luc would come at the first sign of trouble.

"What do you reckon happens when we find the Valan?" Sara asked.

Ella shrugged. "Honestly, I don't know. None of us do. Hopefully, they'll help us figure out how to stop Esme once and for all."

Sara shivered, pulling her coat tighter. "I thought it would be an adventure to try to kill strange beasts, but it's kind of scary too."

Ella nodded, knowing the fear all too well. She hadn't slept well in weeks. It seemed like months since she'd first opened the gate and set off the chain of events that had led them to all being fugitives. Ella and Luc still had an age-old curse hanging over their heads if they failed to stop the Esrac this time. "I appreciate you coming with us, but I wish you had stayed in the city."

"This is my fight, too," Sara added. "That thing killed Griffin, and I'm immune to magic, so you still need me. Don't bother trying to convince me to leave."

"Can't blame me for trying." Ella said. "I don't want anyone else to die because of my stupid mistakes, but one way or another I'll get justice for everyone Esme has killed."

CHAPTER 2

Esme clutched her arm. Red welts and blackened flesh covered the area where that damned girl had touched her. Sara, had they called her? Her name didn't matter to Esme, she'd kill the girl one way or the other, and make damn sure Sara suffered tenfold from the pain she'd inflicted on her.

The pain of her arm had distracted her so much she hadn't paid attention to where she was. She only knew that Ella had opened the gate again and sent her to a different location. Esme's metallic teeth clanked together as she muttered a curse and glancing around, she saw thick trees all around her. She appeared to be in another forest, but where? Where had that damned avatar sent her now?

Esme had heard the avatar and her companions talking before she'd attacked. The elderly avatar woman had called Sara an ungifted, someone who couldn't be touched by magic and possessed the ability to neutralise all its forms. There had been legends of such people even in her own realm, but anyone suspected of having such an ability had been put to death long before they'd ever had a chance to harm the Esrac.

She stumbled and leant back against a tree as rays from the midday sun stung her eyes and prickled her skin. She needed blood to heal herself, yet thanks to the avatar, she had no way of knowing where the nearest food source was. Ella and her companions had proven stronger than she'd anticipated, sending her away before she'd had the chance to do any real damage to them. No matter, they'd only prolong their suffering this way. She *would* kill them, no doubt about that, just as she'd done to Luc and Ella in their past lives.

She pushed all thoughts of death and killing out of her mind as she looked around.

Where am I?

This looked nothing like the hell realm she'd been sent to and forced to hibernate in for the past thousand years, and Esme doubted Ella had the skill to banish her to a different one. That meant she was somewhere in Ella's own realm. But a thousand years had passed since Esme had almost conquered it. She didn't know her way around.

She searched through the fragmented memories she'd taken from Griffin and another man she'd killed during her time here, hoping they might help her get her bearings, but no such luck. Neither Griffin nor the other man she'd killed had been here before.

Ella's mother's memories only extended to Antaria and its surrounding area. So they would be useless here. Ella wouldn't have sent Esme anywhere near her precious mother.

She made her way through the woods. Leaves and branches caught at the bodice of her long leather dress, making her clench her teeth. How she hated trees and greenery! She missed the barren, rugged landscape of her own realm, where she had ruled as queen for centuries. Her hive there had been her home all her life, and she suddenly missed the great sprawling halls and buzz of her people, who had been forced into deep hibernation with her after she had tried and failed to take down the city of Arkadia.

As much as she missed them, she felt no guilt. Esrac weren't at the mercy of such pitiful emotions like humans were. Besides, one failure wouldn't stop her. She'd try again and again until this realm became hers, and she was reunited with her people again to enjoy the rich feeding ground she'd promised them. No longer would they have to endure long centuries of forced hibernation, their bodies weak and decaying.

She broke off a branch and tossed it aside in disgust. She'd burn every forest to the ground when she took full control of this realm, but first she needed somewhere to take refuge out of the sun; preferably somewhere with food, so she could heal her injuries and perhaps set up a permanent base—something she would need if she was ever going to conquer this realm.

The avatar and Valan knight wouldn't come after her again. She knew they'd be too busy trying to figure out how to stop her. That would at least buy her some time to regain her strength and plan her next move.

Esme snorted as she pushed through the trees, envisioning what it would be like when she finally laid waste to this realm. Up ahead stood a small house with pink walls and a small garden surrounded by flowers. This place looked to be what some humans would consider pretty, but it disgusted Esme. She had never understood humans' love for colour. It served no purpose among the Esrac.

She heard the faint thump of two heartbeats inside. The barbs on her hand ached and hunger gnawed at her belly. At least the avatar had sent her somewhere with a food source nearby. What luck!

The sun stung her eyes again as she moved out of the shade.

Wretched sunlight!

She ran, her boots pounding against hard earth and her long leather skirt billowing behind her.

She shoved the front door open, and someone cried out in alarm. Esme grinned, her metallic teeth glistening. She knew her green skin, black eyes, and long blood-red hair appeared terrifying to humans.

"Alan!" the voice called. It belonged to a pale and skinny dark-haired woman, who backed away as her blue eyes went wide with fear. "What are you? Get out of my house!"

Not the way Esme liked her food. Frail meat sacks never lasted long, but she needed sustenance now. Esme flew at the human, grabbing her by the throat.

The woman tried to scream as Esme's barbs cut into her flesh but couldn't. Her arms flailed about as she struggled to get away.

Esme felt warmth flood through her body and closed her eyes, enjoying the ecstasy for a moment. The throbbing in her arm lessened as some of the pain faded.

"What the hell are you doing?" a man's voice yelled.

Esme let out a low growl as she released the woman, who slumped to the floor. She turned around to see a dark-haired man standing in the doorway. His heartbeat quickened, and Esme breathed deeply. The smell of fear was almost as delicious as the taste of blood itself.

"It's not polite to interrupt someone when they're eating," Esme remarked.

The man pulled out a small, oddly shaped weapon. A stunner, she knew from the memories of others she had killed.

She rolled her eyes as he aimed it at her. "That won't kill me!"

She flew at him as he fired, sending a burst of blue light at her.

Esme didn't know why humans bothered to fight back; they stood no chance against her. She clamped her fingers around his throat, and the stunner clattered to the floor. His eyes bulged as his face wrinkled.

Esme took her fill, then stopped. When she glanced down, her arm still had blackened flesh, but the welts had almost disappeared. She gritted her teeth and let out a low growl. Why hadn't she healed completely? Her flesh should be whole again, not damaged!

Despite the stories of ungifted ones in her own realm, Esme hadn't faced one herself before Sara, and had no idea if this kind of wound would be permanent or not.

Could the ungifted one actually *kill* her?

Impossible! No one could kill her; she was meant to conquer this realm. It was destined.

"Now I will kill *you*, unless you prove to be useful," she said as she released the man.

The man stumbled, no doubt weak from the loss of blood and the life force she had drained from him. All humans withered, aged, and then died if an Esrac took too much from them.

"What...What did you do to me?" he gasped, touching his now-weathered face.

"That's not important. First, tell me where I am," Esme commanded. "What province is this?"

"What?" He gaped at her as if he had no idea what she was talking about.

"Tell me where I am!" Esme hissed. "Or I'll finish off your wife and kill you."

"Elyria," he said, glancing past Esme to where his wife lay. "Moira, are you okay? Answer me."

"Elyria..." She scanned through her memory banks. "That's twenty miles from Celestus."

"What are you?" Alan trembled.

"How many people reside in your village?" Esme needed to know how many she might be up against. If enough humans banded together, they could injure her.

"What?" Alan frowned, mouth agape.

"Answer me!" She raised her hand, ready to grab him again.

"Two, maybe three hundred. What did you do to my wife?"

Esme smiled. Enough food to last her a while, to begin a new hive.

Her teeth flashed. "You shall be the first of my new warriors if you are as strong as I think you are." She raised her left hand and pressed her palm over his chest.

Alan's eyes darkened as Esme released him. He slumped to the floor; his eyes glazed over. Esme knew she'd have to wait a few hours to use him, but at least she had somewhere to hide out.

"Alan?" the woman moaned, coming to. "Alan, what's happening?"

Esme smirked. Time to fully sate her hunger.

She grabbed the woman by the throat. Moira struggled, hitting out as Esme tightened her grip. She felt a rush of satisfaction as Moira's hair whitened and her skin shrivelled, the blood draining from her.

Esme let the woman's withered husk fall to the floor and stared at her arm, where the damaged flesh remained. She gritted her teeth. Why hadn't she healed? Blood and life force could heal even the gravest of injuries. Perhaps Moira had just been too weak to fully replenish her, but she needed to keep a close eye on the avatar and her companions, especially the ungifted one.

She glanced over to Alan. It would be a while before the transformation completed itself.

In the meantime, she'd get acquainted with the neighbours.

CHAPTER 3

Ella and the others spent the day traipsing through dense woodland. Fidget seemed thrilled to be in the wilderness and happily ran around their feet.

"How do you think the Valan will react to us going to see them?" Eric asked.

Luc sighed, running a hand through his short black hair. "In truth, I don't know. The rules say avatars should be put to death, but they haven't always enforced that rule. Some of them believe only an avatar can stop the Esrac."

Adria snorted. "More than one Valan has tried to kill me over the years." She leaned heavily on her stick as she hobbled along behind them. Her skin may have creased with age and her dark hair long since turned grey, but Luc noticed a fire in her sharp green eyes. A determination and will to survive.

Ella stared at her. She had last seen the woman years ago, when her father had still been alive, and Adria had never been welcoming toward Ella or her mother. Ella hadn't given her much thought over the years and had been happy growing up with her parents back in Antara before she'd gone to take a scholarship at Celestus University several ago as an archaeology student.

She wouldn't have sought Adria out at all if they didn't need her help in finding the Valan base. She only hoped the ancient order of knights sworn to keep the peace between realms could help them.

"If they're so bad, why are we going to find them?" Eric wanted to know.

"Because we need the help," Luc answered. "They know things that have been passed down by the ancestors, and they can help us find a way to kill Esme and the Esrac once and for all. Plus, we won't have to worry about troopers finding us so much from the other side of the border."

"How can we stop the Esrac?" Sara asked. "The only way the ancestors could stop them was by banishing them to another realm." She glanced over at Ella. "Could you do that again? Use the gate and send Esme back to the hell realm?"

Ella shook her head. "No, even if I did, Esme would still find a way to come back one day. I know her well enough by to know that."

Banishing Esme in her first life had only delayed the inevitable; she needed to be stopped once and for all.

"Speaking of ancestors, aren't you and Ella the ancestors? Reincarnated, I mean?" Eric said, looking at Luc. "Why can't you to figure out how to stop the Esrac together?"

Ella and Luc glanced at each other.

"We don't remember everything from our past lives," Luc said after a few moments. "Things are different now Esme is free."

"What makes you think the Valan will help?" Eric persisted. "I mean, *Griffin* let the green freak out, and we all thought he was a good guy!"

"Because the other Valan won't want Esme free," Adria replied. "Their ultimate goal is to protect the realm from the Esrac. Griffin was just a power-hungry fool."

Sara winced at this, Ella noticed.

"How do they feel about people like me?" she asked.

Adria gave a harsh laugh. "Oh, no doubt they'll love you, my dear. Just as much as the Senate would love to get their hands on you."

Ella felt a pang of guilt at the mention of Griffin. He'd been the one who led the expedition to the old city of Arcadia in the first place. It was there she had found the gate and unleashed the first wave of Esrac. She had thought Griffin to be her mentor and friend, yet he had only sought to use Ella in his attempt to control the Esrac and ended up releasing Esme in the process.

"What if they don't want help?" Ella prompted. "Will they try to kill me and Adria?"

"Don't you mean 'Gran'?" Adria arched a thin eyebrow.

She pursed her lips together. "I only met you again three days ago. You haven't earned that title yet." Part of her still resented Adria for not being there after her father had vanished. Ella suspected Adria knew a lot more about her dad's disappearance than she let on, and she still wanted answers.

"We should set up camp. It's dark, and we won't make much progress on foot tonight," Luc suggested.

They each had blankets in their packs and pulled them out.

Sara got to work on building a fire but paused as she was about to light it. "It's okay to do this, right?"

Adria pulled out her own blanket and nodded as she sat down. "Just to heat our food on. Put it out as soon as you're done."

Ella glanced around for Fidget, who came over carrying some acorns. He climbed up onto her shoulder and sat there munching.

Oh, to be a dust bunny. They lead such uncomplicated lives.

Luc and Eric wandered off, saying they were going to look for wildlife to hunt in an effort to save their ration packs.

Ella glanced over at Adria. She still didn't know how to talk to the woman who'd been a stranger to her all her life, yet she had so many questions about her dad, and being an avatar.

Ella brushed her hair off her face. "What happened the day my dad died?" she whispered, whilst Sara fumbled through her pack for more food. "You said he helped you cross over the border, and the Chancellor confirmed as much."

Adria hadn't been keen to answer her questions in the days they spent at her cottage, but Ella was tired of waiting. Her grandmother at least owed her some answers.

Adria stared at the flickering flames as Sara moved away to give them some privacy. She sighed and shook her head. "That is a day that's best forgotten."

Ella's hands clenched into fists. "Please, I spent so long wishing and hoping he'd come home. I need to know what they did to him. Why did he help you cross the border?" Even now, part of her still hoped her father might still be alive and out there somewhere.

Adria hissed out a breath. "I lived across the border in Anis. Your father was born there, and my family lived there. Even Luc was born there."

Ella's eyes widened. Luc never spoke of his family. He only told her he'd lost his parents when he was young. She had no idea he'd grown up across the border.

"How come I met you before that?" she asked. "I thought you lived here then too." Her dad had never spoken about Adria or much of his childhood. It made her wonder if she ever really knew him at all.

Adria shook her head. "I came to visit your father via the gate after I sensed you using magic," she said. "The Valan knew about me, of course, but I married one of them, so they tolerated me over the years. That became more of an uneasy truce once my husband died. I only opened the gate once by accident when I was a teenager, before I had any training, but I'm not as strong as you. I could only open it partway without awakening Esme. Some Esrac come through occasionally, but there are those among the Valan who can use the gate too. At least, the Masters can. It helps them stay one step ahead of the troopers."

"So avatars and the Valan still used the gate after Aurelia?" Ella frowned. She'd been under the impression the gate had been sealed for the past thousand years.

Adria snorted. "Of course. It's hard not to be drawn to Aurelia's creation; it's part of who we are. Our role is to teach others magic and ensure that that knowledge is passed on to future generations. At least, it used to be." Adria picked up a stick and prodded the fire. "I came back here that day because your father wanted my help. The day I met you, I realised you were Aurelia. I told Caspian he should remove your magic, that it'd be safer that way and no one would ever know about you, but Cas said no. He thought you were the key to stopping the Esrac."

Ella shook her head. She still had trouble getting her head around thought of being alive once before, but to find out her dad had known proved even more shocking. "Dad knew? Why didn't he tell me?"

"Food?" Fidget prodded her with his paw.

She reached into her pocket and handed him a couple of honey drops.

"Because I convinced him not to. You have no idea what life the other side of the border is like." Adria shook her head and sighed. "Your father never wanted that life for you. He wanted you to grow up in safety, to live like a normal human."

"I have a good idea of what it's like to be hunted." Ella ruffled Fidget's pointed ears.

After her magic was exposed, the Senate had locked her up for over a month and tried removing her powers. When that had failed, she and Luc had managed to escape from Celestus with their friends and former teammates, Eric and Sara, and now they were all fugitives in a place where magic was outlawed.

Adria shook her head. "Being on the other side of the border is far worse than what you faced here."

Ella pursed her lips. She didn't want to argue with Adria. Granted, she didn't seem like the easiest person to get close to, but they shared the same blood and were both avatars. Despite that, Ella had no idea if Adria would teach her anything about magic or how to use the power inside her.

"Cas asked me to come home with him the day we crossed the border together. He feared the other Valan might find out about you. He wanted me to be there if anything happened to him. He asked me to watch over you."

All colour drained from Ella's face. "Are you saying my dad died because of my magic?"

Her heart twisted at the thought. She had enough guilt weighing her down from the mistake she'd made in her past life, and in this one by accidentally opening the gate as she had. She didn't know if she could cope with the idea of her dad dying for her as well.

Adria shook her head. "No, he died because of the Senate and their persecution of magic. *They* killed him. You are in no way responsible for their actions." She reached out and briefly touched Ella's hand for a moment. "Don't even think about blaming yourself."

Ella picked Fidget up and held him close. To her surprise, he didn't try to wriggle free.

"I want to learn more about how to control my magic; about what it means to be an avatar."

Adria hesitated for a moment, her gaze returning to the fire as she pulled her hand away from Ella's. "That knowledge is already inside you. You just need to learn to access it."

"Will you show me?"

Fidget wriggled free of her arms and climbed back onto her shoulder, where he resumed munching.

Adria fell silent for a few moments. "Part of me still thinks it would be safer if you didn't."

"Luc and I are cursed, remember? If we fail again…"

The curse had been placed on them a thousand years ago when their past selves had failed to keep the balance of power between the realms and unleashed the Esrac on an unsuspecting world. They'd been doomed to pay for that failure until they stopped Esme and the Esrac once and for all.

"If you do, you won't die. Not unless Esme succeeds in taking over this realm, which she won't."

Adria rose. "Sara, come on, that food won't cook itself." She glanced back over at Ella. "We'll start practising later, but even if you learn to fully control your magic, it still may not be enough to stop Esme."

CHAPTER 4

Luc moved through the trees, half-tempted to pull out his sabre and cut through the branches. As much as he enjoyed being out in nature, he got a little sick of trees after a while. Still, it was better than being locked up in Celestus and forced to do a job he hated under the constant watch of the Chancellor's spies and lackeys. At least out here he was free to be himself and no longer had to hide his powers or what he really was.

Eric trudged along behind him. "Do you really think the Valan can help?" His green eyes glanced around uneasily. Luc knew he was out of his element here among nature, and most at home around machines.

Luc tried not to sigh. Just because he was one of the Valan didn't mean he had all the answers. He didn't, and in truth, he felt lost without Griffin's guidance. Griffin had been his mentor for over ten years, and a father to him after Luc had lost his own family.

"I hope they can," Luc said after a few moments.

"Seems like a long shot to me." Eric bent and grabbed a few pieces of wood from in front of him.

"It's our only shot. The Valan are descended from the Arkadians; they have their knowledge, and they're among the few in this realm who still possess magic." He pushed through the trees. "Keep your stunner out. If we catch any game, it will be quicker if you shoot it."

"Why not just use your glowing sword thing?" Eric raised an eyebrow but pulled his stunner out and glanced around as if he expected something to appear.

"It will cause more damage and make things less edible."

"Hey, I'm sorry about what happened back in Celestus. You know, when I hit you?" Eric said. "I thought—"

Luc turned to stare at the engineer. "I know you had feelings for

Ella." He hadn't expected Eric to bring this up, and wondered why he'd done so now. Things had changed since they had left Celestus. He and Ella had grown a lot closer, and despite breaking up a few months earlier, their ordeal had strengthened their relationship.

Eric rubbed the back of his neck. "Yeah, she's some girl. I mean, woman," he said. "But you guys are meant to be. I get it now."

Luc shook his head. "I haven't always handled things well," he admitted, "but I hope things will be different now."

It felt odd to be talking about his relationship with Eric, of all people. They'd never really been friends.

"I've been thinking about the green-skinned bitch, and how Sara managed to burn her. Maybe she's the key to stopping Esme." Eric looked at his stunner, which he held between his fingers. "Maybe we could trap her, and Sara could put an end to her."

Luc snorted. "If only it were that easy. Esme can use a whole host of tricks to get herself free." He and Ella had tried defeating Esme in their past lives, but it hadn't worked.

"Didn't I hear her say something about her using you—I mean, the *past* you—to get knowledge about stuff? Like Ella and the gate thing?"

He winced. His capture—or rather, Lucan's capture—at the hands of Esme still haunted his dreams at times. If he hadn't been captured and tricked, Esme may never have learnt the secrets of the gate or how to use magic. "Yes," he grunted.

"So what happened?" Eric prompted.

"Esme came through with some drones. They overpowered me and took me to their realm." He shook his head.

Why am I telling this to Eric, of all people? He hadn't even really spoken to Ella about what had happened to him during that time. Those memories were best left forgotten.

"Esme can project illusions and make people see things that aren't real," he continued. "She got into my head and got whatever she wanted from me." He gripped the hilt of his sword. "I was as much to blame as Ella for the carnage the Esrac caused, maybe even more so."

The guilt still weighed on him at times, but he was learning to put it aside. He had to if they ever truly wanted to stop Esme.

"I get why what you and Ella did was wrong, but I don't see why you have to pay for it now."

"The ancestors believe no bad deed can go unpunished. Avatars keep the balance of magic and the Valan keep the peace. We both failed in our duties."

His duty had been to keep the peace in the realm and Ella's had been to keep the balance of magic for life and death, both of which they had failed to do by visiting the Esrac home world.

"Well, the green bitch can bleed, which means she can die," Eric said. "Still, are you sure we can trust the Valan?"

"Just because Griffin betrayed us doesn't mean all Valan are bad." Luc still believed in the values of the Order that he served both now and in all his lives.

"Maybe not, but I don't want to lead the girls straight into a trap."

Luc opened his mouth to speak again, but froze as a chill ran across his senses. He pulled his sword out; the blade flaring to life, and sent his senses out to scan the area around them.

Eric flipped the switch on his stunner. "What is it?"

Luc raised a hand to silence him. He considered talking to Eric in thought, then realised it wouldn't work. Eric possessed no magic.

"Esrac," he mouthed instead.

Eric gripped his stunner tighter.

A stunner wouldn't do much good against the Esrac, especially if it was Esme. Luc had no doubt Ella sending her away would have kept her from finding them for long. She was too hell-bent on revenge to stop coming after them.

Luc scanned the tree line as his senses went on high alert.

Wind rustled the leaves, and an owl hooted off in the distance. But everything else had gone silent. There were no sounds of animals or wildlife. After a few moments, even the wind died away to utter stillness.

Where are you? Luc scanned the area with his senses, trying to trace the source of the chill. Esrac had to be around here somewhere. He had felt the presence of at least one of them.

"Where is it?" Eric mouthed.

Luc gave a slight shrug, sending his senses out further into the woods. He scanned for any anomalies, feeling the vibrations of different life forces around him. The trees, the surrounding wildlife, and the very earth beneath his feet consisted of energy and gave off their own different vibrations. An Esrac gave off waves of dark and cold, almost like being trapped in an empty space with no lights and no way out.

The Esrac had to be close. The chill slithered down Luc's back like icy water now. Esrac weren't known for their patience, and they attacked on a whim, so why hadn't it attacked them yet? What was it waiting for? Even if Esme had sent someone to watch them, a drone wouldn't just wait around, it would be too tempted by their blood to hold back. Drones didn't possess the patience Esme herself had when it came to prey.

A shadow moved at the edge of a large oak tree, and Luc braced himself, ready for an attack. He gripped his sword tighter and took up a fighting stance. He felt his own energy merging with that of his sword in preparation for any number of drones.

Eric's finger itched against the trigger, Luc noticed, and he spared his companion a quick glance. Part of him hated the fact Eric had been dragged into this at all. His only crime had been helping Luc get information on the Esrac attacks back in Celestus. Other than that, he had been just a member of the expedition team.

A small deer moved out into the clearing, chewing something as it stared at them.

Eric let out a breath. "Ah, I can't believe…"

He laughed and lowered his stunner.

A figure lunged at Eric, knocking him to the ground. He and the drone grappled, Eric wildly kicking and punching his assailant.

Luc muttered a curse as two more Esrac drones dressed in tattered clothes came at him, the second one armed with an axe.

In one swift move Luc's cut off the armed drone's hand at the wrist, making him howl in pain.

The other drone came at Luc with what looked like a crowbar. He ducked and rolled; avoiding the blow, then leapt up and swung his sword at the original drone as it dug its barbs into Eric's chest.

Eric turned and rolled out of the way, coughing.

"Use your stunner!" Luc yelled.

Still coughing, Eric grabbed his stunner and fired. A blast of blue-white light shot out, and the drone ducked out of the way to avoid the blast.

Luc frowned. Since when did drones avoid a direct attack? In all his centuries of fighting them, he'd never seen anything like this. Even when they were injured, they fought to the death. Nothing came between them and their prey.

The second drone came at Luc, as did the third. This time, the third brandished a jagged metal rod. The rod glanced off Luc's blade as metal on metal clashed and sang.

Bursts of blue light lit up the night as Eric fired at the first drone again, which slumped to the ground this time.

Luc blocked another blow, raised his hand, and sent the second drone hurtling against the tree, where it became impaled on a branch.

That should keep you busy for a while.

He continued to clash with Drone Three, and raised his hand, sending the drone stumbling backward. Seeing an opening, Luc spun and swung his sword, slicing off the drone's head. The body slumped to the ground.

Luc turned to dispatch with Drone One, wiping a splatter of black Esrac blood from his face, and found it already on the ground. Its body smouldered with steam from being stunned so many times.

He hurried over to the tree. With a wave of his hand, he levitated his sword and sliced off the head of Drone Two.

Sludge dripped down the tree as the body slumped forward, then fell to the ground.

"Argh, look at my shirt. That thing tried sucking the life out of me!" Eric groaned. "How did those things even find us? Ella sent the Queen away."

"Esme can still sense us and track us with her mind. She didn't become a Queen out of necessity; she's more powerful than you think."

Luc caught hold of his sword as it floated back down to him. He hurried over to the first drone, prepared to slice its head off and put it out of his misery.

"Hey, I killed one of them!" Eric half grinned as he rubbed his chest. "See, I'm not as useless as you thought. Even *I* can fight the bad guys."

"These aren't like proper drones, they're different," Luc snapped, wiping Esrac blood off his face.

Drone One gurgled, and its chest heaved. "Help me!" its harsh voice rasped.

Eric raised his stunner. "Holy crap! I thought it was dead."

"Wait!" Luc commanded, keeping his sword at the ready. Drones weren't known for speech or intelligent thought. Their sole purpose was to serve their queen. He peered down at it.

"Luc, we're supposed to kill those things, remember?" Eric hissed. "He tried to suck the life out of me. What are you waiting for?"

Luc bent and yanked off the drone's black mask. It revealed the face of a man with pale green-tinged skin that had wrinkled.

"Help me," the drone breathed. "She killed my wife." He touched Luc's arm. "Please, help me…"

Luc frowned, still unsure of what to make of this. In all his lifetimes of fighting against the Esrac, none had tried talking to him like this.

"Luc, what are you waiting for?" Eric snapped. "Kill the damned thing!"

"Wait," Luc hissed, staring at the drone. "He must be newly turned. I still sense humanity in him."

"Are you saying humans can turn into Esrac?"

Luc ignored the question and kept his attention focused on the drone. "Who are you? What's your name? Tell me what happened to you."

If he could find out where this man had come from, he'd be able to find out where Esme was. Ella hadn't directed the gate very well during Esme's last attack, so Esme could have been sent anywhere in this realm.

"Alan. She came, the demon. She killed my wife!" Black blood gurgled from his mouth, and his eyes glazed over.

Luc sighed and sheathed his sword, then swore and muttered a curse. "These drones *are* newly turned. That means Esme is starting to change people."

"Wait, what?" Eric yelped. "You've never mentioned that people can turn into…does that mean I'm gonna change too?" He looked himself up and down, examining his body more closely. "Ah hell, I'd rather die than turn into one of those things."

"No." Luc moved over to him and checked the barb marks on Eric's chest. "It's just a graze, you'll be fine. You won't turn into one of them, that would take a lot more than a few pinpricks."

"Graze? *Pinpricks?* I'm bleeding here!" Eric cried.

"It's just a flesh wound. The drone didn't have time to take much. Ella has a healing—"

"*Am I going to turn into one of those things?*" Eric interrupted, gripping his stunner tighter. "If I am, tell me now. I deserve to know the truth."

He shook his head. "I doubt it, but the truth is, I don't know. We never learnt that much about the Esrac other than how to kill them."

"Great, a thousand years later, and you don't know how someone turns into a green-skinned freak!" Eric rubbed his injured chest.

"Let's get back to camp." Luc sheathed his sword and did another scan of the area with his senses to make sure there were no more Esrac around.

"What about them?" Eric motioned to the corpses. "Why haven't they turned to sludge?"

"The transformation into full Esrac must not have completed," Luc mused. "Let's get back to the others. We'll get Adria to check you over, then decide what to do with the corpses."

CHAPTER 5

Ella knew from the grim expression on Luc's face that something bad must've happened. Her heart raced.

"Oh no, not more Esrac?" She thought she'd felt a familiar chill earlier, just like she had the day she discovered the chamber and unlocked the gate. Then the Esrac drones had come through.

Luc nodded. "More drones attacked us."

She frowned. "Esme used the gate again?"

She had suspected Esme might be able to use the gates to some extent, but hadn't thought she would actually be able to release her people from the hell realm they were trapped in.

"No, they were newly turned." He shook his head. "They attacked us with human weapons. I guess Esme is a lot more resourceful than we thought."

"Turned?" She gaped at him. "Turned how?" Realisation dawned suddenly. "Are you saying Esme can turn *humans*?"

She never given much thought to how Esrac reproduced, but it made sense now. Bile rose up in her throat, but she gulped it back down again. She'd never imagined people could turn into Esrac; they looked so different from humans, she hadn't even thought they were biologically related.

"She must inject them with something," Sara mused. "It would be fascinating to study an Esrac up close and see how their bodies worked."

Ella nodded in agreement. She missed working in the lab with bones and specimens as she had done at the University, and if they had a chance to study the Esrac, maybe they could figure out a way of finally stopping them.

"I don't know how she does it, but they weren't fully changed. The one that attacked Eric couldn't drone him," Luc explained.

"Am I gonna change into one of them?" Eric demanded warily.

Adria snorted. "Of course not. Only female Esrac can turn people."

"Are you sure?" Eric asked. "Luc said you don't know exactly how people change."

"I've learnt a thing or two about Esrac over the past fifty years," Adria said. "I assure you, you won't turn into one of them."

Eric breathed a sigh of relief and slumped down onto a fallen log.

Ella frowned at Adria. How much did the old woman really know about the Esrac if the main gate in Arkadia had been sealed shut for the past thousand years? Sure, avatars could still summon the gate, just as Ella had, but it only had a limited effect. She guessed there was a lot more to the gate than anyone had let on. Would she ever really know the true extent of what being an avatar was? Or their history?

She wanted to ask more, but instead picked up her pack and rummaged through it for the healing wand.

"I have the wand." Sara pulled out the device. "Here, let me help," she said, as she moved over to Eric's side.

"I've just had a green-skinned freak try to drone the life out of me." Eric replied, grabbing the wand from her. "I don't need your hands of mass damage touching me too."

Sara rolled her eyes and scowled at him. "I don't hurt anyone unless they're a threat. It usually only happens when I'm frightened or angry. I haven't hurt Luc and Ella, have I?"

"We need to stop her before she turns too many people and amasses an army." Luc's words interrupted Sara and Eric's bickering.

Ella ran a hand through her long hair and glanced at her grandmother. "I've been thinking about that. Maybe we could lure Esme into a trap, and you and I could force her through the gate again. Send her somewhere else, so she's cut off from the rest of her people. Maybe that would weaken her enough so she'd never be able to use the gate again."

Adria shook her head. "No, that won't work again," she said. "Besides, doing that all those years ago only brought you time. Esme *must* die if we are to truly defeat the Esrac."

Eric nodded at Sara. "Why not use her weapon hands? She burnt Esme up pretty good." He winced as the device started knitting his flesh back together.

"Burnt, yes, but not enough to inflict permanent damage. And not enough to kill her, either."

The five of them sat down to eat from their ration packs, and the mood turned sombre as they discussed how to deal with the Esrac problem. Beheading Esrac was the only sure way to kill them, but Esme was much stronger than her drones. Their past attempts had all failed because Esme never let anyone get too close to her.

Ella fell silent. Part of her wished she—or rather Aurelia—had never created the gate in the first place. It had brought nothing but death and suffering for all generations of avatars who followed it, but destroying it wouldn't do much good now Esme was here. Plus, it had proved to be a useful escape route from the Senate's troopers, who were hunting them. Their only hope now lay with the Valan, but Ella had mixed feelings about the Order of knights. Griffin had been one of the Valan, and he had betrayed her. Luc had told her bits and pieces about the Order, though even he didn't know if many of them had survived over the centuries.

Ella waited until the others had all gone to sleep before getting up to go in search of Adria, who'd wandered off.

She entered a nearby clearing, where Adria stood staring up at the night sky.

"No sign of any troopers," she remarked. "Let's hope the luck is on our side." Adria covered her mouth and coughed again.

"Why does the Chancellor fear magic so much?" Ella moved over to Adria's side. "Surely not all magic can be bad?"

"Magic itself isn't bad; it's how people use it that matters," Adria replied. "Humans are the bad ones, magic is a living, breathing thing; a force that exists all around us. You just have to know how to use it." Adria motioned to the ground. "Let's begin."

Ella sat down and shivered against the cool night air, wishing she'd brought her blanket to sit on.

Adria sat down in front of her, seemingly unbothered. "Contrary to what legend says, avatars don't need extensive training. It's all a matter of desire, will, and concentration." Adria picked up a large stick and handed it to her. "Here. Set this alight."

Ella frowned. Of all the things she'd expected, setting a stick on fire hadn't been one of them.

"I already know how to summon my starfire." She hoped Adria wouldn't waste the night talking about things he already knew how to do. She needed to learn how to fully defend herself from the Esrac and how to injure Esme, even if she couldn't kill her yet.

"Yes, but only in anger, from what I've seen. Your father may have taught you to hide your magic, but it will take a lot more than that to use the full power inside you." Adria motioned to the stick. "Everyone has to start with the basics before they can move on to advanced magic."

But I already know the basics!

Ella sighed. She'd expected to practice combat, and this seemed pointless. She gripped the stick and waited. Nothing happened. Narrowing her eyes, she willed it to light again. Still nothing.

"See, you're trying too hard," Adria said. "Magic should be as simple as breathing. We are part of magic, and it is part of us. Let it flow through you."

After a couple more tries, the stick still refused to light. "This is stupid! We need to figure out a way to stop Esme, not set sticks on fire." She tossed the stick aside. "It's not as if that can kill an Esrac."

"Aurelia was known for her impatience, too," Adria remarked. "You can't walk before you learn how to crawl. Now clear your mind."

Ella picked up a different stick and squeezed her eyes shut. It had never been this hard to summon the fire before; why wouldn't the damn thing light? She let out a breath and forced herself to relax.

This would be so much easier if I could remember Aurelia's knowledge, so why can't I? You'd think that stupid curse would at least let me remember everything.

She supposed that would be confusing. Although she had lived as Aurelia before, she wasn't Aurelia now. That had been a different lifetime. She'd had other lives over the centuries, but Aurelia's was the only one she'd seen so far. Part of her wanted to see her other lives and what she had been like then, but it was strange enough seeing flashes of her life as Aurelia; having more memories would only prove even more weird.

Ella gasped as she felt something tug at her mind. She opened her eyes to find Adria, and the forest gone, and herself standing at the foot of a spiral staircase.

What the hell? She ran up the stairs, feeling the soles of her shoes hit the stone.

What's going on?

She looked down to see herself wearing a purple silk dress that had dark stains over it.

Is that blood? Her heart pounded in her ears. *Why covered am I in blood? Is it my blood?*

She ran a hand up and down her chest and abdomen, but felt no signs of injury. Her body felt solid and whole.

She ran faster until she reached a hallway. A man lay slumped against the wall, a trail of blood leading the way to him.

"Lucan!" she screamed. "Lucan?" She ran over, fell to her knees beside him. "Lucan, my love, wake up."

Lucan? Wait, this must be a memory. I'm seeing the past. Still, her heart wrenched at the sight of Luc, bruised and bloodied. Aurelia's pain felt like her own.

Lucas looked up, his eyes half closed. "Lia..." he rasped.

"Oh, Lucan, I've been searching everywhere for you!" She wrapped her arms around him. The gashes on his neck and throat and his tattered shirt made her realise an Esrac had fed on him. "I went back to the Esrac realm, but I couldn't find you." Tears pricked her eyes. "Esme said you weren't there...she lied." Her heart ached seeing him like this.

An explosion from the onslaught of the Esrac attack outside shook the walls.

"Lia, you have to stop Esme."

"Hush, love. I'll find a healer; you're going to be alright." She kissed the top of his forehead and made a move to rise, but Lucan gripped her arm. "It's too late. I love you, Lia..." Lucan touched her cheek for a moment before his hand fell away and he slumped back against the wall.

"No!" Aurelia wailed. "Lucan!" She cradled him in her arms and sobbed.

"What have you done?" A man's voice behind her asked.

She looked up. "Master, do something! He can't die!" she sobbed. "This wasn't supposed to happen."

"You failed, Aurelia. It's your duty to protect and lead our people. You are our avatar, and you brought death."

"No!" she screamed, her hands flaring with bright light.

"No!" Ella screamed. She raised her hands as her starfire shot outwards and exploded a tree behind Adria. Branches and bits of wood shot in all directions, and the sound ripped through the still night air.

"Ella? Ella, wake up," Adria said loudly. She reached down and touched Ella's shoulder. "Breathe, girl. You're safe now. You are not Aurelia anymore; you are Ella."

Ella blinked as the sight of Lucan's body faded, and the darkness of the forest came back into view.

Tears streamed down her face. "Luc!" she croaked.

"Ella." Adria gripped her shoulders. "It's not real. What you saw happened centuries ago. The pain you are feeling doesn't affect you now. Luc is alive and well."

"But he...he was dead. He died in my arms." She buried her face in her hands and wept. Why, out of all the things she could remember, did she have to recall that? She'd known Lucan had died, of course, but never thought she would witness it again now. It felt so real.

Her heart twisted, and her chest ached as she let out heaving sobs. Adria was wrong. Aurelia was still part of her. She could still feel her anguish over losing the man she'd loved.

"Not your arms, Aurelia's arms. You're not Aurelia anymore," Adria said. "Breathe and try to focus."

Ella shook her head, wiping her eyes with the back of her sleeve. "Why did you make see that?" she snapped. "Why?"

"I didn't. Only you can access those memories. Your life and Aurelia's are still bound to each other."

"Ella?" Luc called, running over.

She sniffed and looked up, half wondering if she was dreaming. "Luc!"

Ella got to her feet and threw herself into his arms. She clung to him tight to make sure he was real. "Oh, Luc...I saw you die!"

"She saw *Lucan* die," Adria corrected as she stood and let out a rasping cough.

"What happened?" Luc asked, as he wrapped his arms around Ella.

Ella tried to speak, but no words came out, so she just shook her head. She couldn't speak of what she'd seen. The pain still felt too raw.

"We were practising magic and Ella remembered his death," Adria replied. "It's late, we should all get some rest." She pulled her shawl

tighter around herself. "Ella, it's alright. That life has passed now."
"Yes, but it's still haunting me."

CHAPTER 6

Luc tried to calm Ella down, even opting for them to sleep next to each other, away from everyone else. But he knew she hadn't had much sleep by the dark circles under her eyes the next morning. He had no idea why she would have seen his death now. Perhaps it was a warning? They were running out of time, and the curse still loomed over them.

The sun rose high in the sky. There wasn't a cloud in sight, and it felt warmer than it had for the past few days. It would make their walk much more enjoyable.

"I haven't turned into a green skinned freak yet," Eric grinned as the five of them sat eating from their ration packs that morning. "I'm so relieved I'm not a monster."

"You'd still be ugly even if you didn't change," Sara muttered.

"Hey!" Eric snapped. "Who woke up on the wrong side of the log this morning?"

"Enough, you two." Luc sighed as Ella cast her ration pack aside and walked off. She hadn't said two words to him all morning despite his repeated asking if she was all right.

Eric stared after her. "What's wrong with her?"

"It's been a long night," Luc said as he rose and headed after her.

As Luc drew close to where she stood, Fidget appeared and jumped up onto Ella's shoulder. "La sad?" he squeaked.

She ruffled his ears. "No, Fidge."

Luc moved over to her as he pushed the through the trees. "Hey, you okay?" he asked. "I know last night must've been hard—"

"You didn't have to watch me die," she interrupted, shaking her head. "It's not just my life as Aurelia. Last night I saw other things. So many people died because I—I mean, Aurelia—went to Esme's realm. More people are dying now because of me. How am I supposed to live with that?"

"We both need to stop blaming ourselves for what happened in our past lives. We can't change it, but we can do something about it; stop Esme and make sure she's gone for good this time."

"How are we supposed to do that when even the ancestors couldn't stop her?"

"We aren't the ancestors. Things have changed since then. *We've* changed." He took her hand. "One thing you've taught me is that anything is possible."

"*I* taught you that?" Her eyes widened.

"Yeah, your strength helped me get through Griffin's betrayal. As long as we're together, we can get through anything." He wrapped his arms around her and kissed her. "I know this life is different; we'll make it different. Just because we failed once doesn't mean we'll fail this time. We just have to have faith in ourselves and in our destiny."

She sighed and hugged him. Fidget jumped off her shoulder with a yelp to avoid being squashed.

Luc held her close and ran a hand through her long hair. She rubbed her dark eyes and pulled back, nodding. "You're right. Sorry for losing faith there for a moment."

He laughed. "I haven't seen you cry once since all of this started. I wondered when you'd stop holding everything in."

She gave him a playful shove. "I hate how well you know me sometimes."

He slipped his hand in hers. "Come on, we've got a long day of walking to do if we're ever gonna reach the border."

Ella froze at his words. "Luc, I've been thinking. This started in the old city—all of it. Maybe we should be going back there instead of crossing the border."

Luc's eyes widened. "There's nothing in the old city, and the Chancellor blocked off the citadel. She probably still has men watching the place in case we go there."

"I just feel like we should be there. It's close to the border, after all."

Luc didn't doubt her instincts, but shook his head. "It's too dangerous. We'll be safe on the other side of the border; there will be fewer ships there to track us. At least then we won't have to worry about the troopers so much," he said. "We're more at risk the longer we stay on this side of the border, and the further we are away from

Esme the better."

Ella sighed. "Okay, I just hope the Valan can help us. Nothing I've learned about them so far inspires confidence."

"Not all of them are like Griffin," he assured her, squeezing her hand. "Come on, let's go."

Ella hesitated. "Do you think Esme will send more drones after us? Is there a way to stop her from sensing us?"

Luc shook his head. "She senses us whenever we use our magic. The less we use it, the better." He wrapped an arm around her shoulders.

Another few hours of walking through the dense forest took its toll on them. Adria suffered the worst out of all of them and needed to rest every few minutes.

By midday, they finally pushed through the tree line and out onto an open road that looked to be made of ceramicrete. These types of roads rarely got used in Celestus as everyone travelled by airship.

Luc pressed a button on his link, and a holographic map of the area appeared. He scanned through different routes and tapped the link again to try and work out how long it would take them to finally reach the border. Roads and buildings flashed by as he moved through different towns and villages.

"You shouldn't be using that." Adria made a sudden grab for his arm. "You might as well be lighting a beacon to lead the troopers straight to us!"

Luc jerked his arm back, making the hologram flicker. "My link is untraceable, thanks to Eric." He grinned at the engineer, who really was a genius when it came to technology and machines.

"I disabled the trackers in each of our links. It's not as hard as you'd think," Eric said. "We can use them for basic stuff like maps and communication."

Adria's lips pressed into a line. "I still think it's too dangerous, any form of technology could be used by the Senate to track us."

"There's a village called Casel close by. Maybe we should—"

"No, we can't," Adria insisted. "If someone sees us, we'll get arrested." She doubled over, coughing again.

"Not if we're careful," Luc said. "We've still got fifty miles to cover and are low on food. I still have some coin left from when we left Celestus. It's enough to get us some decent supplies."

"We do need food," Sara pointed out. "We're low on rations as it is. Maybe if just one or two of us go, we won't attract so much attention."

"Maybe you should see a doctor whilst you're there," Ella suggested to Adria.

The old woman shook her head and scowled. "I don't need a doctor, I'm fine."

Ella frowned. "This Senate doesn't know who you are, and I really think you should get that cough seen to."

"Why can't Ella open the gate and get us to the Valan that way?" Eric asked. "I'm surprised she hasn't tried it before now."

Adria shook her head. "The gate will only take us a short distance on this side of the border, and the Valan move around a lot so there's no telling where we would end up. Besides, they have wards in place to stop gate travel."

Ella frowned. "But you said the Valan use the gate as well?"

"They do, but only when necessary, and only the Masters use it. They have endless rules about gate travel."

"Who's up for getting some supplies, then?" Sara asked, trying to diffuse the growing tension. "Do we have enough money to get some chemicals as well? I have an experiment I'm working on."

Adria sighed again. "Fine, you and I —"

"I'll go. I'm an expert at haggling," Eric cut in.

After Ella and Sara went through their own packs, they came up with a few more coins until they'd gathered one hundred in total. It wasn't much, but it'd give them some decent supplies to face the unknown with.

Luc and Eric headed off to the village whilst the others went off to find somewhere to rest, and before long, they moved past a row of tiny houses. This place seemed a world away from the glowing towers of Celestus, much like Antaria had been.

"Hey, what if we used our coin to get a ship?" Eric remarked. "It'd be easier to travel, and we'd reach the border a lot quicker. Adria isn't looking well. It'd help her too."

Luc shook his head and pulled his hood up further to cover his face. "Not after what happened last time we had a ship, it's too risky." He lowered his voice. "The troopers would be able to track us. No one gets over the border undetected—not by ship, anyway.

Plus, we need our supplies."

"An old vessel fitted with GLS can't be tracked. I could find something cheap, and we'd still have enough left over for supplies." Eric held out his hand. "Come on, give me some coin and I'll find something, even if we end up ditching the ship before we reach the border."

Luc hesitated, then sighed. The longer they stayed on this side of the border, the more danger they were in of being found by troopers or more drones. "Fine, but if you don't find anything don't waste good coin." He handed the gold to Eric.

"Awesome. Be back in a few!" Eric scurried off without saying another word.

Luc sighed. At least this place had a decent-sized market.

He wandered past various different stalls selling everything from clothes to weapons and jewellery until he found one selling food.

The old woman with a weathered face and long straggly white hair that manned it beamed when she saw him. "What can I get you?"

"I need around twenty ration packs. Large ones, if you have them," he told her.

She chuckled. "Ain't no ration packs here, boy. I got the best produce in the Republic," she said. "I've got fruit, veggies, nuts…"

Luc's senses prickled as he felt someone watching him. He turned, keeping his hood up as he scanned the crowd of bustling people, yet he found no one giving him so much as a second glance as they bustled by, browsing stalls as they went. Still, the feeling wouldn't go away.

After some haggling, he used all the coin he had left to get as much as he could in the way of supplies. The old woman thanked him and stuffed all the produce in a small cloth sack. After a while, the feeling of being watched faded, but Luc still felt on edge.

Moving on, he picked up a few healing supplies, including a healing wand and some bandages. He had no idea what they might face on the other side of the border, and it was best to be prepared. He didn't remember much about growing up on there; he'd been only five when the Senate killed his parents in an air raid. The Valan had scattered, and one of the Masters had decided to send him to live over the border into at Celestus University with Master Griffin.

Luc wondered what it would be like going back there and seeing the Valan again. He'd always wanted to go back over the border but hadn't had the chance before now. He only hoped the Valan would welcome him back and be able to help.

He glanced around as the hairs on the back of his neck stood up. Someone was still watching him. He cast his senses out, searching for the source. He doubted an Esrac would be out in the open like this, but had no doubt Esme had someone following him.

It didn't feel like an Esrac, but he couldn't find a sign of anyone else.

Where are you? I know you're around here somewhere.

Eric hadn't reappeared yet, either. Luc hoped he hadn't wasted good coin on some wreck of a ship and had used his good instincts.

Luc tapped out a quick message on his link to tell Eric to hurry back. They needed to get out of the village. The longer they lingered there, the more at risk they became of being spotted or arrested.

His feeling of unease grew by the minute, but he didn't want to risk leading any potential pursuer back to the others. Luc moved calmly through the crowded street, past the different rows of stalls, and ducked into a deserted alley with a dead end, though he would get over the wall easily. The smell of discarded waste made him gag as he ducked behind a dumpster, pulled out his sword, and waited.

A few moments later, a cloaked figure appeared. From the height and shape, it looked to be a man, but Luc couldn't make out his face under the hood.

He waited until the man moved further down the alley, then leapt out, drawing his sword. "Why are you following me?"

CHAPTER 7

Ella paced up and down as she, Sara, and Adria sat on benches in a small, sheltered area surrounded by a grove of trees.

"Stop pacing. People will start staring at us," Adria said as she brushed a leaf off her shoulder.

"What's taking so long?" Ella muttered. "They should be back by now. Something must've happened." She continued pacing. "I still think you should go and see a doctor."

Adria waved her hand. "I told you, I'm fine. Seeing a doctor would be an unnecessary risk."

"Can you sense Luc?" Sara asked as she scrolled through the data crystal containing all of Griffin's information.

Ella stopped pacing and paused for a moment. "I'm not sensing he's in trouble if that's what you mean." She sighed. "Why are you looking through the archives again? I thought you didn't find anything that could help us in defeating the Esrac."

"The entire archives could take me years to go through. I haven't found anything *yet*."

"Patience," Adria said, motioning to the bench she had just sat down on. "Ella, come sit. I want to show you something."

"Sara, you're the least likely to draw attention," Ella said. "Would you mind going to look for Luc and Eric? I have an uneasy feeling."

"Sure." Sara rose, shoved the data crystal into her pocket, and hoisted her pack over her shoulder. "I still have some coins left; do you mind if I purchase a couple of things while I'm there?"

"Go ahead, but be careful," Ella told her.

"If they are in trouble, don't linger. Come straight back here," Adria insisted.

Sara made a move to go, then hesitated. "You want me to leave them behind?" Her eyes widened. "I can't do that. They're our friends."

Ella crossed her arms, turning to Adria. "That's not an option. I'm not losing Luc again, and I don't want anything to happen to Eric either."

Sara glanced between them, unsure of what to do next.

"What would Luc want you to do?" Adria asked Ella.

She hissed out a breath. She knew exactly what he'd want her to do, but that didn't make it right. "He'd want us to leave and go across the border without him." She gritted her teeth. "Sara, go!"

Sara rushed off without saying another word.

"We can't just leave them behind." Ella slumped down next to her grandmother. "How can you even suggest that?"

"Do you still have the box your father left for you?" Adria asked. "Don't worry about the boys. They can handle themselves."

Ella's eyes widened. "How did you know about the box?" She'd only taken it out of her pack a few times since retrieving it from her home back in Antaria. She still hadn't been able to open it, despite numerous attempts.

"I gave it to Caspian. I thought you might need it someday."

"So you know what's inside it?" Ella felt a stab of annoyance that Adria hadn't brought the box up before now.

"Yes. Get it out."

Ella frowned as she pulled off her pack and took out the tiny wooden box.

Adria took it from her and light flared between her fingers. With a hiss, the box opened.

Ella gasped. "You can't use magic out in the open like this," she hissed. "What if someone sees? You do know what they do to suspected magic users, don't you? We'll get arrested and burnt alive!"

"I'm too old to care about what they might do to me." Adria coughed. "Here." She reached inside and pulled out a crystal. Of all the things Ella had been expecting, a crystal hadn't been one of them.

"A crystal? What's it for?" she asked as Adria handed it over. It sparkled in the sunlight. She examined it closer and pressed it between her fingers. But nothing happened.

Not a data crystal then.

"When the time is right, you'll know."

Ella rolled her eyes. "Now you sound like Master Griffin. Why do old people have to be so cryptic?" she asked. "Why not just go straight to the point and tell me what it's for?"

Adria laughed, then wheezed. "Because we enjoy it. By the time you get to my age, you'll..." She broke off as she doubled over, coughing.

Ella reached out and touched her shoulder. "Are you alright? That's it! We're going to see a doctor while we're here, even if I have to drag you there myself." She doubted they'd get another chance to find a doctor if they crossed the border. "Your cough is getting worse."

Adria let out a harsh laugh. "I'd like to see you try. I've still got some strength left in this body, mark my words." She shook her head and took a deep breath. "I'm fine."

"No, you're not." Ella squeezed her shoulder. "You're ill, aren't you?" She frowned at her grandmother. "Why won't you let me help me help you? I guess I get my stubbornness from you."

"You're more perceptive than I thought," she wheezed. Her lips curved into a smile. "Yes, stubbornness is a family trait."

"I may be inexperienced when it comes to magic, but I'm not stupid," Ella said and took Adria's hand. "Why didn't you tell me you weren't well?"

Adria coughed again and pulled her hand away as she reached down to grab her flask. She gulped down some of the water before speaking again. "Because I don't want anyone feeling sorry for me, especially not you."

Ella stared at her grandmother. This was the first time since they had met that Adria started to let a few cracks show through her facade.

"No doctor can help me now."

"You shouldn't be making this journey. If I'd known—"

"You'd never have let me come with you. I had to watch over you, just as I've been doing all these years." Adria gulped down more water. "You may think I've been absent all your life, but I've been watching you and helping other magic users whilst I can." She reached out and took Ella's hand. "I want to go home when it's time, back to my village. I want to be there when I pass on."

Ella felt tears well inside her eyes.

"Now, none of that. I won't have you weeping for me," Adria said, patting her hand. "Tears won't do any good. I want to enjoy whatever time I have left. One last adventure for this old girl to enjoy."

Ella laughed as she choked back tears and wrapped her arms around Adria. To her surprise, Adria returned her embrace.

"You'll know when to use the crystal. You have everything you need to find a way to stop Esme."

Ella sniffed and looked up as Sara came running back over. "I found Luc in a local pub," she rasped, her chest heaving.

Ella pulled away from Adria and rose. "Is he alright?"

"He's fine. He asked for us to go and join him there."

Adria coughed, then her eyes narrowed. "Why? Luc should know better, it's far too dangerous."

Sara shook her head. "I don't know. He was there with another man. He said the man is one of the Valan."

Adria and Ella glanced at each other.

"What would one of the Valan be doing here?" Ella asked.

"We need to be on our guard." Adria gripped her walking stick as she rose.

"Maybe you should stay here and rest awhile," Ella suggested. "Or better yet—"

Adria waved her hand in dismissal. "Nonsense. I'll not sit idly by. If there's a Valan here, I want to meet him for myself."

As they headed towards the Dancing Pony, Ella felt a pit of dread forming in her stomach. The pub looked like an old-world building, with dark oak beams, slanted ceilings, and whitewashed walls. It reminded her of some of the buildings back in her village.

Why would one of the Valan be here? Luc had told her the Valan preferred to stay on the other side of the border and be branded rebels rather than live in hiding. Ella couldn't blame them. She'd been forced to hide her magic all her life, too.

Still, she wasn't sure she trusted the Valan, despite Luc's assurances. Griffin had been the one to let Esme out a couple of months ago, and she worried how they might react to her presence. She had, after all, been Aurelia in her past life.

Ella spotted Luc sitting in the corner with a cloaked man and hesitated as Sara and Adria came in behind her. The room reeked of ale and sweaty bodies. Why would Luc have even come in here? He knew they couldn't afford to waste time; they had to get moving before anyone spotted them. Something about this didn't feel right. Why would a Valan knight have suddenly appeared now? Luc had tried contacting them countless times since Esme got loose, and no one ever responded to his calls.

Ella glanced around. She knew she couldn't walk around with Fidget. No doubt the Senate would be on the lookout for a young woman with a dust bunny, so she told Fidget to find Luc but to stay out of sight. He was good at getting around unnoticed. Most people never paid much attention to him, anyway.

She kept her hood over her face, hoping no one would spot her, and grabbed Sara's arm before she had a chance to go over to the table.

"What's wrong?" Sara asked, her eyes widening in alarm.

"Look around, do you see any Esrac in here?" she hissed. She scanned the crowd of people herself, but only had a limited view of them under her hood. "Get a good look at the man with Luc. I want to make sure we not walking into a trap."

Ella glanced at the people sitting around the bar, searching for any sign of Eric. Where had he disappeared to? The more time passed, the more she just wanted to get Luc and get the hell out of there.

Ella, what are you doing? Luc's voice rang through her mind. *Why aren't you coming over here?*

Are you sure that man is really one of the Valan? Ella asked. *Something doesn't feel right here. I think we should leave.*

It's alright. I've already questioned him. He's a Valan, Luc assured her.

Ella glanced at Sara. "Well?"

"I don't see any. The man with Luc looks human, but I can't see his face clearly," Sara replied.

"I want you to go and find Eric," Ella told her.

Luc, where is Eric?

He went to find us a ship. He's at the air dock.

"Sara, go down to the air dock. Stay there with Eric until we call you."

Sara opened her mouth to protest.

"Just go," Ella said.

Sara nodded and hurried off.

Ella headed over to the table and moved to Luc's side as Adria slumped into a chair at the table next to Luc.

"Galvin, this is Ella." Luc slipped an arm around her waist. "Ella, this is—"

"How did you find us?" Ella demanded. She didn't have time for pleasantries, and Adria certainly didn't have time to waste either.

Luc frowned at her. *Is something wrong?*

"We received Luc's message. I came to help escort you across the border," Galvin replied, keeping his face covered.

"Then why didn't you respond to Luc's message first?" she demanded. "He's been trying to contact you for weeks. It would have been safer that way."

Ella, what's gotten into you? Luc asked.

"Your suspicions are understandable, but I was sent to help you," Galvin replied, taking a swig of his pint.

"By whom?" Ella's eyes narrowed. "You're putting us all at risk by being out in the open like this."

"Are you the avatar?" Galvin demanded.

"Who wants to know?" Adria interjected, clutching her walking stick. "Pull back your hood and show your face."

"I can't do that. You know what might happen if I'm seen."

"These two are in much more danger than you. Now pull back your hood," Adria snapped. "If you mean us harm, I'll —"

Galvin shot to his feet as Fidget leapt up onto the table.

"Bad," the dust bunny squeaked.

Ella took a step back as someone advanced toward her and a hushed silence came over the room. Every man in the pub had suddenly turned their attention on them.

"The Senate will pay a fortune for your capture." Galvin pushed back his hood to reveal a hard face, long blonde hair, and piercing blue eyes.

"What's going on?" Luc rose and pulled out his sword.

"Oh, he's Valan alright," Adria said, her lip curled. "You're just like that wretch, Griffin. Part of a sect who kill avatars."

"Adria Noran." Galvin sneered. "I heard you escaped to this side of the border, but I never imagined I'd see you here." He motioned to his men. "I guess now we'll kill two avatars instead of one."

Ella dodged one of the men as he made a grab for her. They hadn't come all this way to be captured now, and she wouldn't let anything happen to Adria.

"Sorry, boys, it's time for us to go." Ella grinned and raised her hands as they flared with light. "Luc, Adria, cover your eyes!"

Golden light flashed around the room, blinding everyone in it.

Ella ran over to the far wall and placed her hand over it until the outline of the gate appeared.

Adria shoved at the men and hit them with her stick as she made her way over to Ella.

"Go!" Ella cried.

Adria stumbled through the gate.

"Fidget!" Ella called, dodging an attacker as he lunged for her

Protect my gran! she told Luc before he went through. *I'll be fine.*

Luc gave her a hard look, but reluctantly ducked through the portal.

A blur of white fur scurried across the floor toward her, dodging a man as he tried to stamp on it. Ella felt heat flow between her fingers and sent him crashing into several other men.

She bent and picked Fidget up. "This avatar won't die so easily!"

With another blast of magic, she sent every person crashing to the floor and ducked through the gate.

CHAPTER 8

Luc breathed a sigh of relief as Ella and Fidget emerged through the glowing gate and the portal vanished behind her. He couldn't believe what had just happened.

He'd been surprised when Galvin had revealed himself back in the alley, but after some questioning, Luc had believed he'd been sent to help. Galvin had known the dates and times Luc had tried to relay messages to the Valan asking for help after Esme killed Griffin.

They had reappeared inside a dark room with broken windows. Light shone weakly through the green glass, rubbish littered the floor, and trees had already made their way up through the broken roof.

"How did you know Galvin couldn't be trusted?" Luc asked Ella.

"I've learned not to trust anyone after what Griffin did." She touched Adria's shoulder. "Are you okay?"

"Yes, don't fuss over me. I won't have that," Adria wheezed.

Luc glanced around and realised they were inside what looked like an old warehouse. "Ella, where did you gate us to?"

"An abandoned building close to the dock. I spotted it as we went through earlier."

"Maybe finding the other Valan isn't such a good idea." Luc ran a hand through his hair. He had thought Griffin was alone in wanting avatars put to death or handed over to the Senate. What had happened to the once noble Order of knights? Had they turned against everything they once believed in?

"Nonsense, of course we're going over the border," Adria said. "We'll find Master Oswald. He is the head of the Order, and will help us."

"Or he'll just have us put to death. When was the last time you encountered a Valan?" Ella asked. "My dad disappeared over ten years ago."

"Not all of them are bad, look at your father." Adria took a deep breath. "I've kept tabs on the Valan over the years. I'll know where to find them once we cross the border."

"Are you alright?" Luc asked Adria.

"I'm fine. It's just dusty in here. I need some fresh air." She stumbled and coughed. "Go find the others."

"Luc, go find Eric and Sara. We'll stay here. I can open the gate again if anyone comes after us." Ella wrapped an arm around Adria. "Hurry!"

Luc took off, passing piles of rubbish and bits of debris on his way through the warehouse. He pulled his hood back up to hide his face. No doubt Galvin and his cronies would be on the hunt for them here. He had told him about Eric procuring a ship for them.

Damn, how could I have been so careless? He pushed the thought away quickly. He didn't have time for self-pity, he had to find the others and get the hell out of this place fast. He tapped the link on his wrist. "Eric, where are you?" he asked as he engaged the call.

"Down at bay four. I've got a ship," Eric replied. "I got a really good deal. She'll be up and ready to fly within the hour."

"I doubt we'll have time to use it. Listen, we need to get out of here. There are Valan close by who want to turn us over to the Senate," he said, scanning the throngs of people at the dock. "Ella and Adria are in an abandoned warehouse close by. Do you think you can get there?"

"Luc, I got a ship, did you not hear me?"

Luc spotted Galvin and several other men up ahead and darted off in the opposite direction.

"Luc, are you still there?"

Luc broke off the connection as he ran. He passed bays filled with different ships, then darted into bay four, where Eric and Sara stood wide-eyed.

"Damn it, we don't have time to run back to Ella and Adria," he cursed. "There are Valan after us. No time to explain."

He glanced up at the Pegasus—Eric's ship of choice. It looked rusty and clunky compared to the ships back in Celestus, even older than the ship they'd flown in from Adria's.

"Will this fly now?" His eyes narrowed. As much as he wanted to make a quick exit, this didn't look like a very safe or effective escape route.

"Only one way to find out." Eric unfolded the ramp and hurried inside. Luc and Sara dashed in behind him. Eric took his place in the pilot's seat. "I haven't had time to do a systems or diagnostics check…"

"We don't have time," Luc snapped. "Just make this thing fly."

"What about Ella and Adria?" Sara asked. "We can't leave them."

Ella? Luc reached out to her with his mind. *Ella, you need to use the gate to get to me right now. I'm at the dock, bay four.*

I can't get the gate to bring us to a place I've never seen before! Ella protested. *I only got into the warehouse because I had a look inside as we went by earlier.*

Yes, you can just focus on me. Hurry!

But…

Just do it! Come on, you can control the gate better than anyone.

Light flared on the wall outside as the gate appeared and formed into a solid archway. Ella came through a few moments later with Adria clutching her arm and Fidget sitting on her shoulder.

"There they are!" a voice yelled as Galvin and his men rounded the corner.

"Crap!" Luc said. "Eric, get this thing online." His heart pounded as Galvin drew a glowing sabre.

Luc jumped down the ramp and grabbed Adria's arm. In one swift move, he picked the old woman up and carried her over to the ship.

Ella raised her hand and hurled a ball of starfire at the men. Galvin deflected it with his sword.

Luc helped Adria inside. "Put me down and go help, Ella," she snapped.

Setting her on her feet, Luc drew his sword and leapt down from the ship. "Eric, hurry!"

"I'm trying!" Eric yelled back.

Luc raced over Ella's side as Galvin tried to strike her. He blocked Galvin's blade, causing a clash of steel on steel to ring through the air.

Get to the ship! he told her.

Her eyes flashed, and more fire flared in her hand. *Not without you! Will that even fly? It looks worse than Adria's old ship.*

I hope so. He parried Galvin's next blow.

More men surrounded them on all sides, all wielding glowing swords.

Luc glanced around at them, but he didn't like the odds. Ten men against one Valan and an avatar didn't seem like a battle they could win, especially when all ten of them had Valan blades that could deflect their magic.

"You're coming with us," Gavin said. "If you come quietly, we'll spare your friends."

Ella snorted. "Why don't I believe you?" She raised her hand as more glowing purple flames flared between her fingers.

"Quiet, witch. It's your fault the Esrac scourge is back in our realm," Galvin growled.

"Witch?" She scoffed. "I'm an avatar, you should know the difference." Ella waved her hand, causing gold light to explode around them, just as it had in the pub.

All the men shielded their eyes just in time.

"Your parlour tricks won't work this time," Galvin smiled.

"Damn it!" Ella muttered and glanced at Luc. *Please tell me you have an idea to get us out of this.*

I'm thinking! He glanced at the men, his blood pounding in his ears.

Why can't you move them with your mind? I've seen you do it with the troopers before.

Ella sent one of the men flying as he lunged toward her.

These are Valan. Whatever magical force I use against them, they can deflect back at me.

Luc backed up a step.

I could open the gate if I can reach the wall, Ella suggested. She hurled another blast of starfire at two of the men, making them cry out in pain as the fire leapt at them, but they each snuffed out the flames before her magic could do any real damage.

They'd stop you before you had a chance to try. Luc gripped his sword tighter, parrying another blow as a dark-haired man came at him.

The whir of engines filled the bay as the ship came online. With a boom, the ship took to the air, hovering over them.

Luc shielded his face from a rush of hot fumes and coughed, and the other Valan stumbled as the force from the ship knocked them off their feet.

Ella, take my hand! Luc yelled internally as he held his hand out to her.

She grabbed his hand, and Luc felt energy ripple between them.

They both raised their free hands, and a powerful blast of energy sent all the Valan crashing to the ground.

The bay door opened.

"Come on, hurry!" Sara yelled.

Fidget scurried up onto Ella's shoulder while Luc sheathed his sword and wrapped his arms around her. "Hold on to me."

She wrapped her arms around his neck, and together they rose into the air. Fidget shrieked as he clung to Ella's shirt.

Luc's brow creased as he used his power to levitate them up onto the ship. They landed on the edge, and Ella stumbled inside. Luc gripped the side of the door for support. When he found his balance, he shoved it shut. "Eric, get us out of here."

He, Ella, and Sara quickly took their seats as Eric manoeuvred the ship around the hangar.

The engines groaned as he forced them out of the bay.

"Can this thing stay airborne?" Ella asked.

"We're about to find out," Eric called.

CHAPTER 9

Esme reclined on a sofa as one of her new drones came over, carrying a mug full of warm blood for her. She scowled as she took it from the female drone.

"Is something wrong, my queen?" the woman asked.

"Yes, I tire of this place. It's pitiful." After spending several days holed up in Elyria, she had grown bored. Even her drones and new blood slaves did little to amuse her. The humans in this realm were more defiant than those from her own land. She wanted her own people, not these poor imitations, but they were all still trapped in a hell realm where they had been stuck in hibernation for a millennium.

Her new drones were weak, pathetic. They followed her orders, but she knew from the last attack on Luc that they weren't strong enough to be of much help.

She'd only sent Allen and the other drones to track Ella and her companions, but the stupid idiots had gotten themselves killed and made her look like a fool. That was something she would not abide.

Esme rose, her long skirt billowing behind her.

A black-haired male drone came in and fell to his knees before her.

"Report," she snapped. She didn't feel in the mood for grovelling.

"We followed the avatar just as you commanded. We tracked her as far as Casel," he told her, trembling.

Esme's jaw clamped together. Normally, she enjoyed even drones cowering before her, but these people had tried her patience enough already. "And? Have they crossed the border yet?" she demanded.

"No, but they gained a new airship and…we lost track of them." His entire body shook.

Esme grabbed hold of his hair and yanked off his head in one swift move. She dropped the head on the floor as his body slumped forward.

"Someone clean that up," she snapped. "And find that avatar. I want to know where she's going and what she's doing."

"My queen?" Another male drone stepped forward. "We did capture a prisoner whilst we were there."

"I have enough slaves already." The last thing she wanted was another whining human around. Their tears and pleas for help were beginning to grate on her nerves. She didn't understand why they couldn't accept their new place in this realm with her as their true leader.

"We captured one of the Valan. He attacked the avatar before she and her companions fled," the drone continued.

Esme's dark eyes widened. "One of the Valan? Here? Good. Keep him alive, it's time I moved on with my plan."

She stormed out of the room. She'd spent enough time in this village and had enough drones for the next stage.

"Are the airships ready?" she asked another drone.

"Yes, my queen," the drone replied.

"Good. We are bound for Celestus, but we have to make a quick stop first. Let's move."

The drone helped her aboard the strange vessel, and Esme felt a buzz of excitement. She had commanded a whole fleet of vessels back when the Arkadians had been in power. She loved watching Arkadia smoulder and burn at the hands of the very weapons created by its people.

Esme winced as the ship's engines whirred to life and the vessel took off. Despite how much she had enjoyed commanding the fleet back then, she never liked flying. It made her feel out of control, and control was something she liked to have over everything back in her own realm.

She watched out of the window as Elyria became smaller and smaller. She was glad to see the back of that place; now she had several dozen drones, she wouldn't need to return there.

A couple of drones complained about the sunlight hurting their eyes and burning their skin.

Her teeth clamped together. *Be patient,* she told herself, *you only need them awhile longer.* Soon she would be reunited with her own people, her true brethren.

Trees blurred below them until the great white stone towers of Arkadia loomed in the distance. Esme smiled as she leaned closer to the window. There it was, the site where she'd been defeated a thousand years earlier, after she'd killed Lucan and Aurelia had forced she and her brethren through the gate.

How she had longed to come back and lay waste to the city she had failed to destroy. This time, she wouldn't fail.

The ship landed a few minutes later. Esme wrapped a shawl around her head that covered her face and arms, protecting her skin from the worst of the sun's rays as a drone helped her down from the ship. She stared up the at the citadel with its white stone walls. Strange, they hadn't blackened with age and looked almost as bright as when she had come here a millennium ago. Now, the Arkadians were gone, and she was standing in their precious city of magic.

She smiled. "I told you I'd be back."

"My queen, what is it we are looking for?" a young redheaded drone asked.

Esme remembered the last time she'd been here. The night she'd killed Griffin after he released her from her century's long imprisonment. She was grateful to the old Valan; he'd helped her when she hadn't been able to trick Ella into opening the gate again. Funny how a Valan knight of all people had helped release her.

"Bring the prisoner," she ordered.

She moved away from the courtyard, picking up the thump of heartbeats as two men dressed in white armour approached with their stunners raised.

Troopers. Esme knew they were from Celestus, no doubt sent here in case Ella and her companions came back.

"Hold it right there," the first trooper commanded. "Who are you people?"

Esme glanced over her shoulder. Each of the drones wore masks she'd had fashioned for them, and their skin was now covered with their coats. *Good.*

"Is there a problem, sir?" Esme wrapped an illusion around herself to appear as a human female.

"What are you doing here?" The trooper demanded. "This is a restricted area."

Esme felt her patience run out and grabbed the man by the throat. "I'm here to wipe your people out of existence," she growled.

He screamed as she dug her barbs into his chest.

The second trooper readied his stunner as the first one slumped to the ground, dead.

Esme flicked the stunner out of the way, then grabbed him, digging her barbs in until the man fell unconscious.

"Keep hold of him." She shoved him toward one of her drones. "We might need him later."

Esme marched away from the main part of the old city, and the drones dragged the prisoners along behind her.

She moved through the paved streets, her mind flashing back to when she had almost conquered this place.

She and the other Esrac had spread through the streets like the plague, and the blood had run freely that day. The Valan had fought back to with their weapons and magic, but not before they'd wiped out thousands of them.

Esme smiled at the memory. She soon would again.

She pushed her way through the overgrown trees until she reached the edge of the cliff face. Esme leapt from the edge, her long skirt billowing around her as she fell through the blackness. She kept control of her body as she fell, avoiding rocks and sharp branches that jutted out on the way down. Esme landed easily, her eyes adjusting to the gloom until she could see as clearly as if bright sunlight illuminated the cavern. Her boots crunched against the ground as she made her way to what had once been the gate room; the place she'd faced Aurelia all those centuries ago. She winced at the memory of when Aurelia had struck her and forced her through the gate.

Esme moved over to the far wall, reaching up and touching a crystal orb that hung there. It flickered, then illuminated the chamber with cool yellow light.

The drones dragged in the first prisoner as Esme stared up at the massive gateway; an arch set in stone with symbols above it. The very thing that had brought her to this realm was here. This was where the main gate existed.

Esme ran her fingers along the runes, feeling static prickle against her skin from the wards that framed them. Wards meant to stop anyone from travelling to Esme's own realm and the hell realm she'd been imprisoned in.

The gate shimmered like a dark mirror as she touched it, and she felt connection in the way she supposed an avatar did. "Bring the Valan over here," she ordered.

Two drones dragged a man with long blonde hair over to her, forcing him to his knees. He stared up at her with hatred in his eyes.

"What luck. I never expected to find a Valan on this side of the border given that Luc is with the avatar and I already killed Griffin." Esme grinned, her metallic teeth flashing in the low light. "What do they call you? Are you a Master?"

She had to hand it to her drones; capturing one of the Valan had been pure genius, although she suspected they had only grabbed him in an effort to placate her after their failure. Still, it was the only good thing they'd done for her so far. Perhaps they weren't *completely* useless.

"His name is Galvin," one of the drones answered. "He led the assault against the avatar."

"Answer me yourself." Esme pressed her barbs against his throat, but didn't break his flesh. "Or I'll kill you."

"You'll kill me anyway, Demon. Just get it over with," he spat.

Esme's teeth clanked together as she clenched her jaw. "Tell me, or I will force it out of you. How would you like to die repeatedly? You see, we can drain life, but we can also restore it. I can keep you alive indefinitely. Imagine that." Her barbs dug in, and she felt a rush of blood flow through her. Esme closed her eyes as Images flashed before her mind. "Galvin, yes. You *are* a Master, one who turned against the Valan on the other side of the border." Her smile widened. "You're going to help me free my people." She yanked him up. "Open the gate."

Galvin stumbled and rubbed his throat as blood trickled down it. "Never. I can't break—"

Esme pressed different runes, using the knowledge she'd stolen from Luc in his past life. The gate flashed as she activated each symbol. "Open it," she commanded.

"Go back to your—"

Esme shoved him forward, pressing his palm against the glowing rings.

Galvin tried to struggle free, but she held him firm. The gate flared with light as the wards broke, one by one.

With the edge of her barbs, she sliced Galvin's throat.

He fell to the floor as the gate opened into the blackness beyond, half of his body lying on the other side of the open portal.

Esme stepped over him, then reached down and sent enough energy into him to heal part of his wound so he wouldn't bleed to death. She moved into the chamber, feeling iciness sting her flesh.

"Bring the trooper, but don't let that Valan move," she snapped.

She didn't want to risk being in this realm longer than she had to for fear of becoming trapped here once again, but she needed to be the one to awaken her people. Her drones dragged the trooper and several of her blood slaves through the gate after them.

Esme went over to the first pod she found and ripped through the fleshy exterior of it. Inside, one of her helmsmen, Storm, lay deep in hibernation.

She grabbed the trooper and ripped into his flesh, letting blood drip down onto Storm's withered body.

"Rise, my children. Our imprisonment is over!" Esme cried.

One by one her people began to wake, dragging themselves out of their pods.

"Come, we have a date in Celestus," Esme smiled. "Time the other realm knew we walk their lands once again."

CHAPTER 10

After flying for most of the day, they stopped in another set of woods that night so the ship could recharge.

Luc prepared to fall into an uneasy meditative state after doing a final sweep of the area. It helped keep his senses alert and replicated sleep in a way that was easier and safer than actual sleep nowadays. He would be alert and ready in case anything came at them during the night.

"Hey, how about you actually sleep for real for a change?" Ella rested her head against his shoulder.

He opened his eyes and wrapped an arm around her. "I can't. I need to stay alert in case something goes wrong."

"Hey, I'm trying to sleep here," Eric grumbled. "If you're thinking about doing any funny stuff, go somewhere else."

Ella giggled, and Luc stifled a laugh.

"Sleep is important, too," Ella whispered, snuggling against him and closing her eyes.

Obediently, Luc closed his eyes too, and sleep soon claimed him.

When he awoke, Luc found himself back in the past. People were rushing past him.

"Prepare to raise the shield!" someone yelled.

A growing bubble of blue energy glowed overhead. He didn't know how such a thing was possible, but it seemed familiar to him somehow.

An airship loomed overhead, light bursting from its cannons.

It felt so real, so familiar, just as the other dreams he'd had of the past had done.

Light flashed as an Esrac came running in firing a stunner.

Their own warriors carried them?

The Esrac fired on the men around him, then a woman swept into the room, her long leather skirt billowing behind her. Her blood-red hair and teal skin shone in the light. Esme had breached the city walls.

Luc felt the familiar weight of his sword in his hand and raised it as she advanced toward him.

The image of her faded as he prepared to strike. In her place stood Aurelia—his heart, his love.

"Come, let's get out of here." She held out her hand.

Luc hesitated, confused by what had happened. "Esme..."

"Is gone, it's me. Come, let's leave this place."

Luc let her lead him away.

The image changed, and he found himself chained to the wall. His arms and legs felt heavy, like dead weights. He didn't have the strength to remain standing, but the chains held him in place.

"Tell me what you know of the gate," said a voice.

The figure before him looked and sounded like Aurelia, but deep down he knew it wasn't her.

He wanted to close his eyes and escape into his mind, but he felt too weak.

"How does the gate open? Is it physically there or can it only be conjured by me?"

"Both..." he croaked. "We use them to travel to different places, but only an avatar or a Valan Master can get through. They're trained..."

Luc jolted awake, sweat dripping down his face, and scrambled up. The only light came from the faint glow of stars. He marched off, needing to somehow clear his mind. Why would he dream of that? He and Ella had both failed and died the first time Esme had raged war against this realm. Was the past telling him it would happen again now? He didn't want to consider that. He and Ella were different people, and they wouldn't be defined by those lives anymore.

But could they really escape the past?

He walked toward the old temple Ella had mentioned finding earlier. Such places had once been used to worship and remember the ancestors in.

Luc believed in the ancestors, and knew they were real. Their magic allowed him to see glimpses of his past life, unlike the knowledge of the avatars, which were passed down through their bloodline.

"Why am I still haunted?" he demanded. "Do you still want us to pay for our past sins?" He stared at the statue. "I'm to blame for giving away the knowledge about the gate and allowing the Esrac into this realm. I accept I betrayed my vows, but don't blame Ella for that." He ran a hand through his hair. "One way or another, I'll keep my oath. I will find a way to stop and kill Esme."

"Luc?" He heard a soft voice, and for a moment thought the ancestors had heard him. Instead, Ella walked in behind him.

Luc sighed. "Sorry for waking you."

"I saw it too," she said, wrapping her arms around him.

He looked up at the statue. "Looks like they're still punishing us even now." He shook his head. "I didn't want you to have to see what she did to me."

"What you feel, I feel too. It's not your fault. What she did to you...anyone would have broken under that kind of torture."

"The Valan aren't supposed to break, and I was a Master back then. I should have been stronger, fought harder." He pulled away from her. "I haven't had the dreams for a while. I don't know why they're happening again now." He stared at Ella. "Don't you ever wonder if we're just doomed to repeat the same mistakes over and over again?"

"No, I believe we are free to make our own choices. I know I messed up when I first opened the gate again, but I know we'll fix it together."

Luc pulled her close. "I do love you, you know."

Ella nodded. "I love you too."

He leant down to kiss her, but stopped as he noticed a blur of white hurrying toward them.

"Bad," Fidget squeaked.

Ella spun around, frowning at him. "Bad what?"

Luc closed his eyes, sending out his senses. "Ships are here. Damn it, I shouldn't have—" he muttered, reaching for his sword.

"Wait!" Ella hissed. "Maybe we can catch them off-guard."

She had a point, and he knew better than anyone not to go rushing in headlong. Gripping his sword, he moved back toward the camp. Sudden light lit up the dark forest, and shouts rang out as flares from stunners shot through the air.

Luc quickened his pace, spotting the first troopers surrounding the camp.

Ella raised her hand, sending two troopers flying as she hit them with a blast of starfire.

Luc punched another one in the face as they lunged at him and raised his sword as a third fired at him, using his Valan blade to deflect the strike.

Small cylindrical shaped airships appeared overhead, and Luc frowned, recognising them as the vessels the Esrac had used to attack cities from the air during the first Realm War.

No, it couldn't be. How could Esme have procured such vessels?

It's a trick, he realised.

"Ella, aim your magic at those things," Luc called as he ran toward the nearest Esrac.

The creature lunged at him, fangs glistening. It made a grab for Luc, then used the other end of its stunner, which had been carved into a blade.

Luc parried the blow, and light flashed as they danced around each other, both trying to gain the upper hand.

"Hey!" Sara appeared, grabbing the drone's arm. The drone screeched as its flesh smouldered.

Luc used this distraction to his advantage and sliced its head off.

"Yuck!" Sara cringed and backed away as black blood covered her robes.

"Thanks," he said, knocking one trooper to the ground, then another.

Esme herself appeared, surrounded by drones, and to Luc's horror, more troopers.

They're with her? Why the hell does she have troopers?

The drones spread out, and Luc prepared for another attack.

"Avatar, come with me now or I'll kill them," said Esme.

"Not happening," Luc growled.

Light suddenly exploded around them.

"Luc, Ella, everyone get inside the ship!" Eric's voice rang out from somewhere within it.

Luc winced against the brightness and ran, avoiding the drones as he went.

He saw Sara jump in first, then Adria grabbed Ella's arm and shoved her in.

Luc got in last, followed by Fidget, who had stuck close behind him since they had left the temple.

The door slammed shut and Eric gunned the engines, shooting off into the night.

"What's to stop them following us?" Sara asked.

"I blew it up. That light display wasn't just a distraction," Eric replied. "It may not have destroyed their ship, but at least we have a decent head start on them."

There was a sudden bang, followed by a sharp jolt and the wrench of metal, and everything went black.

"Luc!" The sound of Ella's voice brought him out of oblivion, and she came rushing over with Fidget scurrying behind her. "Are you alright?" she asked, falling to her knees beside him.

"I think so." He rubbed his head, and his hand came away bloody. "Or maybe not."

Bits of debris and burning rubbish lay scattered around them.

"What happened? Are you hurt?"

"I'm fine, just a few bruises. Esme attacked the ship, but she's gone—for now at least."

A blonde-haired man came over. "You must be Luc; I am Master Winslow. Pleasure to meet you. It's an honour to meet the knight who—"

"You're a Valan?" Luc frowned. "How did you find us?"

"I asked the same thing," Ella whispered in his ear as she gave him a quick hug.

"Master Oswald sensed you were in trouble and sent us to aid you." Winslow knelt to examine Luc's head. "I will have a healer come to help you. My men are searching for your friends."

"Just give me a bandage. I'm fine," Luc insisted as he got up. "Have they found anyone else?"

"Not yet." Ella took his hand.

Winslow brought out a healing wand to patch up Luc's head as more Valan appeared, announcing they had found Eric among some burning wreckage. He had severe burns, but he was alive. Sara had alerted them to where he was, emerging with only a few cuts and bruises herself. They had found Adria at last, unconscious and unresponsive.

"Come, we can do more good for you once you reach our compound." Winslow motioned them over to a ring platform, and light flashed as the rings rose from the ground.

A few seconds later, they all appeared in a courtyard surrounded by stone walls. A white building loomed ahead.

"Your friends will be taken to the healing wing," Winslow told them. "I'll show you to your rooms, where you can get some rest. Later you will be bought before the Valan council."

"What is this place?" Luc asked. He hadn't expected to find the Valan staying somewhere like this.

"It is our base here in Kyrila. I know it must seem a surprise, but gone are our days in hiding," Winslow replied. "We use old magic and some technology to create a safe haven for magic users on this side of the border. The Senate may continue to hunt us, but we're done running and hiding away in caves."

"I've tried calling you many times since Master Griffin died, but I never received a response. Why?" Luc asked.

Winslow shook his head and shrugged. "I'm sure Master Oswald can answer all of your questions."

"I need to be with my grandmother," Ella insisted. "Where is she?

"She in the healing wing being worked on as we speak. You'll only be in the way now, but you can see her later."

Luc put his hand on Ella's shoulder. "She's in good hands. Let's go freshen up."

Winslow took them to their rooms, and Luc got washed and dressed in the fresh clothes that he found on the bed.

As he towelled off his hair, Ella came in. "Don't you think it's odd that they appeared just where we ended up?" she said, frowning.

"No, the Masters here are said to be gifted enough to sense things from miles away. We're lucky they came when they did," he said. "Why are you so suspicious?"

She shrugged. "I'm just nervous. I don't want anything to happen to Adria or Eric."

"The healers here are the best. They'll do whatever they can to help." He paused. "I don't know how the rest of the Valan will react to our presence, especially mine. They may want someone else to be your knight."

"You're my knight. I don't want or need anyone else." She hugged him and sighed. "I hate being unable to see them. Adria wouldn't wake up."

"She's a tough old bird. I'm sure she'll be fine. Eric will miss having a ship though." He returned her hug.

"Let's go check on them. I'll go mad if I have to sit around waiting."

Luc took her hand and led her back out in search of the healing wing. After everything that had happened, he decided he didn't care if anyone found out about their relationship. He loved Ella, and nothing—not even the Valan—would part them now.

Once inside the healing wing, they found Eric, who was now awake, as two healers worked on him.

"Hey, glad you two are okay," Eric said. "How are Sara and Adria?"

"Sara went off with Winslow once he told her about the library they have here," Ella answered. "We probably won't see her for a while. We're not sure about Adria," she added after a moment's hesitation.

"She'll be okay." Eric said, squeezing her hand. "Have you seen this place? It's mag-ow!" He winced as one of the healers applied something to his shoulder.

"I'm going to sit with Adria," Ella said. "Get better soon, Eric. We still need you around."

"Right, you can't kill the green buggers without me," Eric grinned.

Ella left, and Luc stayed, relieved when the healers left too.

"Told you you wouldn't get rid of me that easy," Eric said.

"It will take more than falling from the sky to keep you down." Luc chuckled.

Eric craned his head toward the door. "Are they gone?"

Luc glanced out into the corridor and nodded when he saw no one there. "Why?"

"Check my pack over there." Eric motioned to the floor. "Sara and I have been working on a formula to try and kill the Esrac. It's not much, but Sara thinks her blood might—"

Luc heard footsteps and put a finger to his lips. "Great, why didn't you tell us sooner?" he whispered. "How did you even come up with the idea?"

"It was Sara's idea. Genius, that one—don't tell her I said that though," Eric said. "We've been messing around with it for a while, but we haven't had the chance to test it. Take it out, I don't want anyone else finding it."

Luc slipped a file into his pocket. "Thanks."

"Friends help friends, right?"

"Are we friends now?" Luc arched an eyebrow.

"I thought we already were," Eric said.

Luc nodded and smiled. "Good. Keep this safe."

Eric slumped back onto the pillows. "Wow, whatever they gave me feels good." Seconds later, his eyes drooped shut.

Luc walked out and went to find Ella, who was in a room down the hall from Eric's. She stood watching healers hook Adria up to machines. "They won't tell me anything," she said, "but I know it's bad."

Luc wrapped an arm around her shoulders. "She's strong. She'll be alright."

Ella shook her head. "No, she won't. She told me she was ill before we left that town. She and my mum and the only family I have left. "

"That's not true, you have all of us too."

"Ella, Luc, pardon my intrusion," Winslow said as he appeared. "The council has convened and wishes to see to you both."

Ella shook her head. "I'm not leaving Adria."

"There's nothing we can do for her now," Luc said, squeezing her shoulders.

"I'll have someone send word if there is any change," Winslow said.

Luc's heart pounded as he and Ella were led into the council's meeting chamber. Luc had never been present at the council meeting before; Griffin and Caspian had been the only Masters he'd ever known. He had no idea how these people would react to him or Ella.

"I present before you Lucas Flynn and Ella Noran," Winslow announced. "Ella is an avatar and the daughter of Master Caspian. Luc is a former apprentice to Master Griffin."

Luc bowed his head in respect, as was customary, but Ella didn't.

"I am Master Oswald, head of the Valan council," said a white-haired man. "It's come to our attention the Esrac Queen has been released from the realm from which she was imprisoned. How is that possible?"

"I let her out," Ella admitted. "But by accident. I haven't known about being an avatar very long."

She went on to tell the story of how she had discovered the buried gate and let the first wave of Esrac free. Luc chimed in to tell them of how he defeated them, and Ella explained how Master Griffin had tricked them and forced her to open the gate.

"Winslow tells us you displayed signs of unusual power," Oswald said to Ella. "I sense that magic flows strongly in you. May I see your power?"

Ella glanced to Luc, and he nodded.

She held up her hand, and her fire formed, then shifted from blue to red.

"You have an exceptional talent for magic," Oswald said and turned to Luc. "Did Griffin assign you as her protector?"

Luc nodded. "Yes."

"Unusual, the first avatar in fifty years to be partnered with someone so young. Why didn't we send a more suitable knight?"

Luc opened his mouth to speak, but Ella cut him off. "Luc wanted to strip me of my powers," she snapped. "He didn't want me using magic at all. Plus, he's a trained Master and was Lucan in his first life. I can't think of anyone better to be my partner."

"Masters, we came here seeking your help," Luc said. "We can't fight the Esrac alone, and Esme wants to use Ella's powers to free all of her brethren."

"You've brought the Esrac straight to our doorstep," said another Master.

Oswald stood. "We'll adjourn to discuss your proposal. You may wait outside until we reach a verdict."

CHAPTER 11

Ella paced up and down outside the council chamber. "They had better not try taking you away. I'm not working with anyone else."

They hadn't come all this way seeking Valan help, only to have them deny them any now.

"They can't. I'll never leave you; you know that." Luc leant back against the stone wall.

"Yes, but you're still a Valan, which means they have the power to take you away if they wanted to." She continued pacing. "I say a bunch of strangers has no right to dictate our lives."

Worry threatened to consume her, but she wouldn't let it get the best of her. Despite her concern for Adria and fear of losing again, she'd find a way to get the Masters on their side. They still needed an avatar, didn't they?

"I'll leave if I have to," Luc said. "They may not be happy we're together in this life since we failed our duty before in our past lives."

She stopped pacing and stared at him, wide-eyed. "You'd do that? Being a Valan is who you are. I wouldn't ask or want you to give up part of yourself because of me."

"I've already broken the rules just by being with you. I'm not sure I am cut out to become a fully-fledged knight, anyway."

"Do you think they'll help us?"

Luc shrugged. "I don't know. Griffin is the only Master aside from your dad who I've ever worked with, and your dad left the Order so he could be with your mother."

"I still don't understand why he never told me about any of this. He must've known—"

"He wanted to keep you safe. You can't blame him for that."

Ella scowled at the closed doors. "If their meetings are anything like the Senate ones, they could be hours yet." She sighed. "I'm going to sit with Adria for a while."

"Go, I'll stay here and let you know when they call us." Luc gave her a quick kiss.

Adria still lay with her eyes closed when Ella walked into her room and sat down beside her.

It was quiet now except for the drone of machines.

Ella took her grandmother's hand. "I know we haven't known each other for very long, but you're part of my life now," she said, sniffing. "I don't want to lose you. You have to stay, even if you decide you don't like me. You didn't have to help me, but I'm grateful you did. I know you thought you were protecting me by staying away, but I wish I could have known you sooner." She wiped her eyes with the back of her hand when she felt tears threatening to fall. "Please wake up."

She waited and felt Adria squeeze her fingers.

Ella smiled and squeezed back. "You'd better come back. I need you to help me handle the stuffed shirts." She sat talking to Adria for a while, speaking about nonsense at times, but it felt comforting being there beside her grandmother.

After she had finished, she glanced over to the window. Outside, darkness had already fallen. Ella sighed. "I can't believe Esme managed to free her people. Luc's hiding it well, but I know he's worried about the curse and what might happen to us if we fail again." She blew out a breath. "Will the Valan high-ups help us? I'm beginning to wonder if coming here was the right thing to do in the first place. I know how much you wanted to go home to your village, but I don't think anyone can help us get there now."

Adria suddenly squeezed her fingers again, and her words echoed through Ella's mind. *"You have all you need to find a way to stop Esme. You will know when the time is right to use the crystal."*

Ella fumbled around in her pack until she found the box that contained the crystal. She'd picked it up a few times since Adria had told her about it, but nothing had happened, even when she'd using her magic on it. She wished she had asked Adria more about it when she'd had the chance, but Adria had always seemed so sure Ella would know what to do with it.

She pulled the crystal out of the box and rolled it between her fingers. It didn't look like much, just an ordinary crystal.

Why would my dad even want me to have this?

"Why didn't you tell me more about this thing?" Ella asked. "If it can help us, why didn't you tell me how to use it?" She sighed again. "I'm trying not to lose hope, but everything seems so impossible right now."

The building suddenly vibrated with a loud boom, and the floor underneath Ella's feet trembled as she stumbled over to the window. Outside, lights filled the night sky, but these were no stars. They were ships, Senate airships, by the look of it.

Damn it, how did they find us again?

Ella's heart started pounding in her ears, and she glanced back at Adria, who still lay there, unmoving. She couldn't just leave her here to die.

"Gran, you need to wake up now. There are ships here. Please, Gran." She reached down to grasp Adria's hand, but this time Adria didn't respond. On impulse, she gripped the crystal in her other hand and gasped as energy jolted through her. Ella's eyes snapped shut as images blurred through her mind and all her memories from her previous lives flashed before her. They showed each and every life she'd lived as an avatar and how she'd fallen in love with Luc and fought different Esrac through the centuries. Being an avatar was who she was. Magic was in her very soul. She was sworn to keep the balance and walking through the gates and using magic were as natural to her as the very air she breathed.

Sharp pain stung her chest as she felt tendrils of power wrap around her—the curse! She felt it reaching out for her. She remembered it all now. Her lives, how to use her power, everything, but people had already died. Was it too late?

No! she thought, her hands clenching into fists as the curse squeezed tighter. *Not this time. I haven't failed yet. I still have a chance to stop Esme once and for all.*

The crystal fell from her hand and clattered onto the floor. She let it stay there; it had served its purpose now.

She glanced at Adria again. As much as she wanted to stay, she knew she couldn't, and nor would Adria want her to. Her grandmother would never forgive her if she stood idly by while innocent people were killed. She had to go. That was her duty as an avatar.

"I will make you proud of me." She kissed the top of Adria's forehead and hurried out of the room to find Luc, Eric, and Sara running toward her.

"The Esrac are here," Luc said.

She nodded. "I know, but we're not running away this time. It's time I faced Esme." She took Luc's hand. "That we faced her together. Let's go."

Hand-in-hand, she and Luc hurried outside to find Esme. Eric and Sara ran along behind.

"We haven't had a chance to test out solution yet," Sara said.

Ella frowned. "What solution?"

Sara glanced at Eric.

"We've been working on a way of killing Esme using a solution of chemicals that distort molecules and Sara's blood. We figured it would work the same way her touch does, and it might be enough to kill her," Eric explained. "We haven't had a chance to test it yet."

Ella looked at Luc. "Did you know about this?" she asked.

He nodded. "Yes, but I didn't want to mention it, since we have no idea if it will actually work."

"We have to try it. If it doesn't kill Esme, perhaps it will at least slow her down."

Around them, blasts of light lit up the night sky and people screamed as parts of the compound exploded around them.

"How did Esme get so many ships?" Sara asked. "I know she turned people, but…"

"She must have gone to Celestus and infiltrated the Senate. Damn, I warned the Chancellor," Luc cursed.

"We'll worry about that later." Ella gripped his hand and glanced around at the Valan fighting off different drones.

Esme had to be around here somewhere. She wouldn't stay far from the battle. Ella knew her well enough to know that.

Eric pulled out his stunner and fired at the first drone he saw, and Luc rounded on another as it came at them. Ella moved away from them, reaching out with her mind to search for the Esrac Queen.

Come on, Esme. I know you are around here somewhere. Where are you? I know you can hear me.

A harsh cackle echoed around her as Esme stepped out of the shadows, her fangs glistening like silver. "Clever little avatar," she grinned. "I see a power and confidence in your eyes you haven't had before."

Ella smiled. "Let's just say I've remembered a few things."

"My people are destroying your realm, just as I promised they would, but this is only the beginning. Once the Valan are gone for good, I plan on laying waste to this land and turning it into my own realm. Perhaps I will even take the gate for myself. No doubt it can visit other realms aside from my own homeland and that wretched hell realm."

Ella shook her head. "You didn't win last time, and you won't win now." Blue fire flared between her fingers.

Esme rolled her eyes. "Must we go through this again? You know that can't kill me."

Ella hurled her starfire straight at the Esrac's feet, causing the ground to shake beneath her and set her off balance. She fired again before Esme had a chance to react, this time hitting the Queen in the chest, then again in the face. Esme yelped as the fire singed her skin and rubbed her cheek in disbelief, stunned to see blood there.

Sara appeared and threw a vial of black liquid straight at Esme. The glass smashed, and smoke rose up as it hit Esme's chest.

Esme screamed as her skin smouldered, but remained very much alive. Ella had been right: it wasn't enough to kill her. Eric turned and fired his stunner straight at Esme, hitting her with multiple bursts of blue-white light.

Luc spun, slicing off the head of the nearest drone, then turned and thrust his sword through Esme's chest. Sara grabbed hold of Esme's arm, causing the Esrac Queen's skin to smoulder with white heat. As she held fast, Luc dug his blade in deeper, and Eric continued firing.

"You have failed, Esme." Ella waved her hand, and the gate appeared on the wall behind them. "From now on, neither you nor any of your people will harm this realm again." Behind Esme, the glowing portal of gold light flared to life.

She raised her hand and sent Esme stumbling backward. Esme gripped the sides of the gate, just as she had done a thousand years earlier. "No, I won't go back to that hell realm!"

"You're right. This time you will die." Ella raised both her hands and let all the power she had inside of her flow outwards in a surge of glowing purple light. Sara kept a firm grip on Esme's arm as Ella's magic hit the Esrac head-on, and Esme gave one last scream as her flesh melted away.

Luc twisted and sliced off Esme's head in one fell swoop, and her body disintegrated into blackness. Around them, unholy shrieks shattered the night air, echoing over the roar of engines and blasts of light as one by one the Esrac disintegrated into nothingness.

EPILOGUE

Ella stared at the shining towers of Celestus City as the ring platform transported them to the Senate meeting chamber. The Chancellor herself sat inside, surrounded by the rest of the Senate. Esmeralda looked up, mouth agape as Ella, Luc, Eric and Sara all piled into the room.

"You!" the chancellor gasped. "Guards, seize them!"

Ella held up her hand. "Wait, at least let us have the chance to speak first," she said. "We know you're still recovering after the Esrac invasion."

"And you're trying to cover it up, no doubt," Eric added. "You'll probably give the public some lame excuse and say it was an attack by the rebels."

"We thought you'd like to know the Esrac threat is over," Ella continued. "After a thousand years of plaguing this realm, the Esrac Queen is dead, and her people are no more."

Luc pulled out Esme's head—the only part of her to have survived — and dropped it on the table in front of the shocked Senators. "We wanted to give you this as proof. You can't deny magic exists anymore."

"How did you...?" The Chancellor asked.

"That's not important. What *is* important is that we are not going away. You can outlaw magic all you like, but it's a part of this realm. A part of our world," Ella said. "You can't just make it disappear anymore. We're done hiding. We're done running."

"Magic is all around you, whether you choose to use it or not," Sara said. "Even Master Griffin understood that. It's a part of our history, part of what the ancestors passed down to us. You can't erase that any more than you can erase magic itself."

Master Oswald moved in behind them. "I am Oswald, head of the

Valan. I came to tell you that without these four young people, all of you would either be dead or living as blood slaves under the Esrac Queen's rule. As they said, we will not hide away anymore. We've taken up residence in the old city of Arkadia again. It's the home of our ancestors, and our home. No matter what you say or do, you will not take our land or our magic away from us."

Ella smiled at the stunned expression on the Chancellor and Senators' faces and turned to the others. "Let's go home."

Since her grandmother had woken up, she had started taking some of the Valan's remedies, and was gradually recovering from her illness. Ella couldn't wait to see her.

The others left the room first, and Ella took Luc's hand and began to let him lead her away.

"Wait," the chancellor called, standing. "Perhaps we can come to an agreement."

Ella's smile widened, and Luc wrapped an arm around her shoulders.

"We'll do that soon enough," Ella promised. "But first, like you, we have a lot of rebuilding to do."

Hand-in-hand, she and Luc left the shining towers of Celestus behind them, and she looked up at the sunset. She'd finally kept her promise, the vow she made all those centuries ago. She'd stopped the Esrac and saved thousands from dying in the process.

Today was her twentieth birthday. The first one she had seen in centuries. And all she would remember from it was love and the promise of a better future.

**If you enjoyed reading this book be sure to leave a review!
For more news about my books sign up to my newsletter on
tiffanyshand.com/newsletter**

ALSO BY TIFFANY SHAND

ANDOVIA CHRONICLES

Dark Deeds Prequel

The Calling

ROGUES OF MAGIC SERIES

Bound By Blood

Archdruid

Bound By Fire

Old Magic

Dark Deception

Sins Of The Past

Reign Of Darkness

Rogues Of Magic Complete Box Set Books 1-7

EVERLIGHT ACADEMY TRILOGY

Everlight Academy, Book 1: Faeling

Everlight Academy Book 2: Fae Born

Hunted Guardian – An Everlight Academy Story

EXCALIBAR INVESTIGATIONS SERIES

Denai Touch

Denai Bound

Denai Storm

Excalibar Investigations Complete Box Set

SHADOW WALKER SERIES

Shadow Walker

Shadow Spy

Shadow Sworn

Shadow Walker Complete Box Set

THE AMARANTHINE CHRONICLES BOOK 1

Betrayed By Blood

Dark Revenge

The Final Battle

SHIFTER CLANS SERIES

The Alpha's Daughter

Alpha Ascending

The Alpha's Curse

The Shifter Clans Complete Box Set

TALES OF THE ITHEREAL

Fey Spy

Outcast Fey

Rogue Fey

Hunted Fey

Tales of the Ithereal Complete Box Set

THE FEY GUARDIAN SERIES

Memories Lost

Memories Awakened

Memories Found

The Fey Guardian Complete Series Box Set

THE ARKADIA SAGA

Chosen Avatar

Captive Avatar

Fallen Avatar

The Arkadia Saga Complete Series

ABOUT THE AUTHOR

Tiffany Shand is a writing mentor, professionally trained copy editor and copy writer who has been writing stories for as long as she can remember. Born in East Anglia, Tiffany still lives in the area, constantly guarding her work space from the two cats which she shares her home with.

She began using her pets as a writing inspiration when she was a child, before moving on to write her first novel after successful completion of a creative writing course. Nowadays, Tiffany writes urban fantasy and paranormal romance, as well as nonfiction books for other writers, all available through eBook stores and on her own website.

Tiffany's favourite quote is *'writing is an exploration. You start from nothing and learn as you go'* and it is armed with this that she hopes to be able to help, inspire and mentor many more aspiring authors.

When she has time to unwind, Tiffany enjoys photography, reading, and watching endless box sets. She also loves to get out and visit the vast number of castles and historic houses that England has to offer.